HEART

By the same author:

THE INSTITUTE
PARADISE BAY
OBSESSION

HEART OF DESIRE

Maria del Rey

First published in 1994 by
Nexus
332 Ladbroke Grove
London W10 5AH

Typeset by CentraCet Ltd, Cambridge
Printed and bound by Cox & Wyman Ltd,
Reading, Berks

ISBN 0352 32900 9

This book is a work of fiction.
In real life, make sure you practise safe sex.

1

Westerham looked up as the secretary marched breezily into the office again, still wearing the look of haughty disdain that had greeted him first thing that morning. He held back his smile, knowing that he had to return her iciness, degree for degree; it was part of the game. Her eyes, very blue and very cold, flashed at him for a moment then turned away again; there was a faint sneer on her glossy red lips. She walked across the office, pulled a file from a filing cabinet, then walked back.

'No sign of Mr Christie, I take it?' Westerham said, waiting until she was back by the door before speaking.

Louise hesitated then turned slowly to face him. Her hair was cut short at the back but a long fringe fell down to almost cover her eyes, as if she wanted to hide behind the shock of brilliant fair hair. 'No, Mr Westerham,' she said coldly, 'there have been no phone calls.'

'You will tell me,' Westerham smiled patronisingly, 'won't you?'

She inhaled sharply, narrowing her lips a fraction and fixing him with a look that could kill. 'Of course I will,' she said tartly, then slammed the door before he had a chance to follow up.

Westerham stood up and walked across the office

to the window. Louise's anger, and it was genuine from what he could tell, was the least of his worries. He had been going round in circles, chasing his tail in the search for whatever was going on in the company. Someone was making an awful lot of money out of the company; unfortunately it wasn't the directors or the shareholders. It should have been a simple investigation: in and out quickly with a minimum of fuss and as little blood on the carpet as possible. It should have been like that but it wasn't, and Westerham was getting restless, though not as restless as the board of directors that had appointed him.

He waited by the window, the blinds slicing the pale wintry light that filtered through. The traffic was crawling along the street outside, and the congestion of the cars and the miserable overcast sky made him turn away. Was Christie the man to go for? He was Director of Operations at the company and so in an excellent position to line his own pockets. And the fact that he had gone on holiday the moment that Westerham had started nosing around was not a good sign, not a good sign at all.

But what about Louise? She was good, very smart, very capable and obviously in the know. It never failed to amaze Westerham how close some men were to their personal assistants, closer than wives, closer than friends, closer even than lovers. And Louise was like that; her fiercely protective manner was not contrived in any way. If anything was going on then she had to know about it, and most likely in full glorious detail.

Westerham went to the door and stuck his head out. She was there, waiting at her desk, sitting tall and straight, her short skirt stretched tight over long stockinged thighs. 'Can I have a word?' he asked, allowing a smile to pass across his lips.

Silently she stood up, her eyes still as cold as ever, head held high, challenging him with an expression of utter disdain. He held the door open for her, breathed her perfume as she slid by. She walked with a natural elegance, more like a model than a bureaucrat.

'You were in films before?' Westerham suggested, watching her glide into the seat in front of Christie's desk. Her skirt, short and tight, had surely been designed to display her thighs to perfection.

'How did you know?' she replied, looking at him suspiciously.

'There's a lot that I know,' Westerham smiled, secretly pleased that his informed guess had looked like solid research rather than gut instinct.

'Am I supposed to read something into that?' she asked coolly, her eyes still hard and confident. But there was something more than just hostility behind her expression; her eyes sparkled with something else, something that he felt within himself too.

'What made you give it up?' Westerham sat on the edge of the desk, one hand resting on his knee. She wore a smart black jacket to go with the short skirt, and a simple white blouse that did nothing to hide the rounded shape of her breasts. It was an outfit designed to draw the eye, very sexy but standoffish at the same time, just as she was.

'It got boring,' she shrugged.

'I see. Appearing behind the cameras got boring so you decided to do something exciting, like working in an office. Doesn't sound very likely, does it?'

Louise shifted uncomfortably. 'Where is this leading, Mr Westerham?' she asked.

3

It was a good question. He leaned forward, staring directly at her, into her crystal blue eyes. Her lips were slightly parted, glossy, red, inviting. 'Did you work with Christie before you came here?'

'What's that got to do with anything?' Louise demanded, and this time the hard edge of confidence was blunted. For the first time Westerham saw doubt in her eyes.

'I want answers, Louise,' Westerham said quietly. 'I want to know what's going on. I want to know what Christie is up to. I want to know and you're going to tell me. Aren't you, Louise?'

She swallowed hard, looking directly into his eyes, too afraid to turn away, caught in the hypnotic gaze that tore away the arrogant self-confidence that had protected her until then. 'I don't know anything, Mr Westerham,' she managed to whisper, her tanned face turning pale.

'That's not true, is it, Louise?' he said reasonably, his voice low and insinuating. They were close now, he was almost on top of her, his face close to hers; he was breathing her scent, could feel her warmth so close to him.

'I don't know . . .'

He reached out and touched her cheek with his fingertips, tracing a slow circle on her soft skin. She turned into his touch, closed her eyes softly, a sigh escaping from her lips like a whisper. He watched her, fascinated by the expression on her once icy face, her eyelids flickering, lips parted deliciously. She turned further, pressing her face right into the palm of his hand. She was sighing softly, making little animal sounds that seemed to be exhaled with her breath. He took her face in both hands, drew her closer. It was inevitable; the moment their eyes

4

met he had known that they would make love. All the cold glances, the frosty looks of disdain, the barely concealed contempt, all conveyed the exact opposite; nothing was what it seemed.

Louise took his fingers in her mouth, her red lips closing tightly. She sucked and licked, her tongue sliding up and down, caressing his fingers lovingly.

'You're wet,' Westerham stated, his voice level, successfully hiding his own feelings of excitement.

'Yes,' Louise whispered, her lips closing around his fingers once more.

'Is this the desk where Christie fucks you?' he asked, stressing the word 'fuck' so that it was hard and brutal.

'Yes. I want you to fuck me too.'

He pulled his fingers from her mouth and then pressed his mouth against hers, sucking violently, forcing his tongue deep into her mouth. She resisted for a moment, tried to push him away and then responded, clutching at his shoulders and then pulling him closer. His hands were on her chest, gently massaging her breasts, toying with her erect nipples so that she cried out. He swallowed her cries, drinking in her breath as if it were pure sweetness, then he pushed her away.

'Where's Christie?' he demanded coldly, sitting back up on the edge of the desk, his eyes fixed upon her.

'Why are you doing this?' she asked softly, the hurt in her voice matched by the pained expression on her face. She looked betrayed, confused, vulnerable. Her lipstick was smeared, her lips almost bruised, eyes wide and tearful.

'I need to know,' he told her simply. Her nipples were hard points on her white blouse, pressing

5

through the silk where he had rubbed them to erection.

'I don't know,' she mumbled without conviction.

'Are you still wet?' he asked mockingly.

'You're a bastard.'

'So I've been told,' he smiled.

'I want to go.' She stood up, smoothed down her skirt, avoided his eyes.

'Do you really want to leave now?' He reached across and touched her face again. She winced, closed her eyes again. She was excited, trembling as he stroked her soft skin. Her throat was bare, white, alluring; he touched her there, pressing his fingers firmly over the silky smoothness of her flesh.

'Don't do this to me,' she whispered, but her eyes said otherwise.

He pulled her close and tore open her blouse, the buttons flying across the office like bullets. Her breasts were bare, her nipples centred in firm white flesh. He palmed her breasts softly, flicking his thumbs over the nipples to make them harder until she was sighing again.

She fell into his arms and he held her for a second, breathing hard against her throat so that his breath was hot and hard against her skin. He slipped a hand under her skirt and felt the glassy smoothness of her thighs. Her panties were damp and sticky, and he felt her shivering with pleasure as he stroked her pussy through the damp material.

'Do you still want to go?' he asked softly.

'What if I do?' she replied, holding on to him tightly.

'Then you can go.'

'No. I want to stay.'

Westerham smiled to himself. He kissed her on

the neck, sucking at her skin violently, then kissed her on the mouth again. She responded: her breathing was hard and her panties were becoming wetter by the second. His movements became more insistent, his fingers pressing through her panties into her sex, while he squeezed her breast tightly with his other hand.

Louise tried to say something but he covered her mouth with his, exploring her with his tongue. She held onto him weakly, moving her hips back and forth with the rhythm of his fingers. He bit her on the neck again, pressed her nipple between his fingers. Her moans grew deeper, more urgent; she was clawing at him, her painted red nails digging into him.

'Oh Jesus . . .' she cried, arching her back and throwing her head back violently. His fingers were deep inside her sex, straining against the thin silky panties. She climaxed, shuddered, then collapsed into his arms again. He kissed her softly on the face and on the forehead, licking away the beads of sweat that had formed so suddenly.

'I'll be at my hotel,' he told her softly, steering her back into the seat in front of the desk. She looked dazed, her eyes unfocused for a moment. Her breasts and throat were patterned red, her face still carried the after-shock of ecstasy.

'But . . .' She leaned across and pressed her hand over his hard throbbing prick.

'No, I'll see you later,' he told her, taking her hand and kissing her fingers lovingly.

She looked at him, confusion in her eyes. Suddenly she seemed to remember herself and tried to cover her naked breasts with the torn blouse.

Westerham walked out of the office without even

bothering to look back at her, aware that she was looking at him with a mixture of hate and desire in her crystal blue eyes.

Sarah was just about to get up and go when she saw Eddie striding into the place. He looked fashionably dishevelled, two days growth on his chin, black hair greased back, black sunglasses and a black leather jacket.

'Two cappuccinos,' he called to the old man behind the counter, and then slumped into the chair beside her.

'Late,' she said simply.

'Yeah, sorry about that,' he mumbled from the side of his mouth, though she knew that he wasn't really sorry at all. He was scanning the coffee bar looking for pretty faces the way he always did. It annoyed her immensely and he knew it.

'Look, Eddie,' she said sternly, 'I don't have time for this. What do you want?'

The old man shuffled up to the table and parked two cups of cappuccino on the corner. 'Cheers, mate.' Eddie handed him a handful of coins and then turned to Sarah. 'Don't worry about it then,' he said sourly. 'I've only got a job for you, that's all.'

'A job?'

'You got better things to do,' he said, 'forget about it.'

Sarah breathed deeply, doing her best to control herself. 'I'm sorry,' she said finally, checking her growing anger. She hated him sometimes, he could be such a pig about things.

'Forget it,' he said, sulking. He fell silent, sipping

his drink and looking straight ahead, staring at his reflection in the gleaming tiled wall.

'Please, Eddie, it's just that I've been waiting ages and . . .' Sarah continued apologetically, knowing that he was deliberately playing up because he knew she was desperate for work. The leather jacket and shades looked bloody ridiculous, and he was acting like a spoilt child who needed humouring, but there was nothing else she could do.

'It's a film. *Power and Glory* or something like that. A good production by the sounds of it.'

'You're kidding?'

'Nope. I'm on camera again. This'll be good, I promise you.'

'Wow, that's great!' Sarah cried excitedly. She couldn't help sounding happy; her natural optimism always beat her suspicions hands down, even though Eddie Watson was just the sort of man to arouse all sorts of suspicions.

'No big names,' he continued, his voice seeming to have picked up the note of excitement from Sarah. 'But some really juicy parts in it. Good script, and I mean bloody good.'

'And? What about me? What about me?'

'I've put in a word for you,' he told her, slipping his sunglasses off and staring deeply into her eyes. He took her hands and drew them close, kissing her fingers softly.

'Is that all? You've put in a word for me?' Sarah sat back in her seat, her excitement deflated. She snatched her hands away from Eddie's lips angrily.

'They want someone with a bit more experience for the main parts,' he explained seriously. 'I mean there's bound to be some walk-on parts but I put you up for one of the bigger parts. You'd want that, wouldn't you?'

'Sure, but . . .'

'It's about a politician and his downfall. See, he's going places, the man to watch and all of that. Only problem is that he has this weakness . . . He likes the ladies a bit too much.'

'Who's the script by?'

'You wouldn't know him, but he's good. The problem is that this bloke is going to go to the Home Office, except that he gets involved with a prossie. That's your part,' he paused, 'if you get it.'

'A prostitute?' Sarah looked faintly disgusted.

'More than that. This isn't one of those clichéd "whore with the heart of gold" stories. It's more realistic. See, she's a professional dominatrix . . .'

'A what?' Sarah demanded.

'A dominatrix. Whips, chains, bondage and spanking cabinet ministers. You get the picture?'

Sarah pushed her cappuccino across the table. The more she heard about the film the less she liked it. Eddie was well known for his dubious connections, and the film sounded very suspect.

'It's on the level,' he assured her. 'It's the real thing, nothing dodgy, I promise you. The whole thing's about power, you see. Who's got the power? It works on lots of different levels. See, the papers get to find out about it, and then it's a question of who has the power: politicians or the press. And then when he's with the dominatrix, who has the power? Him or her?'

'She does,' Sarah replied.

'But does she? I mean she beats him and all that, but he pays her at the end of it. So who has the power?'

'I see. It's not a porno movie?'

Eddie laughed, his bright white teeth breaking through the grey-green stubble of his face. 'No, it's not a porno movie. It's not being done in some dodgy back room. This is a proper production, in a real studio, with real actors and actresses. It's not dodgy, I promise you.'

'But Eddie, I know you,' Sarah laughed, but already she half believed him. His story sounded convincing, and she knew that he could never have thought of the subtext by himself. And he really was a good cameraman; she'd seen his name on enough credits to convince herself that that at least was true.

'Like I said, I think they want someone who's done a bit more work, that's all.'

'But I've done work. Are they at least willing to let me audition?'

'Sure, but I can see there being a few others up for the part. I mean she's one of the main characters, this is a juicy role. And there's more to it than parading around in leathers and holding a whip.'

'So, there is some of that?'

Eddie shrugged. 'I told you, it's realistic. You'll have to strut your stuff, but it's more than just that. To be honest I think it's based on fact, or at least part of it is. I reckon the only way to guarantee getting the part is for you to do some research of your own.'

Sarah looked at him for a moment, trying to fathom his true motives behind the put-on sincerity of his dark brown eyes. 'What sort of research?' she asked slowly.

'Go and see a real life dominatrix.' He paused, not smiling, his face completely straight. 'Talk to her, see what it's really like. And for Christ's sake, mention it when you get to talk to the casting director.'

'And where am I . . .'

'I've got a number. Her name's Dominique . . .'

Sarah burst out laughing. 'Dominique? Not Madame Whiplash?'

'I don't know what you're laughing at,' he smiled. 'Your real name's not Katya Russell, is it?'

'But that's a stage name . . .'

'There,' he laughed triumphantly, 'you've got something in common already.'

Louise peered into the hotel restaurant, searching for Westerham amongst the small number of thinly scattered diners. She had been debating for hours whether to go in search of him but now that she was at the hotel her earlier resolve had dissipated. She knew that he was a bastard, she had known that even before she had set eyes on him; his reputation had preceded him. But there was something about him, bastard or not, that was difficult to resist. It wasn't that he was particularly good looking; he was in his late thirties, not very fit looking, with a face that looked permanently in pain. His looks weren't it, it was something else, something intangible, like an aura around him. He exuded confidence, and a magnetism that was irresistible.

He wasn't eating so she went in search of the bar. She had changed clothes. Her ripped blouse had had to be binned and her panties had still been damp when she got home. Her lips still felt tender, and her sex still in a state of arousal, the feel of his fingers a ghostly sensation still inside her. She had climaxed, her cries had carried beyond the confines of the office, but Westerham had acted as if it had

12

been nothing. His prick had been as hard as stone when she had touched him, but he had pushed her away, as if he were unaffected by what he had been doing to her. It made her mad to think about it: the way she writhed in his arms while he was cold and unmoved. It made her mad but turned her on too.

The first bar was full of bored looking businessmen; their eyes lit up when she walked in. She saw at once that he wasn't there, she knew that she would be able to feel his presence even before she set eyes on him. That was the way he was, he filled a room just by being there, it was impossible to ignore him.

Louise turned away, catching sight of the eyes following her in the mirrored wall at the entrance to the bar. She was dressed in a tight-fitting black dress, long enough to cover her bare thighs down to the knees, but tight enough to show her body to best effect. There was a second bar in another part of the hotel, and the waiter that directed her to it had leered at her long after she was on her way. She turned back and saw him still looking, his greedy eyes admiring the tightness of her behind, the velvet dress parting her backside so that it was obvious she was naked underneath.

Westerham was there, she sensed it as soon as she walked in. It was a quiet room, filled with isolated corners, the red velvet curtains and oak panelling creating an atmosphere of plush opulence. The barman smiled to her but she ignored him. Sure enough Westerham was there, sitting at a table in one corner, talking with a young waitress. Louise smiled; she could see that the waitress was hovering, unable to tear herself away from him. He was smiling, sitting with his arms across the back of his seat, his eyes fixed on the young woman so that she couldn't turn away.

'What would you like to drink?' he asked when he saw Louise approaching. The waitress spun round and her eyes narrowed, realising at once that Westerham had lost interest in her.

'Rum and blackcurrant,' Louise told the waitress. The bastard, why hadn't he shown the faintest surprise that she had turned up? He had known that she was going to be there, there had been no doubt in his mind and Louise hated him for it.

He gestured to the seat opposite but didn't bother to get up. 'You look very nice,' he said when Louise sat down.

'You ruined my blouse,' she told him, suddenly at a loss for words. Why had she bothered to turn up?

'It was worth it though, wasn't it?' He laughed cockily. His eyes were a question mark, waiting for an answer.

'Yes,' Louise admitted softly, unable to lie even though it was what she wanted to do.

'Doesn't Christie ever tear your clothes off?'

Again the desire to lie, to wipe the superior smile from his lips. 'No. Never.'

'I didn't think so. Do you love him?'

'It's nothing to do with you. You wouldn't understand, your type never understand anything,' she said bitterly.

'Perhaps you're right. My type never understand anything, except plain facts and figures.' He laughed again, an arrogant laugh that made Louise feel disloyal for ever having spoken about Tony Christie. 'I like you, Louise, really I do,' he added. 'You're honest, and that's something I admire.'

'Am I supposed to feel flattered?'

'No, but I'm being honest with you.'

The waitress brought Louise her drink and Westerham hardly glanced at her. 'Were you going to try and bed her if I hadn't turned up?' Louise asked when the woman was safely out of earshot.

'There was no if about it,' Westerham smiled. 'You were going to see me tonight. And what makes you think that I haven't made love with her already?'

'You're a bastard!' Louise spat at him.

'No, I'm honest. People call me all sorts of things, but what they really mean is that I'm brutally honest. If that makes me a bastard then I plead guilty.'

Louise fell silent. He was right, his honesty was brutal; he said what he meant and didn't try to hide behind anything. It should have been refreshing to see such honesty, but the only thing that Louise felt was a sense of shock. Shock and a feeling of desire, hot and urgent the way it had been in the office.

'Shall we go upstairs?' he asked, breaking the momentary silence.

Louise said nothing, just stood and followed him out of the bar, avoiding the eyes of the waitress and the barman who watched them leave.

'You do look very nice,' Westerham repeated when they were in the elevator going up to his room.

'There's one thing wrong with your sort of honesty,' Louise said, following him out of the elevator and into the corridor.

'What's that?'

'It's cold.'

Westerham didn't reply. He unlocked the door to his room and pushed it open. The light was on, and Louise went in first. It wasn't a particularly big room: a good sized bed with an open suitcase on it, a TV, a desk, an adjoining bathroom.

15

Louise was about to say something when he seized her from behind, taking her face and twisting it back to kiss her on the mouth. His touch was electric; she twisted and turned, forcing her mouth into his. She turned completely, taking his head in her hands too, wanting to eat him, wanting to bite and suck and lick. There was something animal about him, and it brought out the animal in her too.

He broke free, threw the open suitcase to the floor and began to strip off. Louise watched him, her eyes feasting on him. In a moment he was naked, his strong hard prick jutting from a dense black bush of hair. She moved closer, kissing him on the chest, running her hand up his strong thighs. Her sex was wet, aching for his prick. She wanted him quickly, violently, to fill her with all his strength.

He fell back on the bed and Louise fell with him, her body pressed against his, her nipples poking against her tight dress and rubbing against the tight mat of hair on his chest. He pulled her higher, took her mouth again. His hands were all over her, moving up her back, up her dress, over her backside. They were a twirl of bodies, rolling wildly on the bed, exploring each other hungrily.

She sat up and he pulled the dress over her head, throwing it to the floor with scarcely a glance. Apart from her high heels she was naked, and for a moment she sat on his chest, letting him eat her nakedness with his greedy eyes. His hands sought her breasts, cupped them, played with her red nipples till she moaned. Her pussy was wet, thick sticky cream spreading from between her thighs to his chest, scenting him, marking him like an animal.

He pulled her down and round, he was on her, his prick pressed hard against her belly. She was breath-

16

ing hard, aching to have him inside her; she was dying for it, wanting prick like she'd never wanted it before. She stroked his hardness lovingly, enjoying the contrast of the hardness with the silky feel of his glans. His hands were on her backside, spreading her buttocks and playing with her sex from behind. She moaned, ecstatic when a finger pressed tentatively into her sex.

He moved lower, buried his face in her lovely round breasts while his fingers went deeper into her raging hot pussy. It felt like heaven, and she was gasping for breath. He seemed to know where to touch her, when to tease and when to press forward. His fingers were moving rhythmically while his lips teased a nipple into his mouth. Louise cried out, froze into position as she climaxed powerfully.

Westerham turned her over onto her belly and mounted her from behind, forcing his hardness tight between her arse-cheeks. 'Oh please . . . please . . .' she moaned deliriously, the teasing of his prick in her backside too much for her to bear. She arched her back, forcing her backside apart, wanting him to enter her, to fuck her long and hard. He was a bastard. Why was he tormenting her so much?

He was moving rhythmically, pressing his prick between her arse-cheeks and letting his balls press against her sex. Each stroke was agony, each tantalising thrust making her sex hotter and wetter. She pushed him off, onto his back. His prick was wet with her sex-cream that had been smeared between her bottom-cheeks. She kissed his prick lovingly, worshipping it with her mouth, sucking it deep between her lips.

Then she quickly sat astride him, sitting down firmly over his prick. She cried out, a long cry that ended as a whisper. He was inside her and moaning softly, bucking his hips powerfully as she ground her backside down on him. It felt so good, her eyes rolled and the pleasure pulsed through her, waves of white hot pleasure. His hands were on her buttocks, pulled her down, round, this way and that. They moved as one, lost in the urgency of their fucking, oblivious to everything but the pure physical pleasure.

Louise climaxed again and again, each time being taken out of herself, each time losing everything then coming to with the hard rod still thrusting into her. He cried out once, his face strained, a look of delicious agony on his lips, the look of ecstasy reflected in the powerful pumping of his prick as he filled her with waves of thick come.

Westerham woke up early, glanced at the clock and then at the sleeping body beside him. Louise. He smiled. They had made love intensely, all night long and then when they were both exhausted she fell asleep in his arms. He covered her nakedness and slipped into the bathroom, careful not to disturb her sleep.

He showered slowly, stretching his muscles, washing away the sweat of sex that had bound him so closely to Louise. She was good, and he knew that in her way she was as honest as he was. He had to take her word for Christie's innocence, even if Christie was being incredibly difficult, or stupid, depending on how you looked at it. Her loyalty was wasted on Christie, but Westerham had to respect it.

Cold. She was right too, his honesty was cold. But

it was something pure, something unimpeachable, solid, dependable.

'I'm going to be late,' Louise told him when he emerged from the shower. She was sitting up in bed, the cover held chastely around her chest.

'Will Christie be there to see you?' he asked, letting the towel drop from his waist. She looked lovely, her eyes partly hidden by the fringe of golden hair.

'Look, Westerham,' she said wearily, brushing the hair from her eyes, 'you're after the wrong man. Tony Christie has done nothing, nothing at all.'

'Then why's he disappeared?'

'Because he's scared.'

'Of what exactly?'

'You,' she said coldly.

Westerham laughed. 'Scared of me? It's not me he has to be scared of.'

'Yes, you. He knows what sort of a man you are, you'll find something even where nothing exists. Why don't you just leave us alone?'

'Us? Leave us alone? That's significant, isn't it?'

Louise eyed him with the same look of contempt that she had when they had first met, only this time he felt sure there was something else there. Something beyond contempt – pity. 'You sad bastard,' she said softly. 'It's not us you should be looking at. Look at yourself.'

'I'm not the one in trouble,' he snapped.

'Then look at Peter Bartlett,' she snapped back, and then she put her hand to her mouth; she had said too much.

'Thanks, I will,' he smiled.

19

2

The flat was at the top of a long narrow flight of stairs, and by the time Sarah had reached the top she was quite out of breath. She waited to catch her breath, leaning back against the wall, trying to control her nerves too. Eddie had sort of half convinced her that the film – and she still didn't have a proper title – was for real. What she still wasn't sure about was the type of film it was going to be, but caution was a natural reaction to anything that Eddie was involved in.

She stood up straight, swallowed hard and pressed the doorbell. At least the flat was in a nice part of town, and not in some sleazy dive in Soho or somewhere. And Dominique had sounded nice enough on the phone, very friendly, down-to-earth, and with a sense of humour too. Sarah had expected her to be much colder, and in one way she felt a little cheated that Dominique hadn't sounded more sinister.

'Hi, you must be Sarah,' the woman that answered the door said brightly, her friendly smile inviting Sarah into the flat.

'Dominique?' Sarah asked, hesitating at the threshold.

'Yes, that's right. You look surprised.'

Sarah stepped into the flat. 'I thought you'd be . . . I don't know, I thought you'd be different.'

'Older?' Dominique asked, leading the way into a brightly lit front room.

'Yes, older, much older.'

'Please, take a seat. Do you want a drink? Tea, coffee?'

'Coffee, thanks. White, no sugar.'

'The kettle's on,' Dominique said, pointing to the kitchen that opened onto the front room. 'I don't know why people should think that you have to be a certain age to do this.'

Sarah looked at her. She looked to be still in her early twenties; her face still bore the traces of adolescence, her eyes and lips were childlike, yet to bear the thin lines of maturity around them. Her hair was long, very black, as if it had been dyed that colour; it made her skin seem deathly pale, an effect heightened by her lack of make-up. 'I'm sorry,' Sarah apologised after a moment, 'I'm staring.'

'I'm sorry if I've let you down.' Dominique smiled, then laughed happily.

'I'm being silly, aren't I?' Sarah smiled back weakly. She suddenly wished that Eddie was with her; he would at least know what to do and what to say.

'No, not really. But I suppose lots of people have very fixed ideas about what I do, and you're no different from them.'

The kettle clicked off in the kitchen and Dominique got up to make the coffee, leaving Sarah alone for a moment. It had started badly. Sarah hadn't meant to offend but this was a new experience for her; she had no idea what a dominatrix did or how she was supposed to act with one. It wasn't the sort of thing that drama school had prepared her for.

'Sorry, can we start again?' Sarah asked, taking a steaming mug of coffee from Dominique.

'Sure. Tell me about what you're doing,' Dominique agreed, sitting in the settee opposite Sarah. She was dressed in a baggy sweatshirt and faded jeans, as far removed from a fetish uniform as was imaginable.

'Eddie, the guy that gave me your name and number, might be able to get me a film part playing a professional dominatrix. I just wanted to talk to a real one to get some feel for the part.'

'Eddie Watson?'

'Yes, do you know him?' Sarah asked, wondering just what his connection to Dominique really was.

'Sure, I know him, but not professionally,' said Dominique.

'It's not that I object or anything,' Sarah said hastily, afraid that her unspoken assumption might have offended Dominique.

'That's okay, it was a natural thing to want to know. Is this your first film?'

Sarah shook her head. 'I've had bit parts in a few films so far, but this one could be my big break. It's a good part, central to the whole film really. And I'll play it sympathetically,' she stressed.

'What's the plot?'

'Well, it's about power.' Sarah repeated what Eddie had told her; she hadn't seen a script yet. 'It's about a politician who gets mixed up with a prostitute . . . Sorry . . .'

'He gets mixed up with a professional dominatrix and it ruins a promising career,' Dominique finished the story, making it sound like a tired cliché, her voice the epitome of boredom.

'But it's about power,' Sarah insisted. 'Who has the power? The politician or the dominatrix?'

'Don't you mean the Mistress or her Slave?'

'Is that the right terminology?' Sarah asked innocently.

'Yes. Your question is about power. Who has the power, the Mistress or the Slave? Right?'

'Yes, that's right. She's the Mistress,' she repeated, the words sounding strange but somehow apt. There were connotations; the words echoed with a thousand hidden meanings that Sarah could only guess at.

'But that's the wrong question,' Dominique stated, flashing Sarah a sly smile.

'What is the right question then?' Sarah asked, disconcerted.

'The question is, who has the pleasure? Mistress or Slave?'

'Pleasure?'

Dominique threw her head back and laughed, her dark hair flowing like glistening black oil. 'That's what this is all about, pleasure. Why do you think a man would submit to his Mistress, if not for pleasure? Why do you think a politician would risk everything? Not because it's something to impress his constituents.'

Sarah nodded. She hadn't considered the motivations before. Dominique was obviously correct, and the pleasure had to be powerful, so intense that a man would risk everything for it. 'And what about her? If she's only doing it for the money then he's winning, he gets the pleasure.'

'What makes you think she does it for the money?'

'I see,' Sarah said blankly. She felt embarrassed but managed to hide it. 'So they both do it for pleasure. In that case my question is irrelevant. They do it for pleasure, power has nothing to do with it.'

'I didn't say that,' Dominique corrected. 'Power is all part of it, part of the pleasure, part of the ritual. The transfer of power from Slave to Mistress can be intensely erotic.'

'Erotic,' Sarah repeated.

Dominique laughed again. 'You don't know anything about this, do you? You haven't even thought about it before.'

'That's true. I mean it's never been anything that's interested me, or any of my boyfriends. I don't know, it's the sort of thing that's sordid and dirty, not for normal people . . .'

'Well,' Dominique said coldly, 'you certainly know how to make friends and influence people.'

Sarah looked up sharply. 'I'm sorry. For an actress, I'm pretty hopeless at hiding my feelings. I didn't mean to imply that you're not normal or anything.'

'I'll be honest with you too, Sarah,' Dominique said, leaning forward conspiratorially. 'I'm not sure that I can put everything into words, it's a very difficult thing to explain. How important is this part to you?'

'Very important,' Sarah replied quietly.

'Then let me show you. Let me show you what this is all about. Isn't that what you want? To understand?'

'Yes . . .' she whispered hesitantly.

'Good. Join me at my chamber tomorrow. I'll give you the address.'

'What exactly – '

'Just be there,' Dominique laughed. 'And leave all your preconceptions behind. If you're going to play the role sympathetically, I want you with an open mind.'

A chamber. Sarah had been through the dictionary: a bedroom, a judge's chamber, a torture chamber, an enclosed body, a vessel. Each meaning or phrase conjured up an image, pictures in her mind that frightened her. In truth she had no idea what to expect, her preconceptions had already been confounded by Dominique. This time Sarah wanted to go in without judgements, wanting to understand what it was that Dominique couldn't put into words.

The heavy oak door was nondescript, a solid door like any other in a smart Victorian townhouse close to the heart of London. Sarah knocked and felt the solid brass handle hum and vibrate, the sound echoing through the house. She waited a moment then saw the spy-hole change colour. Someone was there, looking out through the fish eye at the distorted world outside, as if the world inside were the only reality.

'I'm looking for Dominique,' Sarah told the old woman who pulled the door open a fraction.

'She's expecting you, madam,' the old woman said, opening the door slightly more, so that Sarah could squeeze in.

'I'm Jenny, Mistress Dominique's maid,' the old woman explained, gesturing for Sarah to move further into the house.

'Every chamber needs its maid,' Sarah thought, and she wasn't sure whether it was a smart joke or not. The house was dark, the heavy black door blocking out the light of day, the walls painted a dull grey that did nothing to add space or light.

'Is Dominique here?' Sarah asked, entering the first room that led off the passage.

'Yes, madam. Would you like a drink? Whisky? Vodka?'

'No, nothing thank you.'

'Please wait here, madam,' Jenny said, her cool manner betraying no emotion. 'When the Mistress is ready she will see you.'

Sarah watched her leave the room, then she sat down on the heavy black leather armchair. The small room was shrouded in a suffocating darkness; tall rectangular windows were hidden behind thick velvet drapes. The walls were bare, the bare floor of stripped pine stained a dark brown so that it almost obscured the wood. The whole effect was to turn thoughts inward, with nothing to distract the mind, nothing to focus on but what was to come.

'This is more like a cell than a waiting room,' Sarah said out loud. Her voice sounded small and weak, hardly able to fight through the darkness. The interview had been strained and uncomfortable; now Dominique wanted things on her terms, but it still left Sarah feeling lost.

There were muffled voices out in the hallway; Sarah recognised Jenny's voice, then the front door slammed shut and the whole building shook. Sarah swallowed hard and waited, convinced that Jenny was coming to fetch her. She waited, tensed up, but the minutes dragged by with no sign of Jenny. When she failed to arrive after a few more long minutes, Sarah got up and walked to the door, ready to walk out of the house without seeing Dominique.

'The Mistress is ready now,' Jenny said, opening the door and startling Sarah.

'Is that what you always call her?' she asked, following the old woman who was dressed from head to foot in black.

'Mistress will answer your questions,' Jenny said. She opened a door that led to a flight of steps down into a cellar. The walls were of bare stone, illuminated by splashes of red light from discreetly placed spotlights. Sound was dead; it carried no further than the darkness would allow. At the bottom of the steps there was another door, put together from rough timbers, a brass ring for a handle.

'You may enter the chamber standing up,' Jenny said, pushing the creaking door open and making way for Sarah to pass.

'Thank you,' Sarah said. She inhaled deeply and went into the chamber.

It took a moment for the darkness to clear, then the soft red lights focused, and Sarah stared wide-eyed at the chamber before her. The stone walls were studded with rings, hanging ropes, chains, constraints of every description. There was a metal cage in one corner, the black metal bars like a medieval prison cell. A tall wooden post stood beside the cage, a solid piece of wood hung with leather straps and cuffs. Opposite the cage there stood a pair of stocks, with padded holes for the hands and a larger hole in the middle for the head. A torture chamber, something from a nightmare age long ago, buried in the heart of a house in the middle of the city.

'Normally you'd be on your hands and knees,' Dominique said coolly.

Sarah turned and saw her, standing up straight,

27

behind the door. It was only the voice and the long jet-black hair that identified the masked figure. The top part of her face was covered by a black executioner's mask: two slits for eyes, Dominique's hair a long plait poking through a hole in the top. Her upper body was encased in a shiny black breast-plate, a plastic shell that held up a perfect pair of breasts, the nipples parted, exposed with the swell of her cleavage. The leather skirt was short, tight, clinging. Dominique's thighs looked long and smooth, firm fleshed. It looked as if she had been poured into a pair of thigh-length boots, again a shimmering material that was sensuously glossy, and finished with very long, very sharp-looking heels.

'So I'm honoured to be allowed to stand then?' Sarah smiled, managing to sound more cheerful than she felt. She was aware that she was staring, but Dominique looked so different, so . . . so . . . sexy.

'You're also honoured in that I'm allowing you to talk freely,' Dominique said, her mouth forming into a smile that seemed sinister because the top part of her face was hidden by the mask. She moved forward, her hips swaying gently, planting each step down hard so that the high heels crashed and snapped on the stone floor.

'I'd normally have to call you Mistress, and beg for . . . beg for whatever it is your slaves beg for.'

'You can call me Mistress anyway,' Dominique told her. 'I want you to begin to understand what it is that goes on here. This is my world now, my domain. Normal rules no longer apply.'

'Do you have a script?' Sarah asked, her laughter ringing false. Dominique was approaching, a preda-tor stalking, the eyes through the slits glaring with a fire that made Sarah nervous.

'Why are you so nervous?' Dominique asked, her voice strange and insinuating.

'I'm not nervous.'

'Call me Mistress,' Dominique insisted.

'Yes, Mistress,' Sarah whispered.

'Isn't that good? Doesn't that give you a little thrill of pleasure?'

'Yes, Mistress,' Sarah admitted, her heart pounding. Dominique was in front of her, her glossy lips smiling, the eyes behind the mask staring without shame. Sarah wanted to reach out and touch her, to feel with her fingers the sensuous leather garments, the glossy layers that clothed Dominique's exquisite body.

'Here, I am the queen. This is my pleasure chamber, everything here is designed to give me pleasure. But I'm a good queen. A queen-bitch indulgent enough to let my slaves steal their pleasure from mine. Do you understand what I'm talking about?'

'No, Mistress,' Sarah breathed, too afraid to do anything but gaze into the mysterious eyes behind the mask. She felt strange, suddenly afraid, so that she was trembling, her whole body shaking. She felt on the verge of something terrible, something fearful from which there was no possible escape.

'It's good, isn't it? The fear. I can see it in your eyes, those lovely fluttering eyes that are fixed on mine. Are you afraid that I'll eat you all up?'

'Please, Dominique . . .' Sarah said weakly, managing to break away from the hypnotic stare. She turned away, her eyes falling on the whips and chains on the wall beside her.

Dominique moved forward quickly, lifting Sarah's long plain skirt and pressing her fingers deep into

29

Sarah's panties. 'You're wet,' Dominique whispered, her hot breath stroking Sarah's face like a lover's caress.

'Yes, Mistress,' Sarah whispered, feeling her pussy flooding with thick sexual fluid. She felt weak, unable to resist Dominique in any way.

'On your knees, now!' Dominique hissed, pulling her hand away from between Sarah's thighs and then bringing her fingers to her nose. She breathed deeply, taking in Sarah's scent and smiling approvingly.

Sarah fell to her knees instantly. She felt the shame rising up, making her face burn red and her heart pound violently. At the same time, she felt the desire flame inside her, merging imperceptibly with the shame and guilt; a kind of secret pleasure that was raw and sexual and pulsing, like the heat in the heart of her quim. She looked up at Dominique and realised that Mistress was beautiful; there was a hardness and purity in her image that transcended everything Sarah had ever thought about or believed in.

'Do you see it now? What it is that my slaves want from me?' Dominique demanded, snapping her heels hard on the ground. Her legs were parted, one on either side of Sarah, her hands on her hips, her head held contemptuously high.

'Yes, Mistress,' Sarah repeated, staring up with a look of desire burning in her eyes, wanting now to give herself completely to Mistress.

'Well? What is it that you want, slave?'

'Anything, Mistress . . . anything . . . Teach me . . . Teach me how to be your slave . . .' Sarah pleaded incoherently, her eyes filled with tears. A voice in the back of her head was berating her for being stupid, for demeaning herself so abjectly, but it was a voice lost in the muddied swirl of contradictory emotions.

'Undress – now!'

Sarah stood up and pulled her clothes off quickly; it was cold and her nipples were puckering but it didn't matter. It made perfect sense for her to be naked, it represented her true nature; naked before the Mistress clothed in her sensual uniform of power. The Slave had to be naked, powerless. Sarah consoled herself with the thought that she really was learning, that her research was authentic, anything but the thought that she was submitting for real.

'Hurry up!' snapped Dominique, forcing Sarah to move quickly.

In a moment she was naked and on her hands and knees again, on the floor. 'I'm ready, Mistress,' she said quietly, her voice quivering uncontrollably.

'Next time you enter the chamber this is how you'll enter – naked and on all fours,' Mistress declared. 'Now, follow me.'

Sarah crawled after Mistress, her eyes fixed on the beautiful boots and the short skirt that was wrapped tight around Dominique's backside. It was all so new, she had no idea what to expect now. The sheer strangeness of it all made her feel even more at Dominique's mercy.

Mistress stopped by the metal cage. She lifted one leg and rested it on one of the horizontal bars, the steel tip of her heel reflecting the weak light. 'This is where bad slaves are locked. Often they're hooded and restrained, arms behind the back, chained into position, a gag in the mouth. But I'm a good queen, and if I'm feeling especially good they may take nourishment.' She pointed to a plastic dog bowl full

31

of water by the side of the cage. 'Have some. You're thirsty, aren't you?'

'Thank you Mistress,' Sarah said, grateful to be allowed to dry her parched throat and amazed again that Dominique had so much understanding of how her slave felt. She knelt down and lapped at the cool sweet water, lapping at it like an animal, careful not to touch the bowl with her hands. When she sat up she saw Dominique smiling and felt a thrill of pride that she had pleased her Mistress.

'Good. You did that very well. You see it's important at all times to remind the slave of his or her position. And what position is that?'

'On hands and knees, Mistress.'

'Subservient. Submissive. Obedient. Are you still wet?'

'Yes, Mistress.'

'Have you ever had sex with another woman?'

Sarah hesitated: the question was unexpected and too personal. She looked away, unable to answer.

'I'll punish you for that,' Dominique promised coldly. 'Now, have you ever made love to another woman?'

The cold threatening tone, the menace in the partly hidden eyes, made Sarah regret not answering. She didn't know what punishment to expect, but the walls were lined with implements of cruelty and pain, instruments that made her shudder just to look at them. 'No, Mistress. Never.'

'I'm going to come on your tongue,' Dominique told her, 'and then I'll punish you for not answering.'

'But . . . please, Dominique . . .'

The slap was a white explosion of pain that had Sarah clutching her cheek with horror. She looked up and her eyes were full of tears. Dominique hoisted herself up onto the metal cage, clamping her heels behind the bars so that her legs were parted, the short leather skirt creating a dark shadow between the thighs.

Slowly, Sarah crawled forward, staring up at Dominique, who waited expectantly. Sarah moved delicately, afraid to touch her Mistress with anything but her soft lips. Her mouth was dry again and she wished she were allowed to sup the water from the bowl, to drink like a bitch. The leather had perfumed Dominique, her body scented by her fetish clothes, so that body and garment were the same.

Sarah inched closer, dipping her head under the tight band of leather, her mouth close to the naked sex that was partly opened by Dominique's position. Sarah kissed her gently, barely touching her soft lips against the underside of Dominique's smooth thighs. Dominique's skin was cool, soft, delicately perfumed. Sarah kissed her again, brushing her face against the tight curls of hair at the mouth of the sex. She felt the heat, the pussy lips dappled with dew drops of honey. Unable to resist any longer, Sarah pressed her tongue into the wetness, into the opening dripping with thick creamy essence. It was the first time she had touched another woman, but it felt good, the taste of sex on her tongue totally natural.

Dominique moaned softly, and Sarah felt happy, pleased to be serving her Mistress. She pressed her tongue deeper, sucking the juices into her mouth where she savoured the sweet taste that was uniquely Dominique. She sought the fiery cunt-bud, sought it and found it, hard and throbbing. Dominique moaned louder, jerking her hips forward so that Sarah could eat her more. Sarah's own sex was

33

aching, filled with an animal desire that was translated into the movements of her mouth. Her breasts were rubbing against the cool patent leather boots, the nipples brushing against the smooth coolness that was so arousing.

Dominique reached down suddenly, clutched a handful of Sarah's hair and forced her face deeper. Sarah cried out: the way Dominique was pulling her hair was painful, but a different kind of pain. She sucked and licked, her mouth hungry for Dominique's sex, wanting to give absolute pleasure and to derive pleasure for herself. *Stealing pleasure*, just as Dominique had explained.

Sarah's tongue was deep inside Dominique, her mouth open, letting the juices dribble down her throat. Dominique cried out, thrust her hips forward, arching her back, her sex pouring forth into her slave's grateful mouth. When Dominique released her, Sarah understood that her Mistress had reached climax. She lapped gratefully at Dominique's sex, greedy for every drop of come, eager to serve as well as possible. Her mouth and face were perfumed, smeared with nectar, marked for possession.

Dominique disengaged herself and stepped down from the cage. Her face was patterned with drops of sweat, the eyes behind the mask burning as intensely as ever. She stood straight, letting the short tight skirt cover her sex once more. 'Now the punishment,' she remembered, her voice still strong and powerful.

Sarah crawled after Mistress, her eyes fixed on the swaying buttocks, on the heels clicking on the floor, on the play of light on the long shiny boots. Her head was spinning, full of delicious confusion. Every

34

breath was filtered through the scent of Dominique's sex, still suffusing her mouth. Her breasts swayed as she crawled along, the hardened nipples missing the smooth glossiness of the boots, the rubbing together of her thighs sending spasms of pleasure pulsing through her.

Dominique stopped by a padded seat, a short three-legged stool in a corner. She sat down, parted her thighs and motioned for Sarah to crawl forward. Sarah obeyed, swallowing her apprehensions. She knelt low and kissed Mistress on the thigh again, wanting to use her mouth to avoid the punishment.

'Enough of that,' Dominique said coldly, her strong voice sounding nothing but total control. 'Across here,' she said, indicating.

Sarah did as she was told. She slipped between Dominique's thighs and then bent over one knee, her legs held in place by Dominique's other knee. 'Like this, Mistress?' she asked, anxious to know that she was doing well, eager to have confirmation that she was pleasing her Mistress. Dominique made no reply, but Sarah felt her reach for something.

'What are the rules?' Mistress asked.

'Subservience. Submission. Obedience,' Sarah repeated, her voice lost in the semi-darkness.

The snap of leather on flesh was drowned by the piercing scream that tore from Sarah's lips. She kicked and struggled, her backside ablaze, but to no avail; Mistress held her close. She turned, saw Mistress's arm high, a thick leather strap held tightly, a look of iron determination behind the mask. She watched helplessly, screaming even before the leather strap came down hard on her bottom-cheeks a second time. The pain was intense, a white flash that left a red heat on her smooth skin. She knew that her skin would be marked, she could feel the tracks of chastisement burning deep into her flesh. The pain was unbearable; a third stroke of the strap was as intense as the first two.

By the time of the fourth stroke Sarah was out of her mind, her voice hoarse from her cries of despair. The heat from her bottom seemed to be bleeding into her, seeping like lava from her arse-cheeks to her sex. The pain changed in nature, she perceived it differently, filtered it through altered sensibilities. It was pain that was also pleasure, an ache that made her feel breathlessly hot, her sex pulsing like a heart. She twisted again, saw the upraised arm and then she moved into it, lifting her bottom to meet the lick of the strap.

Her cries stopped, hesitated, became softer, more urgent, a gasping for breath, delirium. The sixth stroke bit keenly between her bottom-cheeks, just under her sex. She exhaled heavily; her back was arched to meet the blow and then she wilted. The orgasm had been a blinding explosion of energy, a sudden blissful eruption that had taken her out of herself and into the abyss where her whole body was pure sensation.

Sarah fell to the ground heavily when Dominique released her. She moved as if through a fog, still unable to quite see what had happened. The cold stone floor was heaven. She forced her bottom down against the coolness, the trail of come from her sex smearing onto the ground at the same time.

'Well, Sarah?' Dominique asked, smiling again.

Sarah was silent, searching for the words that would express the hundred different things that she felt. 'Thank you, Mistress,' she said at last.

'Do you understand now?'

'Some of it,' Sarah said softly, looking up at Dominique still seated on the stool, her heels flat on the ground, legs parted, her nipples pressed hard against the breast-plate.

'Enough to help you get what you want?' Dominique asked teasingly.

'No!' Sarah replied decisively. There was still so much to understand. The full impact of what had happened had still to hit home. Her mind was full of questions. She wanted to see more, to understand more, to experience everything.

'You sound very sure,' Dominique laughed.

'I feel different . . . You've done something to me . . . I just . . .' Sarah could feel the heat still on her backside, and her nipples throbbing with the same beat as the desire in her sex. Never before had she felt so sexual, as if her whole being were directed for the first time, all her energy channelled entirely for erotic pleasure.

Dominique saw the confusion on Sarah's face. 'Don't try to put it into words,' she told her softly. 'Just forget that. I mistrust words, they lie and they cheat. It's better to experience things as they are, to let the body do the understanding. Do you see that?'

'I don't know . . . Please, Dominique, will you teach me? I can't see how things can ever be the same again.'

Dominique stood up, the smile gone from her lovely red lips. 'The first lesson, slave, is to kiss Mistress's heels,' she said. 'And do it well.'

Sarah scrabbled forward. Her face was down by the cold floor; she could feel the cold sucking at her heat. The glossy boots were before her, a perfect image, the heels like talons, the instep a perfect geometric line, the toe cap tapering into a point that

37

was made for sucking. She flicked out her tongue, touched it to the cold patent leather; the effect was electric. She had never imagined anything so sexual, so purely erotic. Her nipples were throbbing, aching to be touched, to be handled. Her pussy was seeping droplets of sex-honey. The image of Mistress towering above, looking down scornfully at Sarah's backside patterned red by the strap, made Sarah feel utterly breathless.

Mistress snapped her heel on the ground and Sarah swooned, the fear and pleasure passing like a wave through her body. She pressed her face flat on the stone and took the heel fully into her mouth, sucking it lovingly. Her breath misted on the cold black leather, but still she sucked, out of her mind, overwhelmed by the sensation. She cried out, her cry muffled by the heel on her tongue. Tears poured from her eyes. She was shaking, she had orgasmed again, climaxed powerfully without even once touching her own sex. She had climaxed simply by paying abject obeisance to her Mistress. It filled her with a dark joy that made her want to weep with happiness.

3

Peter Bartlett. Formerly Operations Director, and a very successful one at that, now an Executive Director, and one of the three Executive Officers with direct day-to-day control of the company. Westerham was familiar with the name and with the reputation. They had even met briefly, when Westerham had been summoned by the Board to discuss the problems in the company. The meeting itself had been tense, the Board in two minds as to whether an investigation was required or not. There was the distinct smell of blood in the air, and the feel of egos mortally injured. The acrimonious atmosphere had not cleared when he was called in to listen, in grim silence, while the catalogue of problems was listed in a dull monotone by the Managing Director.

Westerham could clearly remember Bartlett: when he had spoken he held the attention of everyone in the room. Fit looking, fastidious, with grey eyes that scanned the room constantly. He was against an external investigation, and he made that abundantly clear in cool measured tones that were all the more effective because of the absence of emotion. He spoke just once, to reiterate his view, not because he thought he was going to win the argument – that he had lost in the private meeting earlier – but because he wanted Westerham to know what was going on.

Westerham had listened calmly, looking directly at Bartlett to get a measure of the man. The politics of the boardroom, as grim and bloody as any, were clear to see. Bartlett was so obviously the pretender to the throne, staking out his claim in full view, waiting in the wings for the king to die so that he could take control. The decision to call in an investigator had been a closely fought one, and victory had been narrow; the tense faces were evidence of that, as well as the acrid smell of cigarette smoke and sweat in the room. Bartlett had just lost that battle, but perhaps it had been a Pyrrhic victory for the other side, for he spoke with the certainty of victory and it was impressive to watch and listen.

He had spoken once, but it was enough. It gave Westerham fair warning that his job would not be an easy one, and that he should expect interference from the highest levels in the company. Situation normal. He listened in silence to the litany of complaints, the insoluble problems, the measures that had been tried and failed, and finally to Bartlett's ominous statement of intent. Then it was his turn to speak. He simply stood up, looked at them coldly and listed his fee. That was it, no promises, no explanations, no list of satisfied clients, no hard sell. It was take it or leave it. It was the only way to respond to Bartlett, the only way to impress on the Board the urgency of the situation and to let them see what sort of man they were dealing with.

He didn't wait to be asked to leave. He had excused himself immediately, clearing the way for a renewed bout of infighting, letting them slug it out amongst themselves. It was a gamble, his performance could have swayed people in either direction. As he left he was sure that Bartlett's half smile was one of confidence, that Bartlett felt himself certain of instant victory. Looking round at the tired faces, at the faceless old men who constituted the majority of the Board of Directors, Westerham knew that Bartlett had lost the second round too, that there were too many people afraid of him to give him the upper hand – yet.

The call had come to his hotel room barely three hours later. The job was his, and the battle had begun. Bartlett was too powerful to tackle directly, and just because he had wanted things kept in-house, it didn't mean that he was up to no good. Things were never that simple. The place to start was in the accounts, in the reams of computer hard-copy that should have told the story but didn't. It was tedious, time consuming work, but it needed to be done. Westerham worked at it diligently, but there was nothing there, nothing worth knowing anyhow, as the auditors had found out for them-selves. The story lay outside of the reams of paper, it couldn't be reduced simply to tables and columns of numbers. But it was the place to start, it gave background, set the scene.

And from the books Westerham had gone back to the directors, meeting several of them to talk pri-vately. But not Bartlett. Not even with any of Bartlett's allies; it was too early to open a line of communication. It was company politicking for sure, high politics, but in the nature of the job. And from there he had picked on Tony Christie, a relatively junior member of the board, and the man who had walked into Bartlett's shoes when Bartlett had moved up in the world. Except that Christie had suddenly gone abroad, even before Westerham had contacted his office to arrange an appointment.

Darling Louise, her cool features twisting in Westerham's mind; he pictured her spread across the desk while he fucked her furiously. Darling Louise, so aloof, so sexy, writhing as he had entered her; she had uttered Bartlett's name and then regretted it. It was no use questioning her any more, she would no more tell him what she knew than she would have told him where Christie had disappeared to. Such loyalty was wasted, but whereas she was being loyal to Christie she was afraid of Bartlett, that too was clear.

The next move was inevitable. Westerham picked up the phone and dialled Bartlett's number. He caught sight of himself in the mirror across the room, looking slightly dishevelled, stubble on his chin, dark rings under his eyes, hair a mess. The waitress had left her underclothes on the bed, the shimmering silky garments soiled, scented with his body as well as hers. He smiled, remembering that she had been panicky about being late for work. She had showered quickly then pulled her uniform on, chattering all the time. When she had been ready, when her uniform was on neat and tidy, her hair neatly brushed to one side, her lips painted a vivid red, he had taken her again. He had smothered her lips with urgent kisses, sucking away her protests, sucking away her will until she was breathing hard and deep.

He had pushed her onto the bed, pulled her skirt up and forced his prick into the wet heat of her sex. She sighed, melted, opened herself for his thrusting prick. He took her quickly, making her climax just once before shooting wads of thick come over the back of her thighs, smearing her with it, marking her with his essence. She lay in silence for a minute, her eyes wide, staring up at the ceiling, her breath harsh, gasping.

'You'll be late,' he reminded her, using her panties to wipe the thick white cream from her thighs. Her skin was soft and smooth, and his cream glistened on her, dew drops speckled up and down her thighs. He cleaned her quickly, wetting her panties so that they were dark and heavy with his juice.

She let him wipe her clean then rushed across to the mirror again, brushing her skirt down with her hands. 'Can I see you again tonight?' she asked, hurriedly trying to fix herself again, looking at him through the mirror while she brushed her long dark hair into place.

'Maybe,' was all he could allow her, but it was enough. On the way out she stopped to kiss him quickly on the mouth, her perfume mingling with the scent of sex. She went out to work without her silk knickers on, and he liked that, he liked the idea that she would be reminded of their love-making all day; every time she moved she would know that he had fucked her, that he had come on the soft smooth skin of her thighs.

'Mr Bartlett's secretary, how can I help you?' The voice, cool and efficient, broke Westerham's train of thought.

'This is Westerham, I'd like to talk to Mr Bartlett,' he stated, wondering what Bartlett's secretary looked like, trying to put together her picture from the coolness of her voice, from her prim and proper manner. He imagined her without even wanting to, without even trying.

'One moment, please,' she said, putting him onto

hold. A moment later she came back. 'Putting you through.'

'Westerham, what can I do for you?' Bartlett said, sounding relaxed and in control.

'I've been talking to some of the directors, just to get an understanding of how things operate,' Westerham explained. 'I'd like to talk about the film studios. Would it be possible for us to discuss this side of things?'

'Still no sign of Christie then?' Bartlett noted, making it plain that he knew what was going on.

'No, no sign of the man.'

'What do you make of that?'

'It's inconvenient,' Westerham said, unwilling to be drawn further. There was a moment of silence; Bartlett was waiting for more but there was nothing more to say.

'I'm fairly busy at the moment,' Bartlett said, his voice betraying the slightest touch of annoyance.

'I just need some background, that's all.'

'Talk to Jen, she has my diary. I'm sure she can find fifteen minutes for you.'

'Fuck you,' Westerham whispered to the dull ache of the dialling tone.

The ringing of the phone stopped, but it refused to die at once. The faint echo of its insistent shrill seemed to hang in the air until it became part of the silence. The clock on the wall in the sitting room seemed to be ticking slower than the clock beside the bed, the two sounds phasing in and out, in and out as Sarah listened. She listened without caring what the time was; it was just the sound that she sought, losing herself in the rhythm that moved fast

44

or slow, sometimes dissonant, sometimes synchronous.

She was empty, washed out, lying in bed while the sun worked its way into the afternoon. Sleep had come and gone, a fitful sleep that gave no comfort and no respite from the thoughts that spiralled round and round and wouldn't stop. Confusion, shock, anger, fear, all had passed through her, and she had felt each with an intensity that left her numb.

She was wearing pyjamas, soft, warm, white. It had taken some time to find them, buried deep in one of the wardrobes, permanently creased and starched. It felt strange putting pyjamas on again; it felt strange slipping under the covers and not feeling the fresh white sheets against her naked skin. It felt strange, but not as strange as seeing the vivid red marks across her body, the stripes that Mistress had made with the strong leather strap.

The sight of the marks on her skin had made Sarah shiver, and then they made her weep uncontrollably, burying her face in her hands as her body was racked by painful sobs. She didn't want to see herself, she didn't want to remember, she didn't want to know. The pyjamas were retrieved in a tearful panic, but putting them on made her feel better, made her feel warm and safe again, like a child.

What had she done? Why had she allowed herself to be humiliated and punished, whipped with a strap in a dark and damp dungeon by a woman she hardly knew? The questions went round and round, robbing her of sleep and energy. The images crowded her mind, filled her consciousness as she went over it again and again. Marlon Brando, Jimmy Dean, big guys in black leather, danger, excitement, feeling sexy, Mistress. Was that the only conclusion? Was it

45

a natural progression, the thrill of danger leading directly to submission to Mistress?

It had been so good. A revelation. Scrabbling on her knees, abject before her Mistress, submitting to it all with a fire raging in her sex. That was the worst part, the part that was unforgivable, unforgettable, inexplicable. She liked it. No, she loved it. She had accepted it all, sucking Mistress's pussy, crawling on her hands and knees, being beaten, and adoring Mistress for doing it.

Life had changed. What was there to do? One moment she was sane, one moment she was like everyone else, ordinary, everyday, and the next she wasn't. She was suddenly someone else, someone she'd never imagined, a stranger, someone she wasn't even sure she liked or understood.

The phone began to ring again, quickly turning from an annoying tone to a shrieking electronic scream. Sarah waited, covering her ears, closing her eyes until it stopped again. There were too many questions, and she was too tired to think about it any more. She sat up, forcing herself to move from the protective warmth of the covers.

'You've got to get up,' she told herself, secretly checking to see if she sounded the same, almost afraid that her voice had changed to reflect the change inside.

She padded across to the bathroom, her face tight, eyes heavy. She plugged the bath and switched the taps on full, oddly startled by the sudden rush of water, affected by the rising steam and the pure physical presence of the water jetting powerfully from the taps. The steam attacked the mirror, obscuring the reflection that was altogether too sharp. She turned from her reflection, slipped off her pyjamas and waited for a moment. When she turned back, her reflection was opaque, unfocused by the droplets of mist on the mirror. But still it was clear enough to see the dark lines on her backside, thick lattice lines that had been inflicted by Mistress.

Sarah looked at herself until the reflection was nothing but a pale shape in the steam. The questions were stilled, silenced by the thumping of her heart and the hissing of the water. For a moment everything had been clear, there had been a sudden swell of emotion, she felt it for an instant – pride mixed with excitement. She had been punished by her Mistress, and the thought was electric.

She was going to go back. There was nothing else she could do. She had to confront Mistress – to exorcise the demon or submit to it willingly once more.

'Well, how did it go?' Eddie asked, his voice sounding flat and monotone over the phone despite the obvious urgency in the question.

'It was interesting,' Dominique replied after a moment of considered thought. She was taking the call in her chamber, clothed in rubber and leather and shrouded in darkness, the atmosphere just as she liked it.

'And?' he demanded, waiting for a simple yes or no answer, as if a positive or a negative were sufficient to convey everything that Sarah had experienced.

'And what?' Dominique smiled, picturing Eddie's growing exasperation; the dark glasses would be off, the hand would be slicking through his thick dark hair.

'Don't play with me, Dominique,' he warned

coldly, though the telephone made his voice tinny and rendered the threat laughable – not that she was afraid of him anyway.

'But that's what you want me to do, isn't it? Play.'

'Where's Sarah?'

It was an unexpected question. 'Isn't she with you?'

'I told you before,' he said, 'me and Sarah are not an item. There's nothing between us, I'm just doing the girl a favour, OK?'

'I find that very difficult to believe,' Dominique snorted.

'Believe what you like. You don't know where she is then?'

'Obviously not.'

'What happened between you?' Eddie asked.

Dominique smiled at the memory – it had been an interesting experience, and a good one. 'That's between Sarah and myself, you should know better than to ask that.'

'Do you think she can make it on film as a bitch?'

'That depends . . .' Dominique sighed. She didn't want to say more, but after what had transpired she could not see Sarah as a dominant in any way at all. Sarah was a submissive, natural, instinctive, born to it.

'Depends on what?' Eddie demanded, as always wanting simple answers to complex questions.

'She needs more . . . more training,' Dominique decided, certain that the word had different connotations for Eddie, if it had any connotations at all. She wasn't sure that words had connotations for Eddie at all; he was the sort of man that took everything at face value, words could only mean one thing, events have only one interpretation.

'How much is it going to cost?' he asked suspiciously.

'Not a penny more,' Dominique promised, knowing that money was his measure of everything.

'When can you do it?' was his next question, quite naturally.

'That depends on her doesn't it?'

'If she rings you, fix it up,' he ordered. 'If I manage to get through to her I'll get her to call.'

'And what about you Eddie? Wouldn't you like some training?'

'Just sort her out,' Eddie snapped, his irritation breaking through.

'Come on Eddie . . .' Dominique whispered into the phone, 'why don't you let me show you what Sarah's going to learn? Let me put you into harness, how about it, eh?'

'Cut that out. Sort her out, that's all.'

Dominique laughed, her laughter echoing through the chamber. 'What are you afraid of?' she taunted.

'Call me when it's done,' he ordered curtly then put the phone down.

He really was a nasty little insect, Dominique decided. She knew that he was afraid of her, afraid of what she would do to him, and even more afraid of his own reactions. Still, he had his uses, he brought her some interesting clients, and there was a certain sick fascination in watching his schemes unfold. The fact that Sarah had suddenly dropped out of view was definitely worthy of note; the experience had evidently been an unsettling one, and that was good, it was exactly what Dominique wanted.

She suddenly became aware of Vincent, his skin cool under her, his back stretched tight, the muscles

49

standing out taut. He was on hands and knees, immobile, silent except for the soft hissing of his breath, carrying her without complaint and without straining. He was strong, his ebony body perfectly muscled, his skin gleaming as if it had been oiled, making the perfect seat for Dominique to sit on. She ran her hand down his back, pressing her fingers over the tight ridges of muscle, stroking him like a finely bred animal. He shivered and she knew it was from desire and nothing else. His head was shaved, making him look mean and dangerous, but she had gagged him well, and his breath hissed in and out slowly.

She stood up, snapping her heels hard on the floor for good effect. He looked up at her with dark soulful eyes, scanning edgily, full of fear and desire merged into one. His eyes were at the level where her rubber stockings gave way to soft pale flesh, the shining black latex pressing tightly so that her thighs bulged slightly at the stocking top.

'Get rid of the phone,' she ordered curtly, 'then bring me my kitten.' She watched him scrabble across on the floor on hands and knees, carrying the telephone to the door of the chamber where Jenny would be ready to take it away. He was nearly naked, only the leather gag over the mouth and the harness around the waist clothed him. That was how she liked Vincent, hard leather straps around the waist and between his thighs, and a gag to keep his mouth shut.

Sarah needed more work; she was going to be hopeless as a dominatrix, she didn't seem to have the power in her. The only way was to show her, to let her watch while a male slave was punished. How would she react to that, Dominique wondered.

50

'You like my little kitten, don't you, Vincent?' Dominique purred softly, smiling sweetly as he crawled towards her, his eyes wide and fixed on her. 'Answer me!' she snapped angrily, startling him, her voice like a slap across the face. He nodded quickly, his lips tightening around the solid leather strap that held the gag in place.

'What should I do with you, Vincent? I'm too good to you, I'm too soft, you need someone to really keep you under control.' She reached out and took the dark bundle that he offered her, a dark bundle held up in his outstretched hands, a votive offering to Mistress. 'What should I do with you?' she asked again, trying to glean from the look in his eyes what it was that he desired from her. She twitched the dark bundle and the heavy strands of the cat unfurled, long fingers of heavy leather, knotted at the end, the claws of her beloved kitten.

Vincent was still, his eyes luminous in the semi-darkness, silent behind the gag, his supple body prostrate before Dominique. She stepped round him, circling menacingly, trailing the strands of the cat across his skin. 'Do you know, Vincent, I'm not sure you're worthy. You bore me, you bore the fuck out of me. Look at you, look at yourself, on hands and knees like an animal. Aren't you disgusted with yourself? Aren't you? There's no spirit in you is there, you're empty. I'm disgusted with you, even if you're not.'

He stirred, his eyes narrowed, looking at her with confusion and a growing anger. The muscles on his face tightened, his lips shut tight over the damp leather band holding the gag in place. Dominique walked round once more, stepping hard so that her heels were threatening spikes smashing hard on the

51

stone floor. 'Why don't you get up? Why don't you do something, you little shit?' she whispered into his ear, standing behind him and leaning over so that her long hair fell over her shoulders and lightly touched his cold skin. It was enough, the sneering tone, the pure contempt finally goaded him to action. He started to turn and rise at the same time, his hand reaching round to grab hold of her. She straightened up and stamped her heel down into his shoulder. He fell forward, his face hidden in the darkness, the gag unable to hold back the cry of pain that tore from his throat.

Dominique stepped forward, planted one heel flat on his back, pinning Vincent into place. He was writhing, his arm flailing, blindly trying to reach back to throw her off balance. It was good, his anger was real, his breath was harsh and the muscles in his back were pulsing. The first stroke of the cat across his bare back froze him, he was caught unexpectedly. A succession of strokes forced him down, each lash of the cat whistling through the air and then snapping hard against his skin.

Dominique walked slowly back across the chamber, fully in control of the excitement that was burning fiercely inside her. Detached yet aroused, she knew that her pleasure was only beginning. He was watching her, she didn't even have to look back, his eyes were burning into her. She reached for the cuffs and turned back. He was still on the floor, hardly moving, his face turned up in an attitude of pure supplication.

'Here!' she snapped imperiously and was gratified as he hauled himself up and crawled towards her. His dark skin was marked with long thin strands of red, the claw marks that the cat had left on him.

Droplets of sweat shimmered in the pale light, his perfect male body bathed in jewels of salt. He stopped before her, bent low and pressed his mouth to the tip of her boots. He couldn't lick but pressed his lips against the smooth patent leather.

She clamped his arms behind his back, taking a second to snap the cold steel cuffs on his wrists. He moaned; Dominique couldn't tell whether it was protest or approval. Not that it mattered in any way; nothing he did mattered. He sat up expectantly, his eyes drinking her in, feasting on the contrasts between her soft white skin and the glossy alter-skins of rubber and leather.

'Heel,' she said softly, no longer needing to scold or command; he was willingly hers. She could well imagine that the red stripes on his back were burning into his flesh; every sinew and muscle had to ache with pleasure and pain. He followed obediently at her heels, her pet, her little dog to play with as she wished. Her excitement was fever pitch but on the surface she was cool and in control. The heat in her sex, the delicious anticipation of desire to be satisfied, were kept from him. He was lost in his own world, bound in by his dreams and fantasies as much as by the physical constraints that he was subject to.

Dominique stopped at the stool and pointed to it with a gloved finger. He understood, and sat on it quickly, his back straight, his body rigid and waiting for her next move.

'Well, well, Vincent, so you are man enough to try to resist, sometimes . . .' she mused, walking round and round slowly, letting him watch her in silence. Her voice was soft, questioning almost, caressing him with low breathless words. 'If you're good,' she stopped before him and let her smile

53

warm her face, 'I may even allow another Mistress to handle you. Would you like that, Vincent? Would you like to be punished by another Mistress? Would you?'

The sharp slap across the face brought no responsive gesture, but when she reached down his prick was hard and throbbing. She squeezed hard, wrapping her gloved fingers tightly around the solid pole of flesh. His legs were apart, and he was sitting right on the edge of the stool so that his prick was jutting out hard and straight.

Dominique pulled down a zip at the side and the rubber mini skirt that had been wrapped tightly around her backside fell away. She smiled; his eyes had widened with excitement, homing in on the dark triangle of hair between her thighs. She straddled him at once, putting her legs over his so that her sex was pressing right up against the hardness of his prick. Her face was above his, and she took him in her arms, pressing her lips to the smooth dome of his head. His skin was dark against hers, the vivid contrast like that of rubber and flesh. It sent a thrill of pleasure through her, a spike of desire as potent as the cat had been on him. The perspiration rolled from his body, and with it the scent of his masculinity, his maleness.

'I'll have to give you to her,' she whispered, 'and she'll use you like an animal. She'll use you and then cast you aside, worthless, beneath contempt. But that's what I want. It's what Mistress desires, and what Mistress desires, Mistress gets.'

Her hands travelled down from his throat, over his smooth hairless chest, to the finely sculpted tightness of his stomach to the stiffness of his prick. Every touch of her fingers seemed to affect him, his breathing was harsh and his body was tensed. Her sex was hot and wet, rivulets of honey pouring from her open pussy to mingle with the sweat that poured from him. She began to touch herself, to put a probing finger into her sex, to enjoy the warmth and excitement of her own body. 'Can you breathe me?' she asked, pressing her pussy-soaked fingers under his nose.

The pleasure was too strong, she could wait no longer, she shifted suddenly, took his cock in her hand and forced herself down on it. She was impaled on him, his hardness going deep into her, connecting with the pleasure centres of her body so that she held still for an age, not wanting to move, not wanting to do anything but prolong the pure bliss that had surged through her.

She began to move against him, rising and falling urgently on his cock, fucking him quickly, wanting to take his hardness repeatedly, endlessly. His body was like stone, hard and unyielding, but she knew that he would respond. Her hands sought his nipples, two hard buds that stood firm on his chest, dark nodes of flesh that she caught in her fingers. He tensed again, she tightened her grip on his nipples, pulling hard, rubbing her thumb and fingers over and over. He moved, jerked, trying to escape the sharp stabs of pleasure-pain that she was inflicting. Every time he jerked, every time he struggled up, he went deep into Dominique. She was shifting and wriggling, driving herself in long deep strokes over his prick. She was fucking him, screwing him for her pleasure, and pleasure it was, pure animal desire that knew no bounds. She arched her back, her strangled cry escaping from her glistening lips. She climaxed but still he was driving deep into her, moving with a tortured rhythm, his eyes closed to eveything but her desire and her pleasure.

Dominique slapped him hard across the face, her fingers tingling with a pale aftertaste of what it had been for him. His nipples were jutting out like hard points, alive to the merest caress of her rubber-clad fingers. She was bouncing up and down on his hardness, the pleasure flaring like a flame under the breeze. Her nipples were hard but wrapped tightly in leather, and that added to the sensations, added to the sensual whirlwind that swirled around her.

She cried out again and felt the echo of it in Vincent's body. He froze, pressed against her, and then his prick was gushing thick waves of spunk into the wet redness of her pussy. They were frozen in time, wrapped together, two heart beats with one rhythm. Dominique moved first; she stood up, her face flushed pink and her body tingling. She looked down at Vincent, his body bruised and raw, his eyes out of focus as if he hardly knew what had happened.

'I meant it, Vincent,' she said breathlessly, removing the leather band from his mouth and the gag with it. 'I'm going to give you to another.'

He was gasping for breath, sucking in the air because it was sweet and pure and free. 'As you wish, Mistress,' he finally said, his deep voice tinged with excitement.

'When I call you I want you here,' she told him confidently. 'That means you stop whatever you're doing no matter what time or day, and come to me. Understand?'

For a moment Dominique was certain that he was going to protest, but the protest never made it to his lips. 'Yes, Mistress, I will obey.'

'Good,' Dominique smiled. 'Now, my boots need cleaning. And do it well,' she warned.

Vincent fell to his knees, his arms still cuffed behind his back. He obeyed without question, using his lips and tongue to worship the sharp heels that had forced him to submission earlier. Dominique felt the desire flare up again, the desire that she always felt when she had a well-trained slave at her feet, willingly submitting to every whim, undergoing every humiliation because that was what she wanted. It was power, raw and sexual, and that was what Sarah had to see for herself.

4

Westerham waited two days before making an appointment to see Bartlett. It had rankled to wait but he wasn't in a strong enough position to force the matter. As it was, he had been grudgingly allotted a fifteen minute slot, and that was only after haggling like an eager salesman with Bartlett's secretary. In the meantime, Westerham had to make do with going back to the books and interviewing a succession of tight-lipped minions. It was dead time, it didn't move the investigation an inch forward, and served only to blunt his reputation as a man who got results. It was frustrating but largely unavoidable.

Tony Christie had finally left a telephone message apologising for his absence, promising to return as soon as he had sorted out some unspecified family problem. Louise had relayed the message to Westerham in a deadpan monotone; she was cold, her voice betrayed neither excitement nor anger, as if their encounter had bleached her of emotion. Her coldness elicited no surprise. It was as he expected from her; her harsh words still rang in his ears no matter how hard he tried to block it out.

The fact that the investigation had ground to a halt bothered him more than anything else; it nagged at him constantly, eating away at the only thing that he prided himself on – efficacy. He had brooded on it for two days, fighting back his frustration until he could take no more, and then telephoned Jen to arrange a meeting with Bartlett. She had been expecting his call, there was a note of obvious satisfaction in her voice, and he knew that she would be reporting back to Bartlett directly. His manner was as off-hand as could be, but there was no denying that he was in a position of weakness, and Jen was as aware of that as her boss. The meeting, the begrudgingly allotted quarter of an hour, was arranged for an early Monday morning, and it left Westerham with two more days to kill.

He decided that it was better to disappear for those couple of days than to spend the time floundering about and getting nowhere, and getting there quite visibly. There were other things to attend to, and if he was incommunicado for a couple of days he knew that word would filter back to Bartlett fairly quickly. He changed hotel on the first morning, finding that the atmosphere where he had been staying had changed. It was threatening to become too domestic, too cosy. Caroline, the waitress, was becoming annoying; she seemed to want more from Westerham than just sex, even though he had made it clear that that was all he wanted from her. Her behaviour had become difficult, she showed signs of jealousy, being rude to a female guest that Westerham had taken to dinner. When he tried to talk to her about it afterwards it had ended in tears and sex, turning her sobs into sighs of pleasure, making her cling to him even more.

The new hotel had a pool, and soon after booking in he had gone down for a swim. The pool was empty, he dived into the stillness and swam a length under water, eyes closed, enjoying the feeling of immersion in the cold water. He surfaced, gasping for breath, his lungs burning slightly, and floated in the water for a moment before swimming back the way he had come. The rippling of the water echoed through the pool house, the light from the surface of the water shimmered on the white tiled walls. The acrid smell of the water filled his nostrils. It was an old pool, built at the same time as the hotel, just after the war he guessed from the design, and it was built for silence, designed to amplify the quiet, the pure white space carrying the natural light that poured through the glass ceiling.

He swam back and forth lazily, turning onto his back for a while, then turning to breast the water. It was a good place to think; when he felt tired he floated on his back, staring up at the grey sky through the glass and resting. This time, he promised himself, he was going to avoid any entanglements with hotel staff – no chasing after waitresses, chambermaids, receptionists or manageresses. It was better to concentrate on getting his job done, much better. And then he slipped round in the water and saw the lifeguard at the water's edge, her long blonde hair falling loose over her shoulders and contrasting with the bright red of her single-piece swimsuit. He swam towards her, slicing through the water quickly, his energy recovered.

'Hello,' she smiled, dangling her legs in the water.

'Hi,' he said, ducking under the water and pushing against the poolside as he set off swimming away from her. His pace was as slow and as measured as it had been before, even though she was watching him, had been watching him for some time as far as he could tell. He ducked down and swam back towards her, his casual glance taking in her long tanned thighs, the tight waist, her small round breasts, her nipples like points against the smooth surface of her swimsuit.

'Guest or visitor?' she asked as he reached her, blue eyes catching his as she smiled.

'Just booked in,' he said, stopping for a moment to catch his breath.

'I'm Jackie. You weren't supposed to be in the pool without an attendant,' she explained, bending her head so that her hair fell like a shower of gold to one side, reaching down past her breasts.

'I won't tell anybody if you don't,' he smiled, then pushed away, propelling himself forward into the water so that her reply was lost in his movement, carried away with the sound of the water that reverberated from wall to wall.

'Are you going to be long?' she asked when he reached her again, her tone a little colder this time.

'No, I don't think so,' he decided, looking up at the big round clock above the poolside, the hands edging jerkily towards noon.

'I'll be in the office for a few minutes,' she explained, standing up.

Westerham nodded, his eyes on her long legs, the water dripping down in little rivulets where she had been dangling her feet in the water. She turned and padded back into the office by the poolside, where she could watch him through an open hatch.

Waitresses, chambermaids, receptionists, manageresses – were swimming-pool attendants part of the list? He smiled to himself. She had a certain quality, a detached coolness that he liked in women. The lap back to the poolside was slow and unhurried, she was sitting by the hatch and reading something, her face was lowered and as she read she twined her

61

fingers through her long hair. Her face was unguarded and Westerham took the opportunity to study it, to appreciate the translucent quality of her skin, of her wide mouth and sharp chin, of her long eyelashes and deep intelligent eyes.

She looked up when he climbed out of the water, the droplets cascading over his body. 'Tired?' she asked, her eyes registering his interest in her as he walked towards the hatch.

'Yes, it feels good. Is it always this quiet?'

She shook her head. 'It's usually pretty busy. The pool's in use all day, and there's always at least half a dozen people around.'

'I like it like this,' he gestured to the silvery surface of the water, barely rippling so that the bottom of the pool and the surface seemed one and the same.

'Then avoid first thing in the morning and early afternoon,' she advised.

'And when are you here?' he asked, smiling.

'Early morning to late afternoon,' she said. The smile she returned was automatic, there was no feeling in it.

'And what about lunch?'

'What about it?'

'Would you join me?' he asked softly, his eyes connecting directly with hers, catching her so that she couldn't turn away. He saw her eyes flicker, recognised the questions, the doubt, the curiosity.

'I'm still on duty,' she explained hesitantly, tearing her gaze from him and back to the book that she had been reading.

'Do you know what I'm thinking?' He drew closer to her, leaning up into the hatch, the droplets of water from his wet hair cascading down his face and onto his chest.

'What?' she asked, tracing the tracks of the water coursing over his body with her eyes, droplets of water coursing over cool skin that was glistening.

'I want to fuck you,' he said quietly, his voice drawing her in, low and guttural but not quite brutal. 'I'm wondering whether you fuck on duty. I'm wondering how you'd react if I reached out and stroked your breasts with my wet fingers,' he paused for a second. 'And you're thinking, who does he think he is? And you're thinking, I should just slap his face and tell him to piss off. But there's more, isn't there?'

She nodded uncertainly, her face colouring red, her blue eyes unable to look at him directly.

'You're wondering what it would be like, aren't you? You're trying to imagine what it would be like for me to fuck you, aren't you?' He reached out with his hand, curved his fingers, reached out but stopped by her chest, his fingers poised to stroke the curve of her breast. He looked up and smiled, his face twisted slightly, eyes shining, waiting. She nodded almost imperceptibly, as if she could hardly admit to herself what she wanted. He touched her breast softly, felt the warmth of her flesh under the smoothness of her swimsuit. His cold fingers drew the warmth from her skin, made her nipple harden, pucker up into a dark bulge against her costume.

'Do you want to?' he whispered, his hand cupping her left breast, moulding to the shape of her body.

'Yes . . . yes . . .' she sighed, taking his other hand and putting it to her breast. She leaned towards him and parted her mouth for his, accepting and responding instinctively to his long passionate kiss. He pulled the straps from her swimming costume and it fell away, exposing the twin globes of her breasts, her nipples hard and ripe in his teasing fingers.

Westerham stripped off and walked round into the office, his heart pounding loudly in his chest. She was waiting for him, holding up her swimming costume at the waist, her breasts bare and waiting for his fingers and lips. The office was cramped, a stool for her to sit on, some swimming things in a corner, a counter with some papers and the book she had been reading. He took her in his arms and pulled her close, forcing her breasts against the wetness of his chest.

They kissed again while his hands swept down her back, pressing her flesh firmly with his fingers, wanting to feel her body react with his. His prick was hard and pressing into her belly, caught in the warmth of her costume. Her mouth was ready for his again and when he sucked her lips and forced his tongue into her mouth he felt her soften in his arms. Her nipples were hot against the coolness of his skin and he liked that, he flicked his thumbs over them, making her sigh deliriously.

'Now I'm going to fuck you,' he told her, whispering into her ear. He turned her roughly, made her look out at the serene silence of the pool while he held her from the waist. She was unresisting, numb, a dazed look in her eyes. He held her breasts from behind, hands across her chest to pinch her nipples tightly so that they grew harder and more sensitive. Her hair smelt fresh and clean, scented with her smell, an aphrodisiac that made Westerham's prick throb painfully hard. He kissed her violently on the shoulder and on the throat, his mouth devouring her so that she cried out, yet still she leaned back against him.

One hand traced down the valley of her breasts, sliding down the smoothness of her belly, and then he ran his fingers through the dense bush of pubic hair. She parted her thighs and guided his fingers to her sex, at the same time rubbing herself up and down his prick, pressing her backside against him. She was soaked; his fingers dipped into her well and were wet and sticky in seconds. He lingered at the mouth of her pussy, stroking her pussy lips apart, teasing her playfully so that her own fingers found her pussy bud. He let her stroke her clitty for a moment, then brushed her fingers aside; it was his game and he was jealous of her.

'Now . . . now . . .' she moaned, his fingers playing in and out of her sex, stroking her bud when he wanted to, making her squirm breathlessly against him. He read her body like a book, was aware of her breath rising – inhaled, held, exhaled – of her backside pressing insistently against his cock. She came suddenly, her back arched while his fingers teased her pussy bud till she could stand it no more. She fell forward against the counter, her body glistening with sweat and droplets of water rubbed off from him.

She was still half-clothed, the costume was loose around her waist, slipping slowly down her thighs. He held her for a moment, then pressed her flat against the counter, her thighs parted so that the red and shiny swimsuit was stretched from thigh to thigh. He kissed her back softly, his lips sucking up the moisture from her body. Her backside was bared, her thighs emerging from tight round buttocks, the swell of flesh firm and shapely. He teased her buttocks apart and looked admiringly at her glistening pink pussy, and at the darker ring of her anal hole. A finger travelled down her back and between her arse-cheeks, teasing her anal hole before sliding into the receptive warmth of her sex. He opened her and then pressed his prick into her sex.

'That's good . . .' Jackie sighed, suddenly moving again, as if she had only just come round from her first orgasm.

'Is that what you like? Being fucked on duty?' Westerham hissed, pressing her down with his hands, turning her face away. He began to fuck her hard, to thrust his prick in and out with long quick strokes. She was wet and each time his prick travelled into her sex he felt the flame of pleasure heighten. She was moaning and sighing softly, moving herself with his rhythm, opening herself and then clasping his prick with her tight pussy as he penetrated. He was breathing harshly, the sweat running freely from his face and body.

'Stop . . . stop . . .' Jackie suddenly hissed, struggling against the power of his cock. She tried to twist away from him, to slip his hands from her waist.

Westerham opened his eyes and saw the elderly guest dive into the pool. He hadn't seen what was happening.

'I'm going to fuck you . . .' Westerham managed to say, his hands seizing Jackie's nipples once more. The old man was under water, his body a shapeless thing travelling smoothly under the glassy surface.

'No . . . No . . .' Jackie sighed, but her body gave her away, she was lifting herself for Westerham's prick, sighing when he drove down. She arched her back and climaxed again, her cry reverberating and echoing with the splashing of the water.

Westerham's own strangled cry joined hers, he fell over her, his prick gushing come into her sex, flooding her with thick waves of it. He lay over her for a second, breathing in time with her, her heartbeat loud and powerful in his ears. He didn't want to move, he wanted to rest on her, to stay close to her warmth, to enjoy the intimacy of their shared body heat. But then she moved, and he remembered himself, felt the same dark feeling come over him. It was inevitable, the darkness that followed the light, the experience of separation, knowing that he was still one, alone, unutterably alone.

He straightened and saw the old man standing in the water, a look of anger and disgust souring his features.

'Why did you do this?' Jackie whispered, as if she had had no part in it, as if he had taken her against her will. She covered herself quickly, her body flushed pink from climax, glancing nervously at the disapproving old man.

'Get me my things,' Westerham told her, pointing to his swimming trunks and a towel that he had left beside the pool. He leaned against the counter, his body still tingling, but now he was unable to look Jackie in the face. He felt tired, drained of emotion, wanting only to get away to his room, to flop down into bed and sleep away the darkness that had swept him up so unexpectedly.

Sarah stood at the head of the stairs indecisively, waiting by the door, unable to bring herself to knock. She had had the idea of meeting at Dominique's flat, hoping that domestic normality, in stark contrast to the dark and menacing sexual atmosphere of the chamber, would render their meeting safe. That had been her intention, but now she was unsure again, afraid of what might happen when she actually came face to face with Dominique. And it was Dominique, not Mistress, she reminded herself, wanting to make clear the separation in her mind; to divorce the personalities so that one was safe and the other was not. She didn't have the heart to turn away, she held her breath and knocked timidly, resigned to whatever was to follow.

'Hi, I was beginning to wonder whether you'd turn up at all,' Dominique smiled brightly when she opened the door.

'I'm sorry I'm late,' Sarah apologised weakly, thankful that Dominique was clad in jeans and t-shirt, barefoot, her long hair in a simple red clasp.

'You're not late, come on in,' Dominique assured her, taking her by the hand and pulling her into the flat.

The radio was on, the volume turned down low, but it added an element of normality to the atmosphere that Sarah was desperate to find. She followed Dominique into the kitchen, determined to say as little as possible, if only to stop herself putting her foot in it again. The kitchen was warm and light, a big square window catching the light that filtered through the greyish sky. She sat down at the table, glancing out of the window at the roof tops across the street rather than looking directly at Dominique.

'Tea or coffee? I can't remember how you take it,' Dominique asked apologetically, putting the kettle under the tap for a second.

'Coffee please, milk no sugar,' Sarah said, a pensive smile on her face.

'It's alright, I'm in civvies,' Dominique laughed. 'You can relax, I won't do anything you don't want me to.'

'Like I said before,' Sarah mumbled, 'I'm hopeless

68

at hiding my true feelings. I'm sorry, I'll do my best to relax,' she promised.

'Good. Your friend Eddie called the day after you were at my chamber,' Dominique informed her, going across the room to get the milk from the fridge.

Sarah swallowed hard. 'You didn't tell him . . .' she whispered, too horrified to finish the sentence. She didn't want Eddie to know anything; he wouldn't understand. She could well imagine the things that would pass through his mind.

'Don't look so alarmed,' Dominique smiled, putting her hand on Sarah's for a second. 'I didn't tell him anything, nor will I ever. Anything that happens between us is strictly private, believe me.'

'Thanks. What did he want?' Sarah asked, reassured by Dominique's transparent sincerity.

'He wanted to know whether you'd be ready for his film.'

'What did you tell him?' The film – once the very thought of it would have had her talking about it endlessly, plotting in minute detail the career that she was going to build on it.

'I told him you'd be ready soon.'

The film had slipped into the background, it no longer seemed the golden opportunity that Sarah had always dreamed of. 'Do you really think that?'

'I'm not sure,' Dominique admitted, turning her back to the table to make the coffee. 'How do you feel about it?' she asked over her shoulder.

'To be honest I haven't given it much thought,' Sarah admitted glumly.

'Does that mean you've changed your mind about doing it?' Dominique asked, putting two mugs of coffee on the table and sitting opposite Sarah. Her eyes were questioning, looking directly to Sarah for an answer.

'No, not exactly. Things have changed, I'm not sure what I want to do any more,' Sarah said softly, looking down at her drink.

'Did you look at the marks on your skin when you got home?'

Sarah's face reddened; the question had come out of the blue and it was doubly unsettling for being so unexpected. She nodded, drawing breath unevenly, as if about to burst into tears.

'What did you think when you looked at yourself?' Dominique asked, ignoring the discomfort her questions were obviously causing. 'What did you feel?'

Sarah allowed herself a moment's recollection before replying softly, 'When I got home I looked at myself in the mirror. I covered myself up and cried.'

Dominique accepted the statement without comment. 'And the next day?' she asked, with the same disinterested tone of voice, as if the answers were purely of academic interest.

'I felt confused. I couldn't help looking, and this time I felt too many things, too many confusing things.'

'Well, Sarah, at least you're honest enough to admit to the confusion,' Dominique said flatly. 'Some people would have denied that, they'd have pretended disgust, anger, revulsion. You probably felt those things too, but there was more to it. I take it that's why you're here.'

'I don't know why I'm here,' Sarah interjected, looking up sharply and then looking away again. It was she who had telephoned Dominique, it was her idea to meet again, and now she wanted to deny the motives that had driven her to do it.

70

'Let's pretend that you're here because you want to be in the film,' Dominique suggested, smiling.

Sarah hesitated for a moment, then decided that Dominique wasn't laughing at her, that the offer was genuine. 'Do you think I'll be able to do it?' she asked, aware that she could not convincingly feign enthusiasm.

'No.'

'Why not?' Sarah asked, startled by the absolute certainty of the answer.

Dominique's answer was painfully frank. 'Because you're submissive,' she stated bluntly.

'No I'm not,' Sarah retorted, the hurt she felt colouring her voice, the first positive sign of emotion that she had expressed. 'If you're talking about what happened in the chamber then you're wrong . . . That wasn't me, not the real me, that was . . . That was . . .'

'An aberration? I don't think so Sarah. And it's not just the chamber; Eddie likes his women submissive, he doesn't like women who are pushy, who have confidence in themselves. He likes to think of himself being in control, and it happens so rarely that I think he must live in a dream world.'

Sarah said nothing. For a while she just sat and drank the coffee, preferring not to think about anything, avoiding Dominique's level gaze by staring into nothing. The window view was sharp and angular, a minimalist study in grey, the monotonous sky attuned with the slate roof of the building opposite. It was better not to think, better to just look at the shifting patterns in the clouds; that way it was easy not to worry about what Dominique had been saying.

71

'Are you really still interested in doing the film?' Dominique asked after a while.

'Yes,' doubtfully, a pause, and then more positively, 'I do want to do it.'

'Then I want you to have a dress rehearsal.'

'I couldn't, not with you.'

Dominique smiled. 'I wasn't offering myself as your victim. I want you to have a session with one of my slaves. It'll give you an idea of what you'll probably be expected to do in the film.'

'With a man?' Sarah said under her breath, quietly horrified by the idea.

'Yes, with one of my male slaves. You'll learn a lot by doing this, much more than you'll learn from reading books or just talking about it.'

'I couldn't,' Sarah said bluntly, unable even to imagine herself as the bitch-queen to a submissive male.

'It's alright,' Dominique said reassuringly, 'I'll be with you. I can show you what to do and how to act. Trust me.'

Sarah stood up and went into the other room, her mind full of doubts and questions. She wished that Eddie had never told her about the film, that she had never met Dominique, that things had been left as they were. It would have been better if the strange feelings inside her had been left dormant, unknown and unsuspected, because now there was no escape. Dominique came into the room, and when Sarah looked up she felt her heart skip a beat. For a moment, the pale young female before her was the Mistress that she had obeyed so willingly in the chamber.

'Why do you do it, Dominique?' Sarah asked earnestly, gazing up desperately, as if Dominique's reply would be the answer to her own confusion. She couldn't understand her at all; Dominique's manner was direct, detached, yet still friendly, still helpful, as if there were two parts to her personality, two sides always on display.

'What do you want?' Dominique snapped irritably. 'Do you really think I've got some neat little answer, a nicely labelled, nicely packaged explanation of why I am what I am? It doesn't exist. Why do you do what you do? Why is anyone the way they are?'

'I'm sorry,' Sarah whispered timidly. She had hoped for an answer, hoped that Dominique had rationalised and explained before, and so would explain it all to her.

'Come here,' Dominique ordered, her voice hard and unyielding. Her face had changed too, her eyes were harder, her lips narrowed. She sat down on the edge of an armchair, her knees together, back straight, waiting.

The room was spinning, and for a moment Sarah felt lost, but when she looked again Dominique was still waiting. She felt many things at that moment, fear among them, but most of all she felt a thrill of excitement, a thrill that was oddly familiar. Without being asked, she fell to her knees and crawled across the room, her heart beating out the journey in rapidly measured beats.

'Pull your knickers down,' Dominique ordered.

Sarah did as commanded. She slipped her hands under her loose skirt and pulled her panties down to her knees, then she looked up expectantly, waiting for the next order. She was wet between the thighs, the desire had speared her suddenly, an emotional switch had been thrown, so that one moment she was cold and the next she was hot. Desire had never been like that before, she had never known herself aroused so easily. In the past, desire had been buried, hidden under layers of inhibition, and it took time to strip those layers away to get to the pure physical response she now felt.

'Across my knee,' Dominique barked, sitting back so that there was room across her lap. She wasn't giving instructions, they were not proper orders but telegraphic codes, ciphers that Sarah instinctively understood and responded to, like a language that she had known in a past life and in which she had suddenly become fluent once more.

She placed herself across Dominique's lap, legs straight, arms out in front of her for balance. Her nipples were hard, jutting against her blouse which was stretched tight, so that even the tiniest movement was amplified, sending trains of sensation through her body. Dominique took the hem of the skirt and pulled it up, throwing it over the waist so that Sarah's backside was bared, her panties still caught up around her knees. Sarah held her breath, could feel Dominique's eyes, feel the way she was regarding the bared backside, eyeing the tight roundness of the buttocks, the darkness that obscured the pink lips of her sex.

The first slap was hard and loud; the sound seemed to hang in the air, an audible expression of the white heat of pain that burned the soft flesh of her arsecheeks. She had sucked in her breath and held it, fighting back the squeal of pain that was her natural reply to the hard smack on the bottom. 'This is stupid,' she tried to tell herself, 'stupid, stupid, stupid.' She turned slightly, caught the blurred movement of the hand as the second smack fell hard across her backside. This time her cry was loud, as sharp as the stinging pain on her flesh. She tried to move, the third slap stopped her at once.

'Stay still,' Dominique hissed.

It was an impossible order to obey; Sarah's entire body seemed to be aflame, her sex was red and aching, the red heat on her backside somehow merging with the rubbing of her nipples on the blouse and with the desire in her pussy. The pain was intense every time Dominique's firm hand made contact, and yet it was sucked away as pain and returned as pleasure, inverting itself so that what was bad felt good. Sarah lifted herself higher, raising her buttocks to meet the downward stroke, her backside reaching up to kiss the flesh that smacked hers. She could feel where her skin had reddened, all over her buttocks and down at the top of her thighs, and the burning felt delicious. The humili-ation was total, as emotionally painful as the physical pain on her behind, yet she sought that too, she sought it as much as she sought the spanking.

'On your knees,' Dominique ordered curtly, push-ing Sarah to the ground.

Sarah looked up, dazed; she had become lost in the steady rhythm of her spanking, lost to everything but the pattern of punishment that marked her pale skin. She knelt in front of Dominique expectantly, quivering, the burning of her flesh and the aching of her sex a single maddening sensation. Dominique began to unbutton the blouse, her fingers snapping the buttons off quickly. In a moment Sarah's breasts were bare, her heaving chest open to Dominique's steady scrutiny. The hard nipples were yearning to be handled, to be kissed and sucked, to be pulled and pinched.

'Fuck yourself,' Dominique said coldly, her face revealing nothing of her own emotions or desires, her face as much a mask as the leather that had hidden her expressions when in the chamber.

Sarah reached down under her skirt, pulling it up so that Dominique could see the pussy mound, see the parted pussy lips, see the fingers pressing tentatively into the sex. She closed her eyes and gave herself fully to the sensation, revelling in the pleasure of fingering herself, stoking the fires that burned so hot in the wetness of her sex. It didn't matter that she was frigging herself in front of Dominique, it didn't matter, all that mattered was the purity of pleasure.

She screamed, opened her eyes wide. She looked down in slow motion, down at the finger marks that were dark red on the pale white of her breast. A second hard slap caught her other breast, a bullet of pure pleasure-pain shooting through her body. She closed her eyes, sought her clitty with her fingers, the steady spanking of her breasts adding layers of pleasure. It was too much, too much. She cried out suddenly, overcome by the force that seemed to tear her out of herself, her body froze, back arched and muscles taut. She climaxed, fell forwards, and still her body was alive to pleasure.

Dominique reached out and resumed spanking Sarah hard on the behind, making her climax again quickly, her breasts still smarting as her bottom was tanned once more. 'Thank me,' Dominique ordered, pushing Sarah away after her second intense climax.

'Thank you,' Sarah whispered shakily, her body tingling all over, her bottom and her breasts smarting sharply, the skin patterned red and white with finger marks. 'Thank you, Mistress,' she said again, and this time she felt an added thrill of pleasure, as if the very act of thanking Mistress were a sexual act of itself.

Dominique smiled at last, the look in her eyes becoming softer. She lifted her t-shirt up to her shoulders and revealed her own naked breasts, the nipples standing enticingly on end. 'Thank me with your lips,' she whispered, taking hold of Sarah's hair and pulling her closer.

5

Westerham drove slowly down the long tree-lined street, peering at the door numbers from behind the wheel, craning forward and counting down towards the house he sought. He braked and stared for a moment at the house, small, neatly kept up, a large square window on either side of the recessed front door; an anonymous house in keeping with its neighbours. He backed the car up and parked it at the side of the road, glanced at his watch and noted that his meeting with Bartlett was in twenty minutes. The slamming of the car door carried through the silence of the street. He caught a glimpse of a net curtain being pulled discreetly back, a neighbour keeping watch on the stranger in the sleek black car.

He knocked once on the door, one hard knock that shook the door and told the household to answer the door at once. The post had been collected, the house next door still had a mouthful of bills poking out from the letter box, the milk had also been taken inside; two circles of condensation still marked the doorstop. There was a lazy shuffling and the door was pulled open.

'Tony Christie,' Westerham smiled grimly.

'Westerham . . .' Christie whispered, swallowing hard. 'How did you find me?'

'Aren't you going to ask me in?'

'What's all this about?' Christie asked, barring the entrance with his body, his knuckles gripping the door tightly.

'I'll tell you inside,' Westerham insisted. Reluctantly, Christie opened the door and stepped back, making way for Westerham to stride in confidently.

Christie showed him into the front room. The large square window cast a dull light over the typically suburban scene, a newspaper lay neatly folded on the floor, beside a cup of coffee and a plate of buttered toast. The room was dominated by a large framed photograph of a wedding, a bride and groom flanked by the smiling faces of family and friends. Christie's face, looking younger and happier, was there, to the left of the bride, his hands resting on a young child standing in front of him.

'How did you find me?' Christie asked, his voice dull with a sense of defeat. He wanted to know more out of a sense of curiosity rather than any raging anger.

Westerham turned to him and looked him in the face before answering. 'It wasn't your secretary,' he assured him. 'You should be proud of her, she's very loyal.'

'If it wasn't Louise than who was it? She was the only one who knew where I was.'

'No, there were others who knew, and one of them passed on an address. Perhaps they thought they were doing you a favour?'

'Doing me a favour?' Christie repeated scornfully. 'It's not in their language. You don't know what it's like . . .'

'Tell me,' Westerham said, sitting opposite where Christie had been quietly reading his newspaper over a cup of coffee.

'I can't tell you anything,' Christie complained, looking tired and in pain. 'No matter what they've done to me,' he said bitterly, 'I'm trapped. I have to keep my mouth shut.'

'Don't make things harder for yourself.'

'This is just a job for you, when it's over you'll walk away from all of this. It's my life, my career, I'll be broken, there'll be nothing left for me, everything I've ever worked for will be gone. I can't do it Westerham, I can't tell you a thing.'

'I'm offering you a chance to save yourself, you can wash your hands of Bartlett and be done with it for good,' Westerham suggested, keenly aware that Christie's knuckles were white when Bartlett's name came up.

'That bastard,' Christie swore softly, 'what's he told you?'

'It was his idea that you disappear, wasn't it?' Westerham conjectured with all the certainty of hard fact. Christie nodded heavily, slumped back in his seat. 'I'm due to meet with him this morning,' Westerham continued, 'I was going to tell him that I had found you and that you were cooperating fully with my investigation. I was going to give him this address as evidence of that.'

'You wouldn't,' Christie said hopelessly.

'If you help me I'll keep you out of it,' Westerham offered, speaking in a low flat tone that suggested that the offer was not for negotiation. 'I won't mention that I've spoken to you or that I know where you are.'

'That's blackmail. How can I trust you?'

'I'll call Bartlett now, I'll cancel our meeting, you can hear for yourself,' Westerham suggested, glancing at the reproduction clock on the wall.

'I can't tell you everything,' Christie explained plaintively, his voice marked with bitterness. 'I don't know too much of what's going on. I was deliberately kept in the dark.'

'Do I make that call?' Westerham wanted to know, ignoring Christie's hedging. It was a clear choice, he knew that once Christie started talking there could be no turning back.

'I'll dial the number,' Christie agreed, reaching for the telephone by the door and tapping out the number himself. His hands were shaking and little beads of sweat had coalesced on his face. 'It's Jen,' he whispered, covering the mouthpiece and giving the handset to Westerham.

'Westerham. I'm afraid that I'm going to have to cancel my meeting with Bartlett,' Westerham told Jen with a certain satisfaction. 'Please give my apologies for the short notice, but something else has come up, something unavoidable. Tell Bartlett I'll reschedule our meeting for another time.'

'But Mr Bartlett is waiting,' Jen reported anxiously. 'You can't cancel like this . . .'

'I'll call at a later date. I'm sure he'll understand.'

'But . . . but . . .'

'Bye.' Westerham was smiling as he put the phone down, certain that Bartlett's rage would know no bounds. It was a small act of war, an act of revenge, but it would have the desired effect, and it made Westerham very happy. 'Now,' he turned to Christie who had been listening in tense silence, 'where do we begin?'

'He'll hate you for that,' Christie said, flopping down into his seat.

'I know, that's why I did it. I want him to know who he's dealing with.'

'What is this? A personal vendetta? I thought this was business.'

'Right on both counts, this is business, and it's personal. Now, you have your side of the bargain to complete.'

'Do you know, Westerham,' Christie said, shaking his head sadly, 'you and Bartlett are just the same. That's probably why you hate each other, because you're both arrogant bastards.'

'Is that received wisdom or your own observation?' Westerham asked, thinking back to what Louise had spat at him.

'What do you mean?'

'Nothing,' Westerham replied tetchily, putting the thought out of his mind. 'Get talking.'

Sarah entered the room timidly, fully prepared to fall to her hands and knees if Mistress desired her to do so. At the chamber it was Mistress first and Dominique second. Sarah had tried to reconcile herself to the division, forcing herself to accept it, although common sense told her that it was childish to play games. Reluctantly she was coming to understand that common sense and cold rationality were a hindrance to knowledge. Mistress seemed to appeal to something far deeper than that; to something buried in the personality, to somewhere out of reach and out of sense.

Mistress was dressed in a shiny red latex catsuit, clinging sensuously to her body from the neck down to her sharp-heeled red ankle boots. It outlined her body to perfection, clothed it in a sensual red skin that shimmered as Mistress moved. 'Good, you're here,' Mistress smiled. She wore brilliant red lipstick that matched her outfit, as red and as sensuously

82

glossy, making it seem as if her costume and her body were one and the same thing.

'You look beautiful, Mistress,' Sarah said softly, secretly delighted in being able to call Dominique Mistress again.

'Jenny has laid out your clothes,' Mistress pointed to a neatly laid out collection of black garments. 'Remember, you're a Mistress too, keep that in mind as you dress. Think of it as putting on a new personality, it's an armour, a magical armour that gives you power.'

'Yes, Mistress,' Sarah agreed, unable to keep her eyes off Mistress. She hesitated then walked across the room to look at the costume that the maid had selected.

'The slave is waiting down in the chamber,' Mistress informed her, sounding relaxed and confident, positively looking foward to the encounter that she had arranged.

Sarah put her shoulder bag down and gently touched the costume, her fingers lingering for a moment on the cool reflective surfaces. She knew that she had to get changed, but was reluctant to do so in front of Mistress, she wanted time to change by herself, to accustom herself to the look and feel of the rubber. And, more importantly, she wanted time to get into character, to fully become a Mistress herself – powerful, confident, sexual. 'I've brought my own heels, just as you wanted,' she said, stooping down to pull a pair of black high heels from her bag.

'Good, Jenny's picked out some latex stockings to go with them. Now,' Dominique urged her, 'get dressed.'

Sarah turned her back to Mistress and undressed hurriedly, self-consciously aware of being watched.

She had been beaten and fingered, had joyously kissed Mistress's heels and yet she was still slightly embarrassed to be stripping naked in front of her. There was an undercurrent of excitement that she felt, a tingling expectation that she might suddenly find herself on hands and knees in abject worship of Mistress once more.

'What are you doing?' Sarah cried, turning to find Mistress standing directly behind her.

'Just getting you ready,' Mistress explained pleasantly. She poured a handful of talc in her palm and rubbed it softly onto Sarah's thigh, the snowy white powder dusting her flesh. With brisk, expert movements she powdered Sarah's body quickly and efficiently, over the thighs and breasts, down the back and over the buttocks. Sarah stood silently, relishing the feeling of Mistress's hands all over her body, a soft fleeting touch that was erotic and yet unfocused, making her feelings of excitement more pronounced. When Mistress's fingers stroked between the thighs Sarah shuddered, sighed softly, unable to restrain the evidence of her arousal.

When Dominique had finished, the room was filled with the pleasant odour of the talcum powder, an odour that had always reminded Sarah of bath-time and childhood. She gingerly took the first of the stockings, so soft and shiny, gleaming with a polished radiance, and pulled it on slowly. It slipped over her powdered body like a dream, close fitting, pressing tight against the skin. She put the second one on and then stepped into her black high heels.

'How do I look?' she asked, staring down at herself, hardly able to believe the transformation. Her thighs looked fuller, longer, the skin so pale compared to the blackness that sheathed her, the

84

stocking top was tight, making her flesh bulge a little against the rubber.

'You look great,' Mistress laughed, flashing brilliant white teeth against glossily painted red lips. 'Now the rest of it.'

Sarah donned a pair of tight PVC pants, high cut and tight waist, with a zip down past the crotch, studded at the sides with shiny chrome spikes. The top was made of the same clinging fabric, a studded half cup bra that revealed the tips of her erect nipples, the studs at the sides. She turned to Mistress, the physical transformation complete. Mistress took her hand and led her to a mirror that was covered with a dirty white dust-cover.

'Is that really me?' Sarah asked when the cover was pulled away and she stared at the cold hard reflection. Her body was accentuated, her thighs were perfect and slightly unreal, a fantasy figurine that made her head swim with excitement.

'Put some of this on,' Mistress suggested, giving her some red lipshine to apply.

In a second, Sarah looked complete, pouting in the mirror, unable to quite recognise herself in the reflection. She looked like someone else, another woman, a woman more attractive, more powerful, more alluring than she had ever been.

'How do you feel?' Mistress asked.

'Weird. It's hard to believe that that's me. I look so different . . . so sexy. It's just a set of clothes, right?'

Mistress smiled and shook her head. 'It's not just clothes. You've invoked something from within yourself, the devil inside, the real you, it could be anything. Don't try and analyse,' she warned, 'just

85

look at her,' she pointed to the reflection, 'and be her.'

'Do you always feel this turned on, when you're dressed this way?' Sarah asked sheepishly, fascinated by the way Mistress's nipples were jutting hard against the tight red latex skin.

'Always,' Mistress admitted, 'but it's not the clothes. It's when I'm Mistress, whenever I assume her character I'm aroused, whether it's in my chamber or in my sitting room.'

Sarah blushed at the memory of her punishment the last time they had met. 'I'm ready now,' she said softly, her heart racing at the sudden awareness that now it was her turn to punish, and that she was a Mistress too, even if only for one day.

Mistress stepped back to take a long hard look at Sarah, smiled approvingly then leaned forward and kissed Sarah on the mouth. 'You don't have to ask now, you don't need permission,' she said, her tongue tracing the shape of Sarah's lips, 'if you want something then do it.'

Sarah passed her hand up over Mistress's thigh, her fingers pressing against the impervious covering that turned Dominique's body into something abstractly beautiful. The nipples were hard little points, ringed by circles of light on the shiny red surface, and she rubbed her fingertips across them softly.

'Let's go,' Mistress sighed, her eyes misting slightly, her breath faster and deeper than it had been moments earlier. Sarah kissed her on the mouth again, wanting to enjoy the freedom of being a Mistress, helpless to resist the desire growing stronger and stronger inside her.

Mistress led the way, out into the dingy hallway

and then down the stone steps towards the chamber. Sarah stopped at the top of the steps, afraid to start the descent into the darkness. 'Mistress,' she whispered at the top of the steps, waiting for Mistress to stop and look back at her, 'I want to thank you, for this and everything else.'

'There's nothing to thank me for. And today I'm not your Mistress, today you call me Dominique, ok? Especially in front of the slave, as far as he's concerned you are a Mistress too.'

Sarah nodded and followed Dominique, her own heels echoing hard on the stone steps, drawing comfort and encouragement from the staccato rhythm and the hardness of the sound. Dominique pushed the door open and Sarah strode into the chamber, chin up, an unconscious look of disdain on her face. 'I am Mistress, I am Mistress,' she repeated to herself, willing herself into the role, willing herself to assume the attitude and countenance to match the uniform that clothed her body so erotically.

It took a second for her eyes to adjust to the pale light, and another second for her to look away from the whips and chains that turned the chamber into a vision of a nightmare. Dominique touched her on the elbow and Sarah followed her across the room, their heels in unison on the flagstones. She struggled to keep her face impassive when she saw the slave, bound tightly in leather and chains behind the bars of the cage. His skin was dark, glistening, muscles stretched tight against the leather restraints that bound his arms together. He was chained to the bars of the cage, but still he had managed to twist round slightly and was straining to get a good look at the Mistresses as they approached him.

'Well, what do you think?' Dominique asked, barely glancing down at the slave.

Sarah shrugged, her eyes met the slave's, she held his gaze for a moment then he looked away. 'Is he good?' she asked, silently gratified that he had turned away from her.

'Vincent's a good specimen,' Dominique decided without too much thought. She opened the door of the cage and walked in, stepping up close so that her heels were by his face. He strained forward to kiss her boots but he was unable to reach, his neck was taut with muscle and the chains holding him to the cage were stretched tight.

'Is he obedient?'

'Only if chastised regularly.'

Sarah caught him glancing at her again, his dark eyes filled with an intense curiosity. This time he looked at her for a moment longer, challenging her silently. She stepped into the cage, Dominique stepping aside for her, and planted her heels next to his face. He made no movement towards her, instead he turned contemptuously away, a faint sneer on his lips. She turned to Dominique looking for guidance, her heart was beating wildly, she knew that Vincent was testing her. Dominique raised her eyebrows, waiting for a response to the slave's insulting arrogance.

'Let him go,' Sarah ordered, gritting her teeth. She was a Mistress, she told herself, there was no way she could let Vincent's impudence go unpunished.

Dominique did as she was asked, she loosed the chains that held Vincent to the cage and stepped away from him. He rolled forward on the ground, exhaling heavily, his breath misting slightly in the

88

cold dark air. For a moment Sarah watched him, lying on his back, looking straight up at the ceiling as he caught his breath. 'On your knees,' she ordered, her voice controlled so that the threat was clear without being too over dramatic.

He moved slowly, lifted himself up on one elbow, and looked at her, a smile forming on his lips, part amusement and part arrogance. Dominique had stepped back and Sarah knew that she was alone. The anger came suddenly, overwhelming her doubts and confusions, he was laughing at her, smirking when he should have been obedient and adoring.

'What are you laughing at?' she demanded, stepping forward and smacking him hard across the face. The slap filled the room with its harsh retort, her fingers were smarting and Vincent was looking away. She watched him turn towards her, his eyes large and filled with rage, the smile gone from his face. 'Now,' she hissed, 'on your knees.'

He began to lift himself, his arms were still bound together so that movement was obviously difficult, but still there was something lazy about his actions, something deliberately insolent. The second slap was as hard as the first. Sarah clenched and unclenched her fingers for a second, hardly aware of the look on Vincent's face.

'Do you want to use something? A strap or a paddle?' Dominique suggested quietly.

'No, not yet,' Sarah murmured, satisfied now that Vincent was moving as she wanted him. 'On your knees,' she directed coldly. 'I want to see what he feels like,' she explained, glancing back to Dominique.

Vincent obeyed, he managed to sit up on his knees, back held straight, looking up at Sarah with unconcealed hostility. 'Don't look at me,' she ordered. He held her eyes for a moment too long before turning away, his gaze falling on Mistress Dominique's heels. Sarah touched him firmly, passing her fingers over his shoulders, feeling the hardness of muscle under the cool skin. He was strong, good looking in a certain dangerous kind of way, and his passions and emotions were expressed purely and physically. She could feel his anger, feel him fighting against the bonds that wrapped him so securely, feel also the arrogance and the rebellion that seethed within him. He was dangerous, and that single thought made Sarah excited.

'He responds best to harsh treatment,' Dominique remarked impassively.

'Is that true?' Sarah asked him, circling slowly, her fingers trailing his body lazily.

'You're not a Mistress,' he said slowly, his voice was assured, confident despite the restraints that bound him.

'Aren't I?' Sarah asked, grinning. She stepped behind him and grabbed him suddenly, bending down low and forcing his head back with one hand so that his face was close to hers. His breath touched her skin, a hot whisper against her lips. 'Aren't I a Mistress?' she hissed, passing one hand slowly down over his chest and over the ridge of tight flat muscle of his stomach. His prick was hard when she wrapped her fingers tightly around it, hard and pulsing sensitively. 'Why are you hard then, slave? Isn't it because you're enjoying this?'

She released him suddenly and pushed him forward. He could hardly resist, he tipped forward so that his head touched the ground. His back was bent over, the leather bands digging deep into his ribs.

Sarah knelt down beside him, she was fascinated by his body, by the pure masculine power that had been tightly reined in and was now prostrate before her. His thighs were thick and powerful and his buttocks were tight and round; she touched him, playfully stroked the soft flesh of his backside. He tensed up as her fingers explored between his thighs, her finger circling menacingly around the forbidden area of his rear hole. She lingered for a moment, looked up and saw Dominique smiling.

'You seem to have silenced him,' Dominique said approvingly. She moved closer, bent down and kissed Sarah on the mouth softly, holding her under the chin while she did so.

Sarah felt Dominique's kiss as an infusion of desire, as if all that she had been doing had been emotionless, the whole thing had had an abstract, unreal quality. She touched Dominique's thigh, stroking the soft rubber skin to feel the firm flesh underneath. 'I want a strap now,' she smiled, turning to catch the look of horror and desire in Vincent's eyes. She took hold of his balls, cradled the coolness in her hand, squeezing very gently so that he held his breath. 'Am I a Mistress, slave?'

He hesitated, the confusion clear in his eyes and on his lips that quivered with half an answer. 'Yes,' he whispered at last, his voice thin and reedy in the dark quiet of the chamber.

'And what do you want?' Sarah teased, holding him firmly, her fingers encasing his balls and gripping tight the base of his stiff prick.

'I don't know . . . Mistress,' he whispered.

'You want to be punished,' Sarah whispered, delighted that he had succumbed. She was a Mistress, he could no longer deny it, and it felt good.

She had been holding back, but now she was aware of the beating of her heart, of the throbbing in her nipples and the wet heat of her sex. The abstract feeling, the feeling of being disengaged, was gone and now she felt powerful, erotic, a Mistress for real. Dominique came back, holding a long black strip of leather, a tawse with knotted strips of leather at one end. 'What do you want?' she asked, bending low to whisper into his ear.

'I want to be punished, Mistress,' Vincent whispered, and he was pleading, looking up at her with begging, crying eyes.

Sarah took the tawse from Dominique, smiling, her eyes alive with an intense excitement. The tawse felt heavy in her hand, the leather strips long and stiff. 'Have I done well?' she asked softly, certain that for once she had fulfilled all that she had to.

'You've been wonderful, much better than I gave you credit for,' Dominique admitted with a smile.

'Thanks. I think I've surprised myself too,' Sarah confessed. 'Now, I think Vincent needs to be taught a lesson.'

She leaned across and slowly undid the straps that held his arms together, each of the four straps burst loose as she undid them, and then he was free. He rubbed his arms with his hands, trying to get some feeling back into his body, the straps had left deep indents on his flesh which Sarah traced with her finger. She stood up and walked lazily round him, he fell on hands and knees of his own accord, assuming a position of reverence that was her due as a Mistress. She stopped at his head, heels planted firmly in front of him. Instantly he fell to licking her black high heels, his tongue wetting the shiny patent leather.

92

'Enough!' she snapped, passing a happy smile to Dominique. 'Now slave, I'll teach you to question me.' Very slowly she unzipped her pants, unzipping the plastic garment right round so that the darkness of her pussy hair poked through. She squatted down in front of him, knees apart and her pussy exposed to his adoring eyes. 'Suck me,' she ordered, 'and do it well or the strap will bite twice as hard.'

Vincent needed no second bidding, he inched forward and buried his face in the dark groove between her thighs, his mouth and lips kissing her pussy lips; she could feel him breathing deeply, sucking in the pure perfume of her pussy scent. She dug her nails into his back and he moved responsively, his tongue snaking between her pussy lips to lap at the thick sex-honey that was oozing sensuously from within her. The pleasure pulsed through her, his tongue a flame that burned whatever it touched, making her sigh loudly.

'Good, good,' she whispered, edging herself forward so that she was open to him, open to the greedy mouth feasting on her sex. It felt odd to have a man sucking her as she wished, giving her the pleasure as she desired it. She lashed out with the strap, a hard stroke that licked at the rippling flesh of his lower back. It had been unexpected, Vincent cried out with shock and pain, but then he was sucking her passionately, his tongue stroking the walls of her sex.

She beat him again, enjoying the feeling of power and control, the sound of leather on flesh filling the air with all the magic of a peal of bells. He was working furiously with his tongue, sucking and biting, playing on the pussy bud so that she was rocking back and forth into his mouth. She used the

93

tawse again, biting it into his flesh so that his moans were whispered into her sex. The pleasure was reaching fever pitch, she dropped the strap and pinned her nails into his flesh, gripping him hard while she climaxed into his sweet adoring mouth.

Dominique was there to hold Sarah as she stood up shakily, her body sprinkled with dewdrops of sweat, her thighs wet with her pussy cream that dappled the plastic garments and rubber stockings. She looked down and felt a thrill of delight when she realised that her heels were being licked clean by Vincent.

'I don't think you've anything to worry about,' Dominique said softly, kissing Sarah on the lips, 'the film should be no problem at all.'

'The film?' Sarah repeated, too dazed to really think straight. The film had slipped from her mind completely, it was an irrelevancy, something that existed outside of the chamber, and for the moment the chamber was her universe.

'Do you think you can submit to me after all of this?' Dominique asked, pressing herself against Sarah.

'Yes, you know I will,' Sarah replied instantly and without hesitation. She was a Mistress, of that she no longer had any doubt, but for her, Dominique was the ultimate Mistress and she knew that she would submit to her without question.

'But you don't think that today will make you react any differently?'

Sarah shrugged. 'I don't know Dominique, all I know is that I'm still your slave, no matter what happens.'

'Let's make love now,' Dominique sighed, seeming to melt into Sarah's arms. They locked mouths, kissing passionately, arms around each other, the feel of each other mediated by leather and rubber so that layers of sensation were added to the embrace.

'What about him?' Sarah asked derisively, looking down at the silent slave at her feet.

'Slaves are to be used and enjoyed,' Dominique explained, smiling wickedly. 'Get me the big gag, the one Mistress Sarah and I will need,' she commanded, speaking down to Vincent coldly. He looked up sharply, as if to complain or protest, but the harsh glare from Dominique sent him scuttling across the chamber on hands and knees, his body rippling with muscle tone, and yet leashed by the force of his Mistress's will.

'Is he really a typical slave?' Sarah asked, her voice lowered so that he could not hear.

Dominique shook her head. 'There's no such thing as the typical slave, just as there's no such thing as the typical master. Everyone has their own history, their own private landscape of desire. Vincent is difficult though, he needs to be reconquered and subdued every time; I think he can never accept the domination as anything but temporary. You've handled him well, and if you can do that then you're genuinely a Mistress.'

'Aren't you afraid of him?' Sarah whispered, eyeing him carefully as he returned, holding something dark between his teeth.

Dominique nodded. 'A little,' she admitted, 'but then the danger is part of the journey. I'd be more afraid not to confront my own desires.'

Vincent stopped in front of the two Mistresses, waiting like an obedient animal for them to notice him once more. His body was bathed in sweat, and he was breathing hard, heaving powerfully. Sarah

95

touched him softly, traced her fingers where she had dug her nails into his flesh. He accepted her touch without complaint, pressing his face into her palm, eagerly accepting her caress.

'Sit up, where I can reach you,' Dominique told him. He obeyed and she took the object from his teeth and showed it to Sarah. 'This is a gag,' she explained, holding it up to the light. It had the shape of two pricks back to back, with a grip of some sort at the join. Dominique pushed one end into Vincent's mouth. He swallowed the plastic prick without complaint, it filled his mouth fully so that his cheek bulged around it. His teeth gripped tightly at the join and then Dominique secured it with a strap that she tied around his head. The second prick emerged from his mouth, a long, ribbed dildo that was the mirror image of the one in his mouth.

'Down, now,' Dominique snapped impatiently. Vincent lay on the floor, arms at his side, legs stretched out, the hardness of his prick jutting out from the dark tangle of hair between his thighs, a hardness that was matched by the dildo projecting from his mouth like some anatomical monstrosity.

Sarah knelt down beside him, she took his prick in her hands and stroked it lovingly, enjoying the sensuous feel of it in her fingers. A wet rivulet of fluid poured from the glans, it glistened on his thickly veined rod, a silver river on the landscape of his prick. She leaned across him and kissed the glans softly, flicking her tongue over the slit so that she could lap up the almost tasteless fluid that was warm and sticky on her tongue. He sighed softly, tensing his body in an effort to control himself. She smiled, suddenly aware of what it was to have power over a man; he could not give himself to his pleasure, he had to hold back, save himself for her, because her pleasure was paramount. She could lick and suck, torment him wickedly with her tongue, enjoying his prick in her mouth just as she liked, without worrying what he wanted. The joy of it was that what he wanted, what he desired more than anything else, was to serve her, that was all.

She lapped up the fluid from his prick very slowly, tantalised by the sighs that escaped from behind the gag, excited by his squirming and tensing as he fought back the pleasure that she gave him. Her tongue traced a route from the thick hairy base right to the tip, tracing the thick underside of his dark cock with the pink tip of her tongue.

'You want his prick, I take it?' Dominique asked, interrupting Sarah's exploration of the slave's thick hard prick.

Sarah looked up and saw that Dominique was undoing a row of studs around her thighs and waist. In a second she had undone the middle part of her red latex catsuit, exposing a section of white flesh against the red rubber. She looked divine, her body was till clothed in rubber above the waist and from the top of the thighs down, but her middle was exposed, the swell of her buttocks and the fullness of her quim were free. 'Do you mind?' Sarah asked, momentarily distracted by the delicious sight of Dominique.

'Why should I mind?' Dominique laughed, advancing on Vincent with a slight swaying of the hips. 'The penis gag always fills my pussy just as I like it, and I love fucking him this way, I can feel the other prick fucking him in the mouth at the same time.'

Sarah straddled Vincent quickly, she held his prick and guided it to the opening of her pussy, which was wet and tingling with aroused ancipation. She let herself down on his prick, enjoyed the feel of it slipping into the warm velvet sweetness of her sex. She sat for a moment, filled with his hardness, her pussy tight around the shaft that pulsed with his heartbeat against her own pulse. Dominique sat down too, sliding herself down on the rigid hardness that Vincent held in his mouth. Sarah watched, fascinated by the way it entered her, by the way her pussy lips seemed to stretch around the hardness.

Dominique leaned across and kissed Sarah on the mouth, their lips entwined while they pressed down hard on Vincent. They began to move together, timing the slow rhythmic dance so that they were penetrated in unison, so that the pleasure was shared, doubled, savoured. Vincent's prick flexed powerfully, rising up to spear between Sarah's thighs as she ground herself down on him. At the same time he moved his head higher, moving the dildo deep into Dominique's sex.

Sarah closed her eyes; all she wanted was to enjoy the feel of Dominique's mouth and Vincent's hardness. The sensations were hard to tell apart, making her catch her breath, hold it, enjoy the frisson of delight and then exhale with the next stroke. She felt lost, dizzied by the rush of energy. She opened her eyes and looked down at Vincent; he was moving in a frenzy, writhing, bucking his hips manfully while his head thrashed from side to side. The dildo was wet with glistening juices, dripping down from Dominique's pussy and into his mouth. He was being fucked too, fucked expertly by Dominique's pussy, and his mouth filled with her essence; an essence that poured down the prick as if it were come that were filling his mouth. Such a clever punishment,

Sarah thought before the pleasure overwhelmed her, so clever because it was so confusing for him.

'You're being fucked Vincent! Fucked in the mouth!' Dominique gasped, riding up and down to climax over his face, her pussy slipping easily over the smooth polished surface of the dildo, a polished surface that ran with her come.

Sarah felt Dominique stiffen, felt the breath go from her body as she climaxed in a string of convulsive spasms. Vincent froze a moment later, his body caught mid-position, his hips pressed up against her backside; his face buried deep between Dominique's thighs. He climaxed too, shooting thick wads of juice into Sarah's hot quim. She continued to ride him, to slap herself up and down over the pumping hardness. He recovered quickly, pumping harder and harder until she cried out, gripped Dominique tightly and let herself go to the force of orgasm.

'That was good,' Dominique whispered, rolling off the dildo that glistened with the thick creaminess of her pussy juice.

'I haven't finished with Vincent yet,' Sarah smiled, the words whispered between deep heavy breaths. The words had an immediate effect on him, he moaned softly, turning to look at Dominique with pleading in his eyes. 'It's no good begging, Vincent,' Sarah assured him, a cruel smile playing on her freshly kissed lips. 'I'm going to thrash you again, then I want you to clean my pussy with your tongue. Is that clear?'

Vincent's beseeching look to Dominique was to no avail. 'Mistress commands,' she told him softly, 'and you'll obey.'

6

Jackie was sitting at a stool by the bar, facing the girl working there, her long blonde hair neatly plaited and snaking down her back. She was laughing softly, her lips parted over straight white teeth, her eyes sparkling with delight. There was no way Westerham could resist her, she looked so relaxed, and the memory of her body brought an instant physical reaction. He edged his way through the hotel restaurant, winding past the diners who ate in subdued silence, more interested in their food than in their partners or the people around them.

Jackie glanced round and saw him approaching, her laughter was cut short and she turned back to the bar instantly. Westerham saw the bargirl looking at him. She said something under her breath to Jackie, who sat motionless in her seat.

'I suppose you didn't recognise me with my clothes on,' Westerham said good-humouredly, sliding onto the bar stool beside her.

'I'm off-duty now,' she said coldly, looking directly in front of her, affording him a perfect profile, her face ice-cold and beautiful; lush lips and deep blue eyes.

'I was only being friendly,' Westerham told her softly, stung by the unexpectedly hostile tone. 'Let me buy you a drink.' He signalled to the bargirl who was hovering expectantly.

'I've got a drink thank you.'

'Scotch,' Westerham said, looking to the bargirl quizzicaly. She looked away from his eyes, rushing instead to get him his drink. 'Look, if it's about what happened the other day . . .'

'What else could it be?' Jackie snapped, spinning round to glare at him angrily.

'You got into trouble,' Westerham guessed, a smile forming on his lips.

'There's nothing funny about that, I could have lost my job,' she told him angrily, her eyes flared as she spoke, anger bringing colour to her cheeks. Westerham liked emotion, and anger was as good an emotion as any.

'Let me make it up to you,' he offered, gazing directly into her baby blue eyes, into eyes that stared back without warmth and without desire.

'Leave me alone,' she sighed, turning away from him and back to the girl behind the bar.

'What happened?'

'Leave me alone,' she repeated, her face set in stone, looking determinedly away from him.

'You,' Westerham turned to the bargirl, his voice cool and authoritative, 'what happened?'

The bargirl looked at Jackie helplessly, her eyes appealing for guidance but getting nothing in response. 'Someone complained,' she whispered softly, looking down at the polished surface of the bar, 'one of the long term guests. He said he'd never seen anything so disgusting in his life.'

'Did you get reprimanded by the manager?' Westerham asked, turning back to Jackie.

'No, I got a bloody prize,' she spat angrily. 'Of

course I got a reprimand, I was lucky not to get fired, no thanks to you.'

'I'm sorry, let me make it up to you,' Westerham said, his voice persuasively apologetic. He reached out and put his hand on hers, felt her tense but not pull away. 'Let me take you out for a meal, somewhere nice, somewhere better than this.'

'Staff and guests aren't supposed to socialise,' the bargirl warned under her breath.

Westerham shot her a look that silenced her at once. 'How about it Jackie? Let's go to a decent restaurant, or perhaps you'd like to go to a club?'

Her hand was in his and he could feel her indecision, he could see it in her eyes too. 'I could have been fired,' she repeated, the possibility of it still hanging heavy on her shoulders.

They wouldn't have done that,' he assured her softly, squeezing her hand. 'Come on, let's get out of here.'

'Why wouldn't they have done that?' she responded, turning to face him suddenly.

'Because a woman like you is irreplaceable,' he explained. 'Have you looked at the attendance figures of the pool for when you're on shift?'

She shook her head, the iciness melting as she listened to his soft persuasive voice. 'Have you looked?'

He smiled. 'The figures are kept in the little office, on the counter. You tick off every customer that comes in for a swim. Your shift has about a fifty percent higher attendance than the other shift, even when you swap round and work the early evening shift.'

'How . . . why?' she asked, unable to understand why he had checked up on her.

He shrugged, smiled lopsidedly. 'It's my job. Figures are everything, they don't lie and they don't cheat. I guessed that the old boy who saw us might not be too impressed,' he chuckled at the thought, 'so I decided to do some checking, just in case.'

'Have you told anyone?' she asked, lowering her voice and leaning across towards him, her perfume enveloping him, filling his nostrils as he breathed.

'No,' he smiled, recognising the look on her face, 'but it should get you a pay rise.'

'Thanks,' she laughed, 'I hadn't realised I was that predictable.'

'You're not predictable, the thought had occurred to me too when I saw the figures.'

'But that's because you're predictable too,' she assured him, disengaging her hand.

'What do you mean?'

'I am going out tonight,' she smiled, standing up and straightening the tight skirt that clothed her exquisitely long legs, 'but not with you. You've redeemed yourself, but I haven't forgiven you completely. You didn't know about the figures, and if they had been bad I could still have been out of a job.' She started to go but stopped and turned: 'If I get the pay rise,' she informed him coolly, 'I might even buy you a drink.'

'Please, don't go,' Westerham whispered, reaching out to grab her arm. She stepped back and shook her head sadly, pity in her eyes. 'Don't do this to me,' he said, hardly able to believe his own ears. For a moment, for one awful moment, he considered putting his hand in his pocket and pulling out a bundle of notes to offer her. The idea flared and died in an instant, and he was appalled by it, appalled by what it revealed of the desperation that

103

lurked beneath the surface of his soul. He watched her go, and the pain he felt was raw and physical, a sickness in the pit of the stomach that made him want to throw up.

The black leather jacket, mirror shades and grey-green stubble had not changed. Eddie was sprawled across two seats in the cafe, trying hard to look fashionably blank. Sarah breezed through the cafe towards him, aware that his first reaction was going to be outright anger because she'd kept him waiting. The big fat man behind the counter looked up, his surly features flickering with recognition. She flashed him a smile and walked by, glad to see that he remembered her from the last time she had been in his coffee bar; it always gave her a lift when she was noticed. It was the actress in her, or perhaps it was the impulse behind the acting.

'Where the fuck have you been?' Eddie demanded sourly, catching her neatly in the reflective surfaces of his glasses. His arms were locked behind the leatherette seat, staking out the territory that was his and which he would share with her when she had explained herself.

'Busy. The way you always are,' she replied pointedly, looking directly at the double reflection in his glasses, a reflection that was more confident than it had ever been.

'Don't fuck me about girl,' he warned slowly, shifting aside for her to sit beside him. 'There's a lot of out of work actresses that'd jump at the chance of doing this film.'

'I don't doubt that,' she smiled. 'Now, have you got any news for me?'

'What's wrong with you?' Eddie asked suspiciously, peering at her as if the change could be discerned in the sweetness of her young face. He had always been used to her running around him, pandering to his inflated ego, hanging off his every word because he was in cinema and she wasn't.

'Nothing's wrong with me. I'm getting into character,' she explained airily, 'you know, the way actors and actresses do.'

'How did it go with Dominique?' he asked, slipping off the glasses to get a better look at her reaction.

'Oh, I've learned a lot from her,' she explained innocently, her eyes fixing on the glasses resting on the formica table top. 'She's very smart, you know, very smart. You ought to get her as advisor on the film.'

'We decide who's working on the film,' he stated, sitting back in his seat as if to emphasise his importance. 'Now, it just so happens I was talking to one of the money guys just recently, he's putting up most of the cash in fact.'

'And?' Sarah asked, annoyed by the way he always started a sentence and then stopped half way and waited for her to beg him to continue.

'He was saying that one of his colleagues has got a birthday coming up soon, and he wanted to do something for him. This other guy's going to be backing the film too, he's the other major shareholder in fact. Anyway, I suggested a sort of surprise party.'

'Eddie,' Sarah interrupted impatiently, 'what is the point of all this?'

'The point of it is that we want to match the party to the film, you know, a theme party.'

'What's that got to do with me?' Sarah asked with

a terrible sinking feeling, recognising that in his usual unsubtle way Eddie was leading up to something.

'Consider it a sort of audition,' he smiled, taking her hand and kissing her fingers softly.

'What sort of an audition?'

'We want to surprise him, you know, the lights come on and all his friends are there with bottles of booze and party hats on.'

'I still don't see . . .'

'We want to catch him with you. Don't look so shocked,' he laughed. 'It'll all be above board, there's nothing dodgy about it at all. And because of the film theme we want you dressed in leathers. Like I said, consider it an audition.'

'Don't you mean this is *the* audition?' she said coldly. 'If I don't do this I don't do the film, do I?'

'Don't look at it like that,' Eddie chided. 'I only want to do you a favour. These are important people, we're not talking about something sleazy here. Trust me.'

Sarah could not naturally couple the idea of trust with Eddie, he was one of those people who seemed to make a virtue out of being untrustworthy. There were a dozen stories and rumours to attest to his shady dealings, most of them from his own lips, and now he was asking for her trust. 'I can't trust you,' she smiled, 'and this whole thing sounds wrong.'

'Alright,' Eddie laughed, 'don't trust me, why be different from everyone else, eh? But I'm not bullshitting you Sarah, this is for real. You'll be paid for this, and you'll make the job of getting this role much easier. You've got to be cooperative.'

'I'm not sleeping with anyone,' Sarah said flatly.

'I'm not asking you to,' Eddie said defensively,

and for a moment Sarah was sure he was being genuine. 'This is just some joke, like a public school prank for men with more money than sense. If you don't trust me then maybe you should meet the guy who wants to set it up, you'll trust him.'

'This is the money man?'

'The majority shareholder. He's a nice guy, I'm sure you'll like him. You know,' he decided, scratching his chin, 'meeting him might not be a bad idea, you know, it might do our cause some good.'

Sarah laughed out loud, drawing startled looks from the people at the tables around them. 'Our cause?'

'Yes, why not?' Eddie asked in an injured tone that sounded curiously sincere.

Westerham groaned, turned his head slowly and opened his eyes. The clock took time to come into view, the numbers were blurred and when they finally focused he groaned again. He closed his eyes again and willed the room to stop spinning. The bottle that stood behind the clock had been full at one point, but somehow it had been emptied, he had drunk it away without realising what he was doing. Or perhaps he did realise what he was doing but preferred to drink the realisation away with all the other troubling thoughts that Jackie's rejection had triggered.

He forced himself to sit, resisted the lurching of the floor and the screaming pain behind the eyes. It had not been an entirely wasted night; he had been forced to sit and think about his next move, focusing on work in an effort to escape the depression that clouded his mind. For a while it had been a successful manoeuvre, and with a clarity that was shockingly stark for an early morning hangover, the conclusions came flooding back to him.

The new film studio was the key to the investigation, and it had struck him that it was so obvious, that he cursed himself for not seeing it right away. It was there in the internecine politics of the boardroom, in the war that rewrote names on office doors and pensioned people off without a moment's notice. Bartlett had been promoted, the culling of the old guard left a vacuum that he filled, first to the joy of his patrons and later to their disquiet. He had first made it onto the board as Director of Operations, and a year later he had stepped up and Christie had taken his place. Christie was a Bartlett appointee, not a very clever man but willing to do as he was told.

The salient point, and one that Westerham had missed, was that there had been a redefinition of areas of responsibility. Traditionally the film studios fell under the shadow of Operations, but somehow Bartlett had taken part of that particular fiefdom with him. He was still the man charged with looking after the new studio, which was to be the jewel in the company's crown, the future of the company and all that. It was the sort of thing that an aspiring company man would covet, but not a man of Bartlett's standing, his stage was the Boardroom itself. Christie had described how Bartlett had made it a condition of his promotion, insisted that he retain direct control for himself.

The insight had come to Westerham as he had worked his way through the bottle. He had felt good, excited by his discovery, ready to plot his next move, until his mind had wandered. Louise, Christie's assistant had come unbidden into his mind, and her words were still there, echoing round and round his subconscious and emerging when least expected, to stab him through the heart. And with the alcohol warming his veins, Louise had become Jackie, and Jackie had become Louise. Together they had dragged the darkness from within till it smothered him, and he needed the drink to smother it.

'Bartlett, you bastard,' he murmured, his voice cracked and distorted, 'I'm going to get you.' It was supposed to be a threat, but it sounded more like a forlorn hope.

He dragged himself to the shower and cleaned himself up, looking sadly at the wreck that was reflected back in the mirror. Why was he letting himself go? The investigation was back on track again, Christie had given him the details of the internal boardroom battles and with it, unwittingly as it happened, the clue to Bartlett's activities. All he had to do was focus on that, pursue that single line till it turned into a noose that would hang Bartlett by the neck.

'Mr Bartlett's secretary, how can I help you?' Jen spoke with a practised coolness, investing in herself authority by virtue of her closeness to Bartlett; it was his name she spoke not her own.

'Westerham here,' he said, the throatiness of his voice like a whisper. 'I'd like to see him quite urgently.'

'Mr Westerham, I'm afraid that Mr Bartlett is busy at the moment, I can't interrupt him. Perhaps I can call you back?'

'I'm sorry, this cannot wait,' Westerham insisted. He was standing by the window of his hotel room, looking down at the green across the street, at the people taking a walk through the grass, walking the dog, or sitting on a bench and reading a newspaper.

'I'll put you on hold,' she relented, the hesitation kept to a minimum.

He spotted Jackie crossing the green, dressed in jeans and denim jacket, a bag slung casually over her shoulder. She looked relaxed, at ease with herself, her long hair caught in the breeze and fluttering down her back. Had she been with a lover? The question hurt Westerham more than he dared admit.

'Yes, Westerham,' Bartlett said, taking the line, 'what is it?'

There was no pretence at niceties, cancelling their previous meeting had put paid to the formalities once and for all. 'I need to talk, Bartlett.'

'Talk now.'

'No, I think we ought to do this face to face.'

'I don't have time for games, Westerham,' Bartlett warned testily. 'If you've got something to say then say it, otherwise stop wasting my time.'

'It's about the film studio,' Westerham said, pushed into broaching the subject when he had planned only to do that face to face.

'So, you've talked to Christie,' Bartlett let drop casually. 'If you've anything specific to say, say it.'

'I'd like a meeting,' Westerham was disconcerted, his meeting with Christie was supposed to have been a secret.

'Christie's with me here,' Bartlett added with the same degree of casualness, the sneering undertone like a knife.

'Who told you?' was all Westerham could ask.

'He did, old boy,' Bartlett laughed.

Westerham put the phone down, cutting off the

laughter before he said something he'd regret. Bartlett had done it again, taken two steps forward for Westerham's one, keeping ahead of the game with consummate ease. Time was running short, he had been brought in because of his reputation for getting results quickly, but it was a reputation that was only as good as the last case. If he failed now, it would put him back years, and Bartlett was the sort of man that made sure that once his enemies were down, they stayed down.

Sarah should have known that she would be given no time to reflect; Eddie didn't work that way, everything was hurried, impulsive, slightly chaotic. She had reluctantly agreed to meet the backer of the film, ostensibly to listen to him talking about the surprise party but, as far as she was concerned, to find out precisely what sort of film they wanted to make. In spite of Eddie's assurances, and he repeated them endlessly, she still suspected that there was something disreputable about what they wanted to do. She had assented to the meeting only to have Eddie arrange it for that same evening, trapping her so that she couldn't back out of it without destroying her chances of appearing in the film.

Eddie had suggested she wear something sexy, something that would catch the eye, and so she had decided on a very long loose skirt and a loose top. It covered her up completely, revealing nothing of her body, and she had applied only a dash of colour to her cheeks; she wanted to appear as demure as possible, to dissociate herself as far as possible from anything remotely suggestive. She knew that if the film was genuine then it didn't matter what she wore, and if it wasn't, she wanted to make it plain that she was going to have nothing to do with it. A part of her had wanted to go along with Eddie's plan, to get the part no matter what, but another part of her clung tenaciously to the idea of principles and integrity. If she hadn't met Dominique then she would have given in, she knew that, but as it was, she felt stronger, more certain of herself than she had done for a long time.

'Aren't you getting dressed?' Eddie demanded urgently when she opened the door to him. He had dressed for the night, the black leather jacket and steel-rimmed shades had gone, he was wearing a smart silk suit and tight black polo neck, only the stubble on his chin remained from the morning.

'I am dressed,' she giggled, flaring her skirt out and hoping that her good humour would deflect his anger for a moment.

'But I told you to do yourself up,' he complained, sliding a hand through his thick black hair. 'You look like a bloody nun. Has the skirt got a slit at the side at least? Can you show a bit of leg?'

'Why should I have to show a bit of leg? Why don't I just turn up with nothing on for goodness sake?'

'It's that bloody Dominique, isn't it?' Eddie cried, face white with indignation

'No, it isn't,' Sarah retorted angrily, 'I make my own decisions thank you very much. If you wanted some stupid bimbo you should have got someone more on your own level.'

'We can't keep him waiting, there's a car downstairs for us,' Eddie sighed, ignoring her cutting remark. 'We'll have to make the best of it. And I didn't want a bimbo, I wanted you because you're

112

smart, girl. Or at least I thought you were. These are film people, they want glamour, they want fun. If you don't want that then stick to doing your stupid experimental plays in front of six people and a dog.'

'I'm sorry,' Sarah exhaled heavily. 'Look I just don't want to get into anything that I'm not happy with. Is that too much to ask?'

'Let's go, we don't want to keep Mr Russell waiting,' Eddie decided, taking her roughly by the hand and pulling her to the door.

'I am sorry Eddie,' she repeated, almost in spite of herself. 'It'll be alright, I'll wow him with the force of my personality.'

'Forget it,' Eddie murmured sulkily. 'Just don't give him the "I'm too precious, I'm an actress" crap, it won't wear any more. I thought I was doing you a favour, I thought you'd be grateful. What do I get? Crapped on is what I get.'

She listened in silence, allowing herself to be pulled along hurriedly. Eddie had a point, she felt suddenly guilty about the way she had been treating him. It was she who had pestered him to get her into film, and his sarcastic crack about experimental theatre had been bang on target.

'Smile,' he hissed when they stepped out into the street and he pointed to the sleek black car waiting for them.

Sarah smiled, a false, nervous smile but a smile all the same. The car gleamed under the street lights, smooth black paintwork and spotless chrome. A uniformed driver had been leaning on the bonnet and now he jumped to attention, his peaked cap was pulled down over his eyes, gloved hands gripped the rear door.

'Good evening,' he said softly as Sarah slid into

the welcoming warmth of the rear seat. Eddie used the other door, and slumped back heavily in the seat beside her, a hand going nervously through his hair as the car moved off.

'Well? Say something,' Eddie said, turning to look at her, his face still set in an expression of anger and disappointment.

'How many times do I need to apologise?' she said softly. He was trying to make her feel guilty, an ungrateful little bitch who was undeserving of his best efforts to help her.

'This isn't what you expected, is it?'

She shook her head. The luxurious car, leather upholstery, mahogany panelling, the chauffeur, all beyond expectation, and, much as she didn't want to admit it, all very impressive. 'No,' she admitted with a guilty smile, 'I didn't expect any of this.'

'Now will you believe me?' he pleaded.

'You can't blame me for being suspicious,' she said defensively.

'But now, you must believe me now.'

She nodded but said nothing, not wanting to commit herself despite the wavering of her distrust. The car skimmed the streets on a cushion of air, a pneumatic glide that swept through the streets of London towards the centre of the city. The bright lights gleamed and sparkled on the black paintwork and on the darkened windows, pale orange merging with bright red and fading to a clean white glare. She watched the play of light on the darkness of the car and let herself drift with it, forgetting about Eddie, forgetting about everything else and just letting herself imagine what life could be like . . .

If the film worked it could be the start of many, it could launch her career in a big way. She'd paid her dues, she'd done local theatre, street theatre, modern and experimental, she'd worked hard and got nothing for it. Now she wanted to move on, to try the commercial stuff, television, film, video. Some of her friends had already trodden that path, moving effortlessly to bigger and better things, and like all of those that had stayed behind, she had derided them, sneering at their commercialism, at their lack of integrity. But now she wanted to take the first step too, and she saw that her cynicism had been masking a growing envy.

'What're you thinking about?' Eddie asked her softly, no longer sounding angry or bitter.

'Nothing,' she said, leaning back into the warm leather seat, 'just thinking about the film.'

'It'll be good,' he promised. 'Real classy stuff. Did Dominique teach you a lot? I mean do you know how to look and how to talk the way she does?'

She nodded, hoping that the swathes of light from the street lamps masked her slight embarrassment. 'She's an actress as well, in her own way,' she explained.

'Mention that tonight, make it sound like you know what you're talking about,' Eddie urged her. 'Remember, bullshit means business here.'

The car pulled up at a smart restaurant off Park Lane, and a top-hatted doorman rushed forward to get the car door the instant the vehicle slowed to a halt. Sarah put her arm in Eddie's and together they walked through the door that was held open for them. The maitre d'hotel was waiting, an attentive looking grey-haired Italian; his eyes scanned Sarah in a single cool sweep that took her in completely and made her feel positively dowdy.

'Mr Russell,'s party, Luigi,' Eddie announced with a familiarity that had the maitre d' visibly wincing.

'This way, Madame, Monsieur,' he said graciously, his accent just the right side of parody.

Sarah followed, her mood dampened by the sight of the other women in the restaurant, impeccably dressed in beautiful designer costumes and looking good in them. She was certain that all eyes were upon her, and her paranoia increased when a sharp peal of laughter broke out behind her.

'Told you to dress up,' Eddie hissed under his breath, the plastic smile on his face directed at the lone diner at the far end of the restaurant.

His face was long, sombre, the solemnity heightened by thin white hair and dull grey eyes. He stood up as his guests approached, his thin white lips forming into a smile that transformed him. 'Katya, my dear, I'm so glad that Edward managed to twist your arm,' he smiled welcomingly. At the table he reached out and gave her a quick hug, his lips barely brushing against her cheek.

'He didn't have to do that much twisting,' she lied, taking her seat at the table. Hearing herself called by her stage name was odd, she so rarely used it herself.

'I'm sure he did,' he laughed, his eyes never leaving her own. 'But I'm glad you came, I like to meet the people I'm going to be working with; a personal touch is so important these days. Don't you agree?'

'Absolutely,' Eddie agreed, cutting Sarah off neatly. 'That's what I told her, Mr Russell.'

'It's refreshing to hear you say that, Mr Russell,' Sarah agreed, unwilling to allow Eddie to do the talking for her.

116

'Please, my dear, call me Thomas,' he said, then turning to Eddie, 'but you can stick with Mr Russell.' Sarah couldn't tell whether he was being serious or not. 'Now, tell me about yourself, what have you done?'

'Fringe mostly, for the last few years at least. I've done some film and video, walk-ons mostly. The last major thing I did . . .'

Thomas stopped her, putting his hand on hers. 'Any television?'

'No,' she admitted, looking up from the thick gold signet ring on Thomas's finger to see Eddie raising his eyes to the ceiling.

'Radio, perhaps?'

'A fifteen minute play,' she said gloomily, 'last year.'

'I see,' Thomas mused, his face cold and impassive, just as it had been when Sarah had first set eyes on him moments earlier.

'She is good,' Eddie interjected desperately, 'I mean she's had honourable mentions in the papers.'

It was damning faint praise, and Sarah's hopes were fast disappearing; the flashy restaurant, the expensive car, the first hints of the good life were going to be the nearest she ever got to making it big.

'I've no doubt about that,' Thomas murmured, not even masking his disappointment. He took a menu from a waiter and glanced at it quickly, distractedly, before handing it straight back.

Sarah wondered what great claims Eddie had made on her behalf. For a moment she felt angry, she gritted her teeth and wanted to smack him in the face for getting her into this mess. She steeled herself and the anger subsided, it wasn't Eddie's fault, not really. 'What angle are you taking on this?' she asked, determined not to give in. 'Is this going to be grand tragedy or high comedy?'

'High comedy?' Thomas asked, looking up suddenly.

'Yes, is the whore going to be a caricature, a cartoon whip wielding bitch, or a real character with her own complex motivations?'

'No, decidedly not,' Thomas stated firmly. 'This isn't kitchen-sink drama, but neither is it going to be knockabout comedy. How would you play her?'

'As a split personality, absolutely strict on the one hand and yet with all her own human failings on the other,' Sarah said, improvising a good deal as she hadn't really considered how to portray the one element of her own personality she had only just discovered.

'How about a trial run?' Eddie suggested, looking first at Thomas and then at Sarah.

'Ah yes,' Thomas smiled, 'our little surprise. To be honest, Katya, the film will never be made unless we get a few more people on board. I have a colleague who's interested, he likes the idea but he's never put his money into film before. Now I know he's got a marvellous sense of humour, he loves the absurd, the out of the way. It ocurred to me that we might play on that a bit. If you could chat him up, get him into your room where you play the dominatrix role, then we put on the lights and jump out with the old champers and balloons, well, it'll appeal to his sense of humour and I've no doubt it'll sway him. If he could fall for it, then why shouldn't a leading politician?'

'So it's not his birthday?' Sarah asked, noting the discrepancies between the scenario that Eddie had described and what Thomas had just outlined.

'Yes, but that's a bit of a sore point, encroaching middle age and all that,' Thomas explained smoothly, really warming to his task. 'He'll probably be feeling a bit down, so the sight of a pretty girl's going to knock him for six. We want to cheer him up as well as butter him up,' he laughed.

'What do you think?' Eddie asked, signalling to the waiter that they were ready to order.

It sounded ridiculous, but Thomas was leaning forward, on the edge of his seat, looking directly at her with his cool grey eyes, eager for her positive response. Sarah looked around, at the dark suited waiters hovering obsequiously, at the glittering chandeliers sparkling with a thousand jewels of light, at Thomas himself, conservatively dressed and cool headed – it had to be right. She nodded. 'When do I have my audition?'

'Good girl,' Thomas smiled, squeezing her hand, 'think of this as being in lieu of an official screen test.'

'I told you she'd be good.' Eddie breathed a sigh of relief, beaming at Thomas like an idiot.

'She hasn't passed the screen test yet,' Thomas said, and again Sarah realised she couldn't tell whether he was joking or not, as if his face were a mask that expressed whatever he wanted it to, and that the ambiguity were deliberate and meant to keep everyone else on edge. She didn't like him, she decided coldly, but she smiled out of necessity, her eyes avoiding his cold searching stare.

7

Westerham nursed his drink and scanned the bar for interesting faces. Jackie had been in earlier. She had honoured him with a smile that was cool and stand-offish, but a smile all the same. He had nodded to her in reply, acknowledging her presence without showing any real interest and had then turned back to his drink, musing about the day's progress. The investigation had become bogged down, with both sides dug in and waiting for the other to slip up before going on the attack.

Christie was back with Bartlett, his fear stronger than his self-respect. The move had been a pointer to the state of the investigation. It was a signal to everybody that Bartlett's hand was stronger than Westerham's. There had been a long and strained telephone call from the company chairman, wanting to know in exact detail what progress had been made. It had not been a long report; Westerham preferred to be blunt than to try and pad out what he had achieved. It wasn't a policy for the faint-hearted, but it was honest and it added strength to his argument for carrying on the investigation. If it had been an easy case to unravel, he pointed out judiciously, then there would have been no need to call him in the first place.

But the news had not been all bad; some progress

had been made at last. The problem had been pinned down to the film studio, and so Westerham had gone back to the facts and figures. Checking through the records he had discovered that the power costs for the studio were incredibly high, and an afternoon on the phone had confirmed the fact. For some reason, the studio was consuming the power of a site twice its size, the place was burning off electricity at an alarming rate. That wasn't where all the money was going, but it was a start, and Westerham had no doubt that further investigation was going to reveal similar odd, inexplicable discrepancies.

He looked up and saw a young blonde entering the bar. She looked around for a second, saw no one that she recognised and so settled for a stool at the bar. She leaned across, her tight grey dress clinging attractively to her curves, and ordered herself a drink. Westerham watched her for a moment, saw her flick her hair back over her shoulder, her eyes scanning the room for a familiar face. Was she waiting for someone, or was she just looking for a likely face? The girl behind the bar, Jackie's friend, started chatting to her, her lips forming words that Westerham could not hear but which he could imagine. He could see the blonde listening to her without really looking, as if the people in the room were much more interesting than the idle chatter of the bargirl.

The blonde seemed surprised to find Westerham staring back when her eyes fell upon him. For a moment they looked at each other, measuring each other up, and then she half smiled and lowered her eyes. He sat still, leaning back in his seat comfortably, waiting for her to look again, knowing that she would look, and that she would turn away once more. Her glance across the room was slow and deliberate, her eyes barely registering him, just to check to see if he was still looking. The coy look half a minute later was just as expected, only there seemed to be some consternation there too, confusion because he was making no obvious move towards her.

'Could you get me another scotch, please?' Westerham asked a passing waitress.

'Yes, certainly sir,' she smiled brightly.

'And could you also get whatever the young lady at the bar is drinking, but bring her drink here.'

'Do you know what she's drinking?' the waitress asked, glancing across at the blonde who was looking at Westerham curiously.

'No, find out but bring the drink here please.'

The waitress turned on her heel and went directly to the blonde who was waiting, perhaps expecting a message from Westerham. Instead the waitress took the order and then carried the drinks back on a tray, placing them on the table in front of him. She smiled sweetly and hesitated, but when Westerham thanked her she turned back to her work.

'It's usually me that plays hard to get,' the blonde explained, taking the seat opposite Westerham.

'It's good to confound expectations sometimes,' Westerham smiled, sliding her the drink. 'Besides, why bother with the formalities?'

'You're very sure of yourself,' she observed, her eyes locking with his.

'That makes two of us. I haven't seen you here before, guest or visitor?'

'Katya Russell. I've checked in tonight.'

'Westerham.' He offered his hand which she took in her fingers just for a second, her eyes still fixed on his. There was something very different about her, something direct in both her manner and her speech.

'Westerham? Is that a first name, a surname or an address?' she asked, her smile of amusement tempered by the purity of her features, smooth pale skin, full lips, finely drawn eyes that sparkled confidently.

'Westerham is all there is, it describes me completely. I'm not sure you look like a Katya,' he told her, intrigued by her directness.

'And what does a Katya look like?' she laughed, throwing her head back so that her throat was soft and white and bare.

'A Katya is more reserved, not so certain of herself.'

'Is that so? And is a Katya usually prey to a Westerham?'

'What are you doing here?' Westerham laughed, surprised at the sound that came so unexpectedly to his lips. He was more than intrigued now. The attraction he felt for her was subtly different from what he'd felt for Louise or Jackie; the physical element was more diffuse, she had blurred the rules of the game.

'What is anyone doing here? Do you mean that physically or metaphysically?'

'You are playing hard to get,' Westerham smiled.

'Why bother with the formalities?' she shrugged.

Westerham paused and tried to fix her in his mind. 'Were you here for anyone in particular?' he asked, certain that he needed to provoke her a little.

'I'm not touting for business,' she said with a brutality that made him blink. 'I just want to enjoy myself. Maybe you're right, tonight I'm not really a Katya, I'm a Westerham.'

'I want to fuck you,' Westerham hissed, leaning forward so that his face was in hers, so that everything was blocked out but his eyes that held hers.

'I know you do,' she smiled, and she didn't waver, she didn't turn away from the intensity of his gaze, she did not tremble or catch her breath or flush pink. 'Let's go to my room.'

She stood up and walked off, leaving Westerham sitting at the table in stunned silence. He felt a little dazed, *all* of his expectations had been confounded, and it left him feeling cheated. He watched her for a second, the tight dress slinkily revealing the perfect shape of her backside, her narrow waist and slender back. Her thighs were long and smooth, her calves accentuated by the high heels that made her legs that much longer and sexier. He felt cheated and confused, but his prick bulged painfully. She made him hard, the desire too strong to ignore.

She stopped at the entrance to the bar and looked over her shoulder. In that moment, she was framed in the light; her long hair was glossy and natural, making her look sweet and innocent, a look so at odds with her almost masculine self-confidence. He followed, wanting to remain detached, to divorce his feelings from the urgent physical desire that she had torched inside him, but unable to do so. He was struck by her casual insight. By rights she should have been his prey, he should have been moving in for the kill with that emotionless and dispassionate manner that sought sexual satisfaction with no strings attached.

'The girl at the bar warned me to stay away from you,' she said casually as they rode up in the elevator. She was leaning back, standing away from him.

124

'You didn't heed her warning then,' Westerham said, glad that she hadn't.

'It's only because she fancies you for herself,' Katya smiled, 'though you frighten the hell out of her. Still, that's what turns her on I guess.'

'Are you always so hot on what goes on in other peoples' minds?'

The elevator stopped and the door slid open but Katya made no move. 'No,' she decided after a moment of consideration, 'only when I'm in control.'

'And what makes you think that you're in control?' Westerham challenged, but then regretted it. She stepped forward just as the door started to slide shut with a faint hiss of air. He lurched forward to block the door, fumbling like an idiot. She pressed the button casually and the door opened to her, at her command, at her control.

He followed silently, angry with himself for being so inept. It wasn't like him, he was never clumsy, it wasn't his way. Her perfume followed her too, trailing a sensuous scent that he breathed, drawn to it inexorably. She slid the key in the lock and strode into her room, not even bothering to look back to see if he was there still.

'Drink?' she asked, flicking on the light in the room.

Westerham was beside her; he reached out and took her in his arms, she was warm and soft, her flesh toned a delicate pink, her mouth wet and open and desirable. 'Forget the drink,' he said coldly, forcing his mouth over hers, pressing his tongue deep into the welcoming wetness of her mouth.

'Not like this, Westerham,' she whispered, disengaging herself from his arms.

'Not like what?' he demanded angrily, releasing her completely. 'What do you want to do, talk?'

'Let's have a drink,' she suggested, crossing the room to the bar beside the bed.

'A drink?' repeated Westerham incredulously, his desire still an aching, throbbing pain between his thighs. He wanted her, wanted to throw her to the ground and bury his prick into the voluptuousness of her sex. Her confidence seemed to have deserted her, and he felt certain that she was playing for time in some way.

'It's scotch, isn't it?' she asked, turning to him.

'What is this? If I wanted to drink I would have stayed downstairs. I thought you wanted sex.'

She laughed and then looked at him strangely, her eyes burning into him. 'I don't want sex, Westerham, I want you.'

'What does that mean?' he asked, his voice losing the hard edge of anger as he was thrown off-balance again.

'Get undressed, I'm just going to slip into something else,' she said, leaving the empty glass on the bar, the bottle of scotch unopened.

Westerham drew breath sharply, irritated by Katya's games and by his own confusion. His instincts told him to make a grab for her, to pull her dress off violently, to suck hard on her nipples and to press his fingers into the sex-heat of her pussy, but something made him hold back. She disappeared into the bathroom, so supremely confident that she didn't bother waiting for his reaction. He went over to the bar, poured himself a drink, and swallowed the amber liquid so that the heat burned its way through his body.

He felt much better for the quick shot of alcohol;

it made him feel in control again. She was a strange young woman, and already he knew that he'd have to see her again, he couldn't let her go, not now. He undressed slowly, uncomfortably aware that he was preparing himself for her when it should have been the other way round, the way it always was. The bargirl would have been on her knees for him, her eyelids fluttering, heart pounding in her chest while she waited for him to make the next move.

He turned at the sound of the bathroom door, saw Katya and froze. She had changed from her slinkily seductive grey dress to an outfit of stark black leather, the blackness in contrast to the whiteness of her flesh. She wore a tight leather mini-skirt over thigh-high boots, a bustier top of leather that held her breasts up to his disbelieving eyes, and her hands and arms were clothed in elbow length leather gloves.

'I take it from the state of your prick that you like this,' she said, pointing to his erect prick with a gloved finger, her voice sharp and brittle.

'What are you doing?' he asked stupidly, unable to take his eyes from her. She marched towards him, her heels digging into the carpet so that each step was purposeful, powerful, her leather-swathed body bearing up on him, a lithe feline stalking her prey.

'Isn't it obvious?' she taunted, pushing him back so that he fell on the bed.

'Look,' Westerham snapped, 'I don't go for this sort of stuff.'

'Shut up!' she hissed, and her hand went across his face with a vicious snap. He put a hand to his face, dabbed his fingers across his lips and looked at the droplets of blood that she had drawn. His face felt numb, a dull ache was all that he felt of the white-heat of pain that had flashed across his face as her fingers had touched him. He looked up at her, looked into the cold eyes that studied his reaction with a detachment that was as unnerving as it was exciting.

'You're drawn blood,' he whispered, telling it to himself more than anything.

'You don't talk,' she ordered. 'Westerham, nothing else, it's not a name is it? It's an object, a thing, an idea of yourself, your pathetic invention. Well, tonight I'm going to treat you like an object, an object that exists for my pleasure and nothing else.'

'I could get up and leave,' he said pathetically, pushing himself up into a sitting position.

'But that isn't a threat, that's a possibility only, a very faint possibility. I'm going to tie you up, and if you keep talking I'll put a gag over your mouth too.'

'Why?' he asked, the question burning in his eyes and on his face. His prick was as hard as stone, and the desire he felt was raw and pulsing like a wound. She was standing over him, the face he had seen as purity and innocence revealed now as the epitome of cruelty. His breath was ragged, uneven, his whole body felt on fire.

'Shut up! You can call me Mistress, and if you beg me hard enough I'll let you suck my pussy. Now, I want your hands behind your back.'

Very slowly Westerham turned his back to her, on the verge of getting up to leave but unable to cross the threshold of decision. The touch of leather on his skin made him sigh, her gloved hand holding him down by the shoulder. Through a daze he felt her bind his hands with tight leather cuffs, felt the warmth of her body on his, the warmth of flesh in

128

contrast to the ice cold emotion. She was cold, imperious, disdainful, but he was on heat, burning with a desire that was total.

'Have you ever been whipped?' she asked, standing straight again.

He turned to her, head bowed, eyes fixed on the join of leather and flesh at the top of her boots. 'No,' he whispered.

'Mistress!' she hissed through clenched teeth, her arm raised for the blow that never came.

'No, Mistress,' he said softly, cowering from the up-raised hand. He looked down at himself, at his throbbing prick that was weeping a silvery trail of liquid the glans. He'd never felt harder, never felt so potent and yet so weak. Why was she doing this? Why was she tormenting him? He tried the strength of the cuffs and felt a thrill of fear pass through him, a weakness that travelled like a wave through his soul.

'I'm going to make you scream, Westerham,' she said quietly, her voice low and even, so cold it made him shiver.

She turned him round and pushed him over. He toppled across the bed, unable to hold his balance with his arms locked tight behind his back. He struggled, and managed to turn his head in time to see her pick up a cane, long and supple and cased in soft leather. Abstractly he watched her raise her arm, saw the perfect line of her flesh, the swell of her breasts, the contrast of golden hair on shining black, the distant look in her eyes. In slow motion the cane whistled and hissed, flexing into an arc as it sliced through the air. The distant quality, the abstractness, dissolved in a single flash of pain that made him scream like an animal. His strangled cry

129

died on his lips, but the pain burned across his naked backside.

'Do you want the people next door to hear you?' she asked derisively, her lips formed into a smile that made him wince with shame.

'Is this how you get your kicks?' he asked, trying to match her mocking tone.

'Yes, but I don't see you going limp,' she laughed, throwing his words back in his face. She touched the arc of fire across his backside, her leathered fingers pressing firmly, the slight coolness sucking away the pain wherever she touched. Without wanting to, he found himself lifting himself up to her, offering himself to her, the sensation of her fingers on his wound making him sigh.

She brought the cane down again, cutting another diagonal across his tensed arse-cheeks. He cried out again, unable to stop himself, the pain was so intense, but when the first flash of pain had subsided, his cock was harder than ever and his balls ached for release. He squirmed, his prick rubbing against the satin cover of the bed, the soft sensations of the satin a tantalising counterpart to the pain that was eating through his rear. Such pain, so exquisite, so powerful, so blissful.

Another stroke followed quickly, a pause while she touched him, explored him wordlessly, indifferently, and then another stroke, hard, fast, powerful. 'Don't . . . Please . . . I can't control it . . .' he begged, forgetting himself, forgetting everything but the pleasure that came from the pain, a pleasure that had him on the verge of climax.

'If you come without me allowing it,' she warned, relishing the power of her command, 'I'll make you eat it up.'

'I can't . . . I can't . . .' he whispered, appalled by the situation he was in. He struggled round, trying to free his cock from the delicious mess of satin that he had pressed himself into. His rear side was alive with a thousand fingers of pleasure-pain, snaking directly from his backside to his balls and prick, directly to the pleasure centres of the body and the brain.

She wielded the cane once more, its whistle through the air exploding into fierce contact with his naked flesh. He struggled hard, tried to tear asunder the binds that held him prisoner, his muscles tense, hard, trying but failing. He collapsed, cried out, her fingers massaging his backside while he spurted thick waves of cream into the satin sheets. It was a nightmare orgasm, a climax so powerful that he felt himself emptied emotionally as well as physically. He turned over on his back, his thighs smeared with warm come that trickled thickly over his cool skin.

'I warned you,' she smiled, her eyes wide with delight. She walked back to the bathroom, Westerham feasting his eyes on her delicious body, her hips swaying as her heels clamped into the thick carpet.

'My God, what am I doing?' he asked himself quietly. While his body seethed with pleasure and pain, he felt numb, the emotions torn from within and abandoned with cool indifference by Katya. The feel of his come smeared over his body was a reminder of the depths to which he had sunk. It was degrading, humiliating and yet immensely exciting. His prick was still hard, drooling thick cream onto his belly.

'Thank your Mistress, Westerham,' she ordered, 'thank me nicely while we're still alone.'

'What have you done to me . . .' he asked mournfully, staring up at her and dazzled by her cool and untouchable beauty.

'Thank me,' she repeated coldly.

'I can't thank you, not for this. Untie me now,' he ordered, turning over on his side to offer her his bound arms.

'No, not yet,' she decided, glancing across the room at the clock by the bed.

'What are you waiting for?'

'Nothing,' she replied quickly, the hardness returning to her voice. 'I said I'd punish you if you shot your load without my command, you're just about to learn that Mistress never jokes.'

'What are you going to do?' Westerham croaked, an involuntary tremor of anticipation passing through him.

Katya held out her hand and showed him a pair of silky black panties, edged with tiny frills of lace. She bent over him and scooped up his juice in the silky garment, then cleaned up most of the come that had splattered the satin bed cover. Her pretty black bundle was soon dark with wet patches, his cream thick and sticky and standing out against the silky panties.

'You make too much noise,' she said softly, leaning close to him. Her lips were moist and open, glossy pink against her bright white teeth. She teased his lips open with her tongue and then sucked at his breath, pushing her tongue deep into his mouth, invading him completely. He felt helplessly excited by her, unable to move because of his bondage, unable to move because he was overcome with desire. Her kiss was long and sensual, her mouth teasing him so that he ached for her, wanting to press his hardness deep into her mouth, to fuck her, to have her the way he wanted.

Swiftly she removed her lips and forced the tight bundle into his mouth before he could turn away. He was gagging, dizzy, slight nauseous, but then he was still, breathing hard and trying to calm himself. His mouth was full of the taste of her sex and of his, his breathing scented with the acrid smell of spunk and the mysterious essence of her sex. The gag filled him, and his tongue pressed hard to push it out so that he could draw breath that was clean and pure.

'That'll stop you screaming,' she explained calmly, turning him over onto his back. 'Now, I'm going to ride this thing,' she touched his prick gingerly, her face a picture of distaste, 'and if you come inside me I swear you'll regret it. And then, if you do well, you can have your reward, you can suck my pussy the way I like it.'

Westerham struggled, tried to back away and to force the words through the sex-scented gag, but she stood and laughed at his helplessness, and the more she laughed the more his arousal heightened. She climbed over him, took his prick in her hand and forced herself down on it, engulfing his prick in the wet heat of her sex, wet with her own desire. The pleasure was too much, she was heaven on him, he closed his eyes and tried to still the clamour in his head. He had to hold back, had to fight the intensity of elation, because that was what she desired.

She began to ride him, moving up and down, twisting herself down on his hard shaft, oblivious to the ecstasy that passed through him. Her eyes were closed, and he tried to fathom her motives, to understand the woman that was devouring him without even trying. Her face was soft and innocent once

133

more, as if the humiliation she had inflicted meant nothing.

He tried to speak again, tried to free his tongue but he only succeeded in swallowing a slow trickle of come. His moans were obviously distracting for her; she dealt him a hard slap to the face that made him whimper with renewed desire. He was hard, his balls aching, but he must not allow himself release, must not, must not, he repeated inside his head. She suddenly teased one of his nipples between her fingers and squeezed. He arched his back and screamed behind the gag, but then his prick was painfully hard and he knew that he was hers totally.

Westerham was woken up by the sharp echoes of pain that pierced him whenever he moved. He opened his eyes in a moment of blinding clarity. He was alone. He sat up, his aching muscles screaming for him to remain still, and looked around the room that he knew to be empty. She had gone while he slept on the floor, wrapped up in the satin cover that she had made him soil. Beside him, on the unblemished grey of the carpet, lay her discarded panties, the silky black glittering with tiny crystals of dried semen.

He stood up unsteadily, his back and shoulders sore, and sat heavily on the edge of the bed. The mirror across the darkened room caught his shape, hunched over in an attitude of utter defeat. The thoughts in his head refused to gel, there was something incoherent about what he had suffered. He waited in the darkness, naked, as the sun rose over the horizon and the light began to filter into the room.

She had gone without saying a word, discarding

him just as she had discarded her knickers. 'I've been fucked,' he said tonelessly. He turned and caught sight of himself in the mirror, his lower back thick with dull red stripes edged with darker bruises.

He dressed as quickly as his bruised body would let him, and then left for his own room. The corridors of the hotel were deserted, saved from total silence only by the faint echo of sound from the kitchens far below. The key to his room refused to work for a minute, his hands were too shaky and it was hard to concentrate. His room was like the one he had just come from, cold, empty, uninviting. He snapped on a shower and watched the water spurt out powerfully, throwing up thick clouds of steam in the early morning chill. He watched it for a minute, lost in the swirling rush of water, then snapped it off again. He was soiled, caked in stale sweat, dried semen and her sex cream, but he didn't want to wash it off. He suffered a distant kind of shock, realising that his prick was hard again.

'Reception, good morning,' an obscenely cheerful voice answered his call on the first ring of the phone.

'Tell me, has Miss Russell checked out?' he asked, his voice deep and dark to his own ears.

'I'm sorry, sir,' the young man replied, cheerily, 'but the name's not familiar.'

'The blonde in Room 207. Checked in last night.'

A pause. Westerham thought he heard the thick pages of the register being turned over. 'There was no Miss Russell in Room 207, not last night or any other night in the last couple of weeks.'

'Maybe it was another room,' Westerham suggested, knowing in his heart that he had quoted the right room number.

'I'm sorry sir, no one of that name's been registered here at all,' the young man stated apologetically.

'Then who was registered in 207?'

'Nobody as far as I can tell. Are you sure that was the correct room?'

'I was there last night, all night.'

'I'll get someone to check the room sir, but there's nothing in the register. I'm sorry.'

'Just check it out,' Westerham murmured.

He put the phone down and poured himself a drink, thankful for the warmth that it induced. Weird things happen in hotels, he tried to tell himself. He had sneaked into empty rooms before, it sometimes added to the sex, the feeling of breaking a few rules. Yes, he poured himself a second drink, she was using an empty room . . .

He sat down on the bed, cradling his drink, aware of the throbbing in his back where the cane had touched him harder or deeper than elsewhere. The empty room didn't matter, a minor detail, irritating but nothing more. All that he wanted was to find her again, to find her and talk to her, because she understood him, she knew him far better than anyone else he had ever met.

Sarah pounded on the door again, her fists beating hard against the wood and glass. Across the street a window went up, an angry head poked through to see what was going on.

'What is it? What is it?' Eddie called from behind the door, fumbling with the latch. 'Oh, it's you,' he yawned when he finally pulled the door open.

'Where were you?' Sarah demanded, pushing her way into the house. Eddie was naked apart from a pair of white shorts, his eyes were still ringed with sleep but now he was smiling a silly adolescent smile.

'Change of plan,' he lied unconvincingly, ambling back into the house.

'You're lying, Eddie,' Sarah said, following him into the kitchen, 'what's going on? Where was the surprise party? Where was Thomas Russell?'

'Give me a break,' Eddie complained, 'I was up all night. Thomas decided that you and Westerham had hit it off so well that it would have been stupid to interrupt you.'

'Thomas Russell wasn't there.'

Eddie opened the fridge, peered inside and slammed it shut. 'No milk,' he sighed. 'I hate black coffee in the mornings.'

'What was going on?' Sarah demanded, her voice suddenly cold and hard.

'Like I said,' Eddie's face a lecherous sneer, 'it was decided to leave the two of you to get on with it. You did really well, really well. You've got the film job, no doubt about that, we ain't seen nothing like it before.'

'What the fuck do you mean by that?' Sarah demanded, advancing angrily towards Eddie.

'Nothing, babe,' he had both hands in the air, in an innocent surrender. 'Just that, er, Westerham called Thomas and said he'd had a really wild time. Yes, really wild. He said he didn't know what hit him.'

'When was this?'

'This morning, only about an hour ago. Thomas called to tell me, he wanted to congratulate you on what you'd done. Yes,' Eddie smiled, 'he said you'd helped him no end.'

'Thomas said that?' Sarah asked sceptically.

'Sure he did. I knew you were a good actress, I told him you could pull it off. And I guess Dominique must have been a good teacher, right?'

'How is Westerham?' Sarah asked, turning away from Eddie, aware that he had picked up on her interest. She hadn't been acting, it had been an entirely natural performance, and her final climax riding Westerham's tongue had been evidence of that.

'He's alright, a bit knackered this morning, I guess,' Eddie laughed knowingly. 'I better give you your cash. Thomas says you deserve a bonus.'

'Money?' Sarah turned on her heels suddenly.

'Sure, we didn't expect you to do this for nothing,' Eddie chuckled at the very idea. He left Sarah for a moment and disappeared into his bedroom.

She moved to the window and looked to the jungle of a garden outside, to the weeds flourishing thanks to Eddie's neglect. She wondered how Westerham really felt; Eddie's story was altogether too slick to be true. Westerham had been sleeping when she left, curled up at the foot of the bed physically and mentally exhausted by the ritual they had played. He had been so certain of himself, it had been hard to imagine him submissive, but once thrown off balance, he had succumbed to the totality of submission.

'Here,' Eddie returned with a grimy bundle of notes, folded over and tied with an elastic band, 'it's probably more than you've ever earned from a single performance. But Thomas is a generous man, to those that please him. We'll be in touch about the film, but if last night was anything to go by you'll have no problem making this sort of money.'

'What do you mean?' Sarah asked quizzically, gingerly taking the money, afraid to dirty her hands.

'Nothing,' he said, turning away from her inquiring eyes.

'If there's anything you haven't told me . . .' she warned.

'I want to get some sleep,' Eddie complained, yawning extravagantly, stretching his body tight so that his prick bulged in his tight shorts.

'I might go and see Westerham,' she decided, her words cutting off Eddie's exaggerated yawn.

'What's the point?' he demanded, his face darkening instantly.

'Why not?'

'Because Thomas wants to work on him, get him involved in the film. If you turn up it could queer his pitch. Just leave Westerham to us,' he counselled earnestly.

'If you say so, Eddie,' Sarah agreed. Eddie exhaled slowly, a great weight off his shoulders. 'Now, I'm shattered,' he said softly, 'I've got to get some sleep.'

Sarah reached out and touched him on the shoulder, tracing a finger nail from his neck down to one of his nipples. He watched her in wide-eyed silence, fascinated but afraid. 'I've still got lots of energy,' she whispered breathily.

'No, I'm too tired,' Eddie said quietly, backing away from her slowly.

'Don't be scared, I won't eat you,' she laughed. He was afraid of her, so obviously afraid, and it marked a complete reversal of roles. She snorted derisively and then brushed past him, her heart beating wildly. Dominique was right, Eddie liked his women stupid, and she was no longer stupid, no longer in awe of him or his work. She was going to see Westerham; what Eddie thought no longer mattered, not him, not Thomas Russell, not anyone.

8

There were three reactions: anger, a sense of betrayal and desire. Westerham felt all three simultaneously, a potent mixture of emotions that seethed and bubbled until he picked up a glass and smashed it against the wall, the explosion of sound and glass followed by a dull silence. He took his face in his hands, and rubbed his eyes despairingly. How could she have done it to him? He sank back into his seat, looking blankly at the TV screen that showed harsh static. It was all there, on tape, from the moment he fumblingly tried to assert himself – the tape showed him reaching for her half-heartedly – to the moment when she had convulsively climaxed with his head between her thighs, the sound of her sighs matched by the sound of his mouth sucking deeply from her pussy.

He paced the room, a caged animal, ready to explode again. How could she do it to him? He felt betrayed, disgusted, wounded in a way the physical beating had never approached. He had believed in her, accepted her as she was, and he had yielded to her because of her insight, because of her knowledge. Sham, all of it a cruel sham; she knew about him because Bartlett had primed her and told her all about him.

It had happened so quickly. An embarrassed

141

chambermaid had knocked on his door and reported that room 207 was empty apart from some personal belongings. His heart had missed a beat, for a moment he had hoped that there was something to lead him back to Katya. The chambermaid had handed over a small polythene bag, her eyes averted in a gesture of embarrassment. He had seized it from her hands and looked inside eagerly, only to find the abandoned panties, still caked with crystals of dried come. The disappointment had showed on his face, because despite the girl's obvious discomfort, she had apologised for not finding anything more.

Westerham had then showered, washing away the disappointment, determined to lose himself in work. There were still the film studio numbers to go through, to see what other costs had been inflated artificially. A second knock at the door revived his hopes that Katya was still reachable. The same chambermaid was there, delivering a package that a courier had just brought into reception. His heart sank as soon as he opened it and saw the video tape. The story fell into place. He knew what was on the film even before he slid it into the machine to play it back.

It was all so clear: Katya's knowledge, her unexplained pauses, her carefully prepared costume. He had watched the tape in mute silence, reacting with desire despite what had happened. The film was well-taken, a clean picture and crystal clear sound. 'Thank you, Mistress,' he had babbled at the end, driven by the experience of pleasure and pain beyond endurance. And she had accepted his thanks by sitting astride his face, opening herself to his tongue, grinding down on him so that her pleasure was complete.

The phone call came while he was still deep in thought, gazing at the film that finished after her climax, after she had graciously allowed him to sleep on the floor, at the foot of her bed like a faithful pet.

'Stop it, Westerham,' was all the unidentified voice on the phone said.

He had flung the receiver across the room, and then the glass that had splintered dramatically. An amber stain had sprung explosively across the light blue-grey wallpaper.

There was no question of stopping the investigation, none at all. How could he? If anything, the film was going to help nail the bastard. Someone had to have made it, the camera had to come from somewhere, the girl had to have been paid. Westerham was going to nail Bartlett no matter what, even it if meant exposing his own degradation to the world. What did it matter? What mattered was winning the case, beating the enemy, destroying Bartlett totally in the process. It hurt, Westerham felt the pain as something unbearable, a gaping wound that seeped with blood and bile, but he swore that Bartlett was going to hurt even more.

And the girl? Was Katya going to hurt too? He tried not to think of her, his target was Bartlett, but the bruising was too deep, the emotional pain too raw. He was going to pay her back too, he was going to make her suffer as he had suffered, emotionally, spiritually. The bitch, nothing she had done to him could compare to what he was going to do to her.

He left for work in a blind unthinking rage, plotting deep, dark revenge. What could they do? Send the film to the newspapers? To his family and friends? To the police? They could do nothing because Westerham was free, there was nobody in his life who mattered, nobody he cared about. He was free and invulnerable, and if Bartlett had any sense then he should have recognised that. Westerham had never won any prizes for popularity, and, in his mind, that was a good thing.

He had let the bitch get to him, allowed her a glimpse into his soul, and this was how she paid him back. Driving through the busy London traffic his mind kept returning to that one fact, to the betrayal above all else. And beneath the anger there was still the desire, the arousal that seemed to grow in direct proportion to the depth of degradation. Where had that come from? He tried to dismiss the idea. Louise had called him a cold bastard. It wasn't an insult, it was something he aspired to, something he aimed for. He should have carried on that way, he should have asserted himself, taken Katya from behind before she had had a chance to play her weird mind and sex games.

He drove directly to Christie's office, dumped the car by the entrance, ignored the receptionist and stormed straight into the complex of offices. Louise saw him, started to say something but then she seemed to shrink back in her seat, too afraid of the look she saw in his eyes.

'Don't call security,' he told her coldly, 'I'll only be a minute.'

He pushed the door open and strode into Christie's office, fists clenched and heart pumping. Christie was on the phone, speaking quietly. He swung round in his seat and looked up with shock written all over his face. Westerham grabbed the phone and wrenched it from the wall, throwing it across the room violently.

'I had to do it . . . I had to . . .' Christie whimpered, rising from his seat.

'Do what exactly?' Westerham hissed, grabbing Christie by the lapels and dragging him across the desk. Everything was black, the sound of voices raised and people running into the office failed to register.

'I had to see Bartlett,' Christie whimpered, hanging limply across the desk, his arms seeking to give him balance but not to push Westerham away.

'What about last night? Did you know about that?'

'Please, Westerham, I don't know anything. He set me up, he's the one who gave you my address, he set us both up. I had to see him, he's too powerful.'

Suddenly Westerham's arms were being pulled away, two uniformed security guards were trying to release Christie. He ignored them completely, their voices lost in the excitement. 'If I find out you had anything to do with last night . . .' he warned, glaring at Christie with a violence that had the guards calling for help.

'I don't know anything . . .' Christie repeated, sinking back into his seat, his pale face bathed in sweat. 'You must believe me, Westerham.'

The office was silent for a moment, the security guards standing off, ready to pounce if Westerham made another move. 'Tell them to fuck off,' Westerham told Christie, with an authority that Christie recognised. He nodded and the guards backed away.

Louise rushed into the office, pushing through the guards and over to Christie. She put her arms around him protectively, her face a picture of anger and concern. 'Why don't you leave him alone?' she

145

demanded, her piercing blue eyes ice-cold with hatred.

'You're wasted on him,' Westerham spat at her. 'You could do much better for yourself than a loser like him.'

'You're a son of a bitch,' she sneered, 'at least Tony's got me, who the hell have you got?'

Westerham glared at her for a moment, stung by her words. 'Tell Bartlett it won't work,' he told Christie, then turned and left, the silent crowd parting to let him through.

By the time Westerham got to the headquarters building the number of security men had been doubled. Forewarned, there was no way Bartlett could allow any sort of confrontation; it would do his reputation no good, even it if ended with Westerham being ejected unceremoniously by the security guards.

He sat in his car and dialled the chairman directly, knowing that his scene with Christie would be all around the company in a matter of hours.

'Tell Mr Gilder that this matter is of the utmost urgency and must be dealt with at once,' he informed the secretary who tried to fob him off.

'What is it?' Gilder asked irritably when he took the line. It sounded as though Westerham had disturbed his sleep or interrupted a golfing anecdote.

'I have been subjected to an attempt at blackmail,' Westerham reported, suppressing his rage as best he could. 'I have been instructed to put a stop to my investigation at once, but naturally I can't do that.'

'What sort of attempt?' Gilder asked, after allowing himself a slight pause while he digested the information.

'I have been filmed in a compromising position,'

Westerham reported through gritted teeth. He could easily imagine Gilder's tired old face forming into a prurient, sickly smile.

'I see,' Gilder said after another lengthy pause. 'To whom do you ascribe this alleged attempt at blackmail?'

'I have no idea. However, various stories about me may yet appear in public. I can assure you that I will continue with my investigation.'

'Can I take it that there is no illegality involved?'

'What?' Westerham was astounded by the question.

'This compromising position. I assume you are engaged in some act that does not break the law? I'm sorry to be blunt about this Westerham, but we have the company name to think of.'

'Listen Gilder, I don't give a shit about your company name. In fact if you don't wake up soon you won't even have a company name to worry about.'

'My question stands,' Gilder said frostily.

'There's nothing illegal about what I was doing. Now, can I have an assurance from you that my position is safe?'

'No you cannot. To be honest, Westerham, I regret calling you into this in the first place. You've created a lot of bad feeling in the company and achieved nothing. And, to lower myself to your level, I don't give a shit about your position.'

'Bartlett's going to have you for dinner,' Westerham warned.

'It sounds like he's had you already. You have one week. If you fail to deliver then your contract will be terminated.'

The phone went dead and Westerham realised he

was sweating, his hand was tight around the phone, his knuckles painfully white. Gilder, stupid and ungrateful, had at least given him one week's grace. It was more then Westerham had hoped for. Telling Gilder what he thought of him had been a crazy gamble but it had paid off. He was sure that if Bartlett had got there first then it would have been an instant termination of contract.

It was a stubborn fact: the power costs were too high and nothing could explain it adequately. The other costs were within reason, the labour costs in line with the personnel involved, the building costs entirely normal. No matter how many hours work Westerham put in, the single fact stuck out like a sore thumb. He had visited the studios, walked around the site, and been shown round by a sullen and untalkative minion that Bartlett had selected as a guide. He watched some filming, a television play he was told, did a quick head count and found the figures a little lower than he had expected but not to any significant extent.

Rumours were flying around, both that he'd beaten Tony Christie up and that his days were numbered. If there were rumours of the blackmail attempt then they had yet to filter back to him directly. The few board members that had been on his side all seemed to be too busy to field his calls. That was expected, it gave him a certain grim satisfaction.

The day spent at the studio had followed twenty hours of solid paperwork, which had in turn followed the half a day lost to drink after he had called Gilder. He returned to the hotel, exhausted but prepared to go through a new set of files. The work was hard but it had the advantage that it left him no time to muse about the mess he had got himself into. Better not to think, better just to work through.

He arrived back at the hotel and headed straight up to his room, hardly noticing the woman sitting in the corner of reception. He waited by the elevator, planning his next line of attack. The elevator door opened and he was followed in by a shadow, the door closed and he pressed the button for his floor.

'You look tired,' a voice said.

Westerham looked up, jolted by the sudden rush of recognition, the hair prickled on the back of his neck, his body tightening instinctively. 'What the fuck do you want?' he hissed, squaring up to Katya who looked at him strangely, as if truly shocked by his reaction.

'I came to see you,' she whispered, backing into a corner. The elevator door opened, she looked out, and watched the door close again.

'You stupid fucking bitch,' he snarled, 'did you really think I would fall for it again?'

'Please, Westerham, I just wanted to see how you were,' she said quietly, the alarm in her eyes widening.

'How do you think I feel? Stupid. Betrayed. Fucking angry. How could you do it, don't you have any respect for yourself, you whore?'

'I am not a whore,' she said coldly. 'If you didn't like it you could have stopped me any time you liked.'

'But then you wouldn't have been paid, would you? It wouldn't be much of a film that way. Get out! Go on, get out!'

'Westerham, I don't understand. Is it Russell?'

'Who the hell is Russell?'

'Your friend . . .' she said.

'No, no friend of mine. Didn't they tell you? Westerham has no friends,' he said bitterly.

'But he was so convincing . . . Please, let me explain. I don't know what's happened but I was set up.'

'What's gone wrong is that everything we did is on film,' he explained, finding a certain satisfaction in telling her, 'in glorious sound and colour, and it's being used to blackmail me.'

'Jesus,' Katya closed her eyes; she looked a little sick. 'I had nothing to do with that,' she said, shaking her head to emphasise the fact.

'Who set it up?' Westerham demanded, punching a button on the elevator.

'Eddie, Eddie Watson and Thomas Russell,' she began. 'They told me you wanted to help in financing a film they want to make.'

'A film?'

'Yes, I'm supposed to be in it. I'm an actress. My name's not Katya, it's Sarah, not half as exotic is it?'

'And no doubt Thomas Russell is not who he says, nor Eddie Watson.'

'No, he's for real. In fact we ought to pay him a visit.'

The elevator opened on the ground floor. 'Have you eaten?' Westerham asked, stepping out into the lobby after Sarah. She shook her head. 'Let's eat and you can tell me exactly what you know.'

'Sure, but there's one thing,' Sarah said, turning to face him.

'What's that?'

Sarah slapped his face so hard the sound drew glances from everyone in the lobby. Westerham rubbed his face, aware that all eyes were upon him. 'Never, ever call me a whore again,' she said evenly.

He nodded, his face red with the imprint of her fingers. The reaction was instant, and not unexpected; his prick was hard, the desire that had lain dormant for two days was aflame again.

Sarah put down her fork and looked at Westerham. He had a rugged, lived in sort of face; eyes that could be captivating, suggesting depth of character and a fine intelligence. His manner alternated between violently passionate and sardonically detached. At all times he was sexual, the chemistry just below the surface, and he had enough self-knowledge to know that it was attractive to women. There was coldness too, best reflected when he was at his most cutting, sarcastic, caustic, the rage barely concealed behind his dangerous eyes. He was naturally a dominating man, in control, powerful, and it made Sarah wonder how he had allowed himself to submit to her.

'More wine?' he asked, as if he had only just noticed that she had been studying him.

She declined with a slight shake of the head. 'This Bartlett,' she began, picking up the conversation where it had left off when the food arrived, 'you're sure that it's the same man as the Thomas Russell I met?'

'Certain. If he was absolutely convincing,' he paused for her to nod agreement, 'then that's him. A tough character, ruthless even when he has no need to be. He likes to win, no matter what the game or the stakes.'

'A bit like you,' Sarah pointed out, smiling.

'You're not the first person to say that,' he agreed,

joining in with a smile. The observation was obviously to his liking, for it was clear that he had a lot of respect for Bartlett/Russell, despite being enemies.

'Does he wear a ring? Big, gold, a bit flashy in a quiet sort of way?' Sarah asked, remembering the signet ring that had caught her attention when she had met Thomas.

'He might do, he's a very tidy man, well dressed, never looks flustered or out of breath.'

That sounded like Thomas, the man that Westerham had described fitted him in every respect. 'Is he really a crook?'

Westerham laughed. 'Any man that resorts to blackmail is a crook. Tell me more about Eddie Watson, is he a boyfriend?'

She hesitated to answer. 'No, he's not a boyfriend. I suppose I'm no longer his type,' she added.

'Who does he work for, normally?'

'He's freelance, and usually in work. He is good at what he does, Westerham, but you'd never believe it from looking at him.'

Westerham seemed to muse on the point for some while, sipping wine, scanning the room all the while, watching the guests coming in and out of the restaurant. Sarah noticed the way he homed in on the women, his alert eyes evaluating every one in turn, with barely a flicker of emotion on his face.

'May I see the film?' Sarah asked. 'I assume you haven't destroyed it?'

'No, I haven't destroyed it.'

'Have you watched it again?'

His eyes flicked, widening slightly and fixing on her coldly. 'No, I haven't watched it again, though it does hold a certain sick fascination for me.'

'How charming of you to put it like that,' she sniffed, feigning disinterest in his reaction, where, in reality, she was dying to know what he felt.

'From the angle it was taken I imagine that your friend Watson must have enjoyed himself immensely. He can't have been more than a few metres away from us. I'd say he'd been hiding in the closet during the entire scene.'

Sarah swallowed hard; she hadn't considered the mechanics of making the film. It made her feel sick to think of Eddie watching them, hiding away in the darkness while she and Westerham performed like an act from a freak show. 'He's a sick bastard for doing this,' she said slowly, completely disgusted by him.

'Perhaps I'm the sick bastard for letting you beat me,' Westerham said under his breath, turning away from her.

'This isn't guilt, is it?'

'Do you find that strange?' Westerham asked, sounding surprised by her tone.

Sarah shook her head. 'I felt it too, the first time. Now, well, now I'm trying to accept what I am. But I have to admit, I still feel a little bit uncomfortable.'

'This will sound stupid, but really, what's a nice girl like you doing involved in all of this?'

Sarah laughed, a full throaty laugh that drew glances from people at the neighbouring tables. Westerham merely smiled, letting her laugh without interruption.

'Forget all that,' she said, regaining her breath, 'what do you suggest we do about this?'

'It depends on how far you want to take this,' he explained. 'I'm not bothered about this film getting out to the newspapers, you might not be so relaxed about that. We can go to the police, but then the story, and most likely the film too, will get out. Or we could try and confront Bartlett with the evidence, threaten him with exposure as a blackmailer. I'm certain he's already covered himself, he's not a stupid man by any means.'

'We could get the film back,' Sarah suggested hopefully, the idea of public exposure making her feel distinctly uneasy.

'There could be dozens of copies around already,' Westerham pointed out quite reasonably.

'Eddie would know that. Besides,' she said, the idea just occurring to her, 'Bartlett might have himself covered but I doubt if Eddie has, he isn't clever enough.'

Westerham smiled agreeably. 'I think you're right. Perhaps we can get at Bartlett, via Eddie. Where can we find him?'

Sarah shrugged. 'He works a lot at night, most nights in fact. I'm not sure what he's working on at the moment, but we can try him at home.'

'Good,' Westerham rose from the table, 'we can call from my room.'

Sarah followed him out of the restaurant and through the lobby, and, although he was leading the way she still felt in control, lagging a pace behind him so that he had to slow down for her. She wondered how Dominique would react in similar circumstances; how would she deal with Bartlett, Eddie and Westerham? She hadn't spoken to Dominique about Westerham at all, not even obliquely, but she had been to see her since the session with Vincent, just to sit and talk. At first she had been afraid that Dominique would try something on, but that fear had soon turned to hope, and then finally to an urgent desire that she had confessed guiltily. Dominique had smiled, and just carried on talking, purposely refusing Sarah's desire in order to emphasise the power relationship between them.

Perhaps it had been better that Dominique had acted the way she did, teaching Sarah by example what it was to be Mistress. The physical side was easy, natural even, the sexual domination was the most sublime pleasure she had ever experienced. It was the psychological side that was more difficult to fathom. For Sarah it had been like regaining consciousness, discovering power in herself where she had imagined none existed. The transformation was still in progress; new facets of her personality were being revealed by every new experience, and the more she unfolded her wings, the more she felt alive.

'Were you just acting, when you did what you did?' Westerham asked suddenly, pushing open the door to his room.

'Acting? Of course. I was acting the way I wanted to act, and you, you were acting the way you wanted to act,' Sarah said, slamming the door behind her and following Westerham into the room. 'A little accident?' she asked, pointing to the whisky stains that still marked the wall.

'I didn't want to act that way,' Westerham said, and his voice was too controlled for Sarah to take him seriously.

'Well, I did,' Sarah stated flatly, with a childish petulance that made Westerham smile.

'Call Watson while I pour some drinks,' he directed, pointing to the phone by the corner of the bed.

Sarah threw herself flat on the bed and picked up the phone; there was a card by it with instructions for dialling external calls. She selected a line then punched in Eddie's number. It rang twice and then she heard the hiss and whirr of an answering machine. Eddie's voice sounded slow and mechanical, a tranquillised version of the real thing. 'He's out,' she called across the room, waving the receiver in the air before putting it down.

'Working?' Westerham asked, bringing her drink over.

Sarah sat up, threw a pillow against the headboard and leaned back. 'Yes, he does do an awful lot of night-time filming,' she said, taking her drink.

Westerham adopted the same position, sitting beside her at the top of the bed. 'Doesn't that strike you as odd?'

She shrugged. 'Why should I? I mean in a studio, with all the lights and cameras, daytime and night-time are meaningless.'

Westerham smiled. 'Exactly. That's it,' his voice grew louder, more excited, 'that is it. The lights, that's why they burn so much bloody power, they're filming all night. Sarah, you've done it! You've cracked it for me.'

'Done what?' she asked excitedly, his excitement feeding hers.

'All the time it's been staring me in the face. They use the film studio at night to shoot their own films. They use the studio and all the equipment to make their own pirate productions, and the costs are all picked up by the company. It's clear profit, clear bloody profit.'

'The film, I mean my film, that was going to be one of these pirate films . . .' Sarah added, filling in the missing pieces. She didn't know what was more

156

surprising, the fact that the film was real, or the fact that it was crooked in some way.

'Yes, that's right, they wanted you to appear in one of their productions. Just think how much it must cost to make a film. Think of all those production costs, of the overheads, of the equipment. They got all that for nothing, and then, with no investment to recoup, everything that comes in is pure profit.'

'Westerham,' Sarah said softly.

'Yes?'

'I want to see the film,' she told him softly.

'Why?' he asked, his good humour evaporating instantly.

'It's as much mine as yours. If it gets out then yours won't be the only career ruined,' she said, putting her drink down on the cabinet and turning to face him.

He ruminated for a second, his eyes examining her face minutely, then very slowly he walked across the room. His silence was dark and ominous, but not threatening. She knew that he feared his own reaction more than anything else. The tape was still in the bright yellow jiffy-bag it had been delivered in, his name and room number stencilled neatly on a white label on the front. He carried it as though it would explode, carefully placing it beside the video player before removing the tape from the bag. She leaned across to get a better look: the tape was unlabelled, a simple black rectangle with white spool holes on the underside.

He inserted it into the machine before switching it on. The static roared for a moment before it congealed into a picture of two people, standing to one side of an empty bed, holding each other for a second before she slipped from his arms. The sound was booming, echoing above a faint electronic hiss. 'Let's have a drink,' the woman suggested, moving across the room, her grey dress looking dull and flat on her body as she moved across the camera.

'What is this?' the man demanded, and his voice was more confused, more edged with anger than Sarah remembered.

'You're right,' Westerham said softly, talking over his own recorded voice, 'Eddie Watson is good with a camera. He positioned it perfectly, there was nothing he didn't capture.'

'It makes you wonder how many other people he's done this too,' Sarah agreed, putting a hand on Westerham's shoulder and pulling him softly back onto the bed.

'Tony Christie no doubt,' Westerham guessed, shaking his head sadly.

'Let's watch this now,' Sarah suggested, turning her attention back to the video. On screen the man, and it was hard to really think of him as Westerham, was naked, standing at the bar, his attention directed off-camera. Sarah recognised that it was the moment when she had first emerged from the bathroom, swathed in the leather-Goddess outfit that Eddie had supplied.

'I'm going down for a drink,' Westerham decided, shuffling off the bed, unable to face the pictures on the screen.

'No,' Sarah said coldly, putting her hand firmly on his shoulder, 'we are going to watch this together.'

'You can't stop me,' Westerham stated softly, turning to face her.

'No, you can't stop me,' she corrected, and her voice carried with it an edge of threat, an edge that

158

dared him to oppose her because she was certain that he would submit.

'You haven't got your other self on,' he smiled, trying to make light of the darkness in her eyes. Her hand was still on his shoulder, and he made no attempt to move it away.

'I don't need the leathers,' she purred, smiling seductively. 'I'm your Mistress, no matter what. Now stay and watch the film.'

'Look,' Westerham sighed, exhaling heavily, 'I can do without this. You can join me downstairs when this is finished.'

Sarah swung hard, a sudden impetuous slap, but she wasn't fast enough; he caught her by the wrist, her open hand a whisker from his face. 'I told you, I don't want this,' he hissed.

He held her tightly while she struggled for a second; intent on wiping the grin that was forming on his face. She was the Mistress, she told herself, he *had* to obey. For a second it was deadlock, and then she relaxed, let her hand go limp and then, when it was obvious the fight had gone, he released her.

'This doesn't change anything,' she told him, masking her disappointment behind a look of cool indifference.

'I think it does,' Westerham disagreed. 'It means you'll never repeat that with me again,' he said, pointing to the picture of his subjugation.

Sarah looked to the screen, at the picture of a stern young woman, her body a shimmering contrast of black and white, wielding a long supple cane. She looked so sensual, her face cruel and intent, her concentration totally on beating the bound male body before her. The video seemed too abstract,

159

robbing the scene of the quiet intensity that had been so erotic. The people on the picture were strangers, going through an arcane and obscure ritual, whose meaning was relevant only at that time.

'You can see how that looks now, can't you?' Westerham commented drily, breaking the momentary silence.

Sarah nodded. It looked unreal, cheap and nasty, a vile sequence of bodily actions without meaning. 'And you won't be bothered if this gets out?' she asked, even more horrified by the idea.

He shrugged. 'It won't make any difference to me,' he said.

Sarah looked at him and saw the sadness that lined his face, the sadness he tried to hide behind a facade of cold insouciance. She felt the sadness reflected in herself, felt it as a pain that stuck in her throat. Very slowly she reached across the bed and kissed him on the lips, touched her mouth to his in an unspoken wish to share her warmth. He was frozen into place, his lips cold and unresponsive. She kissed him again, forcing her mouth harder against his, her tongue pressing between his lips, her hand curling round the back of his head. At last he responded, opened his mouth to her tongue, and accepted it, his breath mingling with hers.

'It will make a difference,' she said breathily, still holding his head close, her eyes inches from his. 'It'll make a difference because I'm involved, it's not just you. We're in this together.'

She kissed him again harder, pressing her lips against his so that it hurt them both. Her weight was pressed against him. He slipped back and fell onto one elbow. He was hers and she was not going to release him. His prick was erect, she felt it against his trousers, her fingers stroking it to perfect hardness.

'Can you remember the taste of me?' she whispered, slowly unbuttoning his shirt and sliding her hand across his chest.

He nodded, closing his eyes and drawing a sharp breath when she took one of his nipples in her fingers, the point of flesh puckering painfully as her fingers teased it. She liked that, she liked the idea of caressing Westerham's nipples, injecting sharp daggers of pleasure-pain and stimulating him the way he would stimulate a woman.

'Call me Mistress,' she urged, gritting her teeth and squeezing hard on his nipple. He cried out, an ache, a sharp exhalation of breath, but he left her hand where it was. 'Mistress . . .' she whispered, touching her lips on his half-open mouth.

'Mistress . . .' he repeated, and she felt the tremor in his voice. He lay back completely, resting on his back while Sarah sat astride his lap

'Undress,' she ordered, 'and then undress me.' She killed his protest with a sharp pinch of his nipples, pressing hard so that the points of flesh were nice and red, as if they had been sucked and licked to full arousal.

Silently Westerham undressed himself and then knelt at the side of the bed, on his knees before Sarah, and undressed her too. Her dress fell to the floor in a bundle, and her panties he pulled down quickly, his eyes falling on the prominent damp patch that stained the red lace. She stood before him, naked herself and looking down at his nakedness. Even without her leathers she was Mistress, she knew she had it in her, no matter what.

He was looking up at her, waiting for her command, sullen but silent, as if he were being taken against his will. 'You want this, don't you?' she taunted, wanting to hear him beg.

'I don't know what I want,' he murmured, making as if to stand up.

'Beg,' she said coldly, making him stay where he was. 'Beg!' she repeated, the anger loud and clear.

'I can't,' he said hopelessly.

Sarah pushed him back against the bed, so that his head and shoulders were flat while his legs were still on the ground, his back arched uncomfortably. Quickly she straddled him, forcing his head between her thighs, forcing him into position so that she could feel his breath against the gaping wetness of her pussy. His lips touched her, a fleeting touch under the sex that made her ache to feel his tongue deep inside. He wasn't ready, he hadn't begged but she could wait no longer.

'Suck,' she ordered, pressing herself down on his head. He was obedient, his tongue lapping the puffed-up lips of her sex, caressing her softly but urgently. His arms were locked under her and she saw that he was uncomfortable, forced under her, his back straining and muscles aching. It hurt him and yet his tongue was deep inside her, licking and sucking with feverish abandon.

She moaned softly, began to rock back and forth, riding his tongue to her own rhythm, making him lap her pussy bud or tongue her deep inside. Her hand ran through his hair, caressing softly or gripping tightly when a spasm of pleasure shook her body. Soon she was crying out wordlessly, the juices running thickly from her pussy onto his lips and into his mouth.

She released him suddenly, pushed him down flat

162

on the floor and straddled his face again. His mouth was inside her again; he knew what it was she wanted and gave it willingly. His prick was hard, sticking out from a thick bush of hair, the reddened tip seeping a silvery trail that marked his belly and ran down his prick. She lay across him, her nipples brushing hard against his flesh, her thighs parted and above his face while her mouth was inches from his delicious looking cock.

'Fuck me with your fingers,' she ordered, taking his prick in her hands and lavishing a flurry of kisses across its glistening length. He tasted good and she was going to enjoy teasing his hardness, playing with it in her mouth till it was agony for him not to come. The feel of his fingers inside her made her go suddenly dizzy, sending shocks of pleasure pulsing through her.

She gorged herself on his prick; her tongue licking wildly at the base, her lips rubbing up and down the length, her mouth sucking on the dome and lavishing it with a long wet kiss. The taste of his pre-come filled her mouth, a ghostly substance on her tongue that suffused her mouth with male essence. Her pussy was burning, his tongue and fingers were making indescribable patterns of pleasure in her velvet sex. She held his prick tightly, pulled at the base so that it was tight and the glans was a sensitive bulb for her to play with. Westerham was bucking, his prick throbbing and twitching in her hands; he was on the verge of climaxing and she wanted it, wanted to swallow his thick juicy cream.

'I want it in my mouth,' she whispered, not sure that he could even hear her. She felt herself falling, his tongue was teasing her clitty while he fucked her with two wet fingers, frigging her faster and faster.

163

The twin pleasures of sucking and being sucked meshed, became one and the same thing, a glorious confusion of the senses that filled her with joy.

She fell on his prick once more, taking it deep into her mouth and running her tongue over and over the glans. He bucked suddenly, jerked his hips so that his prick was buried in the back of her mouth and released waves of hot spunk onto her tongue. She swallowed it eagerly, feeling it go down her throat, smooth wads of juice that made her shiver with pleasure.

It was what she had wanted, to swallow his semen drop by drop while she creamed into his mouth. She cried out suddenly, bucking her hips down on his mouth wildly, oblivious to everything but the force of orgasm that took her completely. She rolled aside and lay there breathlessly, her body pulsing with ecstasy, a mad rush of energy that filled her and emptied her at the same time.

'Was that good, Mistress?' Westerham whispered, softly, some time later. He sounded ill at ease, guilty and furtive but trying hard to cover it up with a nervous smile.

'Next time,' she sighed, turning to face him, 'I'll make you beg for it.'

9

Sarah awoke to the smell of fresh coffee and toast. She stretched languorously, turned and opened her eyes. Westerham was sitting on the edge of the bed, fully dressed, freshly shaven, watching her with a wry smile on his face.

'Good morning,' he said, reaching out to pour her a cup of coffee from the breakfast tray on the bedside cabinet, 'I figured fresh coffee was a kinder way of waking you up than a shove in the ribs.'

She yawned. 'How considerate,' she smiled, sleepily, sitting up in bed. 'What time is it?'

'Before six, it's only just started to get light.' The light had begun to filter through the curtains, a thin, pale light that was absorbed by the softer orange light of the bedside lamps.

'Oh no . . .' she moaned, yawning again. 'What are you doing up at this hour? Let's get some more sleep . . .'

He shook his head and passed her the coffee. 'There's no time. There's less than a week left; if I don't have something concrete by then my contract will be terminated.'

'But the tape?' Sarah said, looking across the room to see that it was still in the video player.

'The tape means nothing. If I don't have anything by the end of the week then I'll have no choice but to go to the police. If I can pin Bartlett down some other way then perhaps the tape can be quietly forgotten.'

'We've got to get him, Westerham, I don't want that tape getting out,' Sarah said gravely.

'I thought guilt was meaningless to you,' he smiled, a little cruelly perhaps. 'If that's the case, why worry about the film getting out?'

'Because I've got a family,' she said passionately, 'that's why. And friends, and people I care about. I don't feel guilty about what passed between us Westerham, you enjoyed it as much as I did, but that doesn't mean I want the world to see just what it is that turns me on.'

'I don't understand that at all,' he admitted. 'I feel guilt but don't care what the world thinks of me, you don't feel guilt but care what other people think. Still, we don't have time to go into all that, we've got work to do.'

'I'm glad you're including me in this,' she said, putting her hand on his. He was a strange man, always operating on different, and seemingly contradictory, levels. But then, as he had pointed out, perhaps she was strange too.

'You're right in what you said before, I am like Bartlett in a lot of ways,' he smiled. 'Right now I have one single aim, and that's to get him, to make him bleed, to have him suffer and then to destroy him completely. I want you, no, I need you, to help me. I can't do it without you.'

'I assume there's a plan,' she laughed, putting her coffee cup down and yawning away the last vestiges of the heavy sleep that had followed the long and energetic bout of love-making they had enjoyed the night before.

166

'Plan is too strong a word for it,' Westerham laughed, drawing closer to her.

'What is it?' she asked, disconcerted by the sudden look of pain that had darkened his face.

'My chest,' he said softly, sitting beside her more comfortably, 'I'm still sore.'

'Didn't you like being hurt?' she whispered, her nipples hardening with desire. She reached out and touched him, felt the hard throb of his prick, confirmation that even the echo of pain was enough to arouse him.

Eddie stood at the door, bleary-eyed, unshaven, dressed in dirty jeans and sweatshirt. 'What is it this time?' he scowled.

'You bastard!' Sarah spat, stabbing him sharply in the chest with her finger. 'What have you done?'

He looked at her blankly, rubbing his chest with his palm. 'What do you mean?'

She pushed him aside and marched straight into the house, cursing loudly and angrily. He slammed the door and chased after her, trying to calm her down with soothing words and apologetic noises.

'I saw Westerham,' she finally admitted, flopping down at the kitchen table, the anger making her hands shake uncontrollably.

'What did he say?' Eddie asked, sitting opposite and leaning across the table. It was hard to fathom what was going on in his tiny little mind. Sarah couldn't tell if it was fear or excitement that made him whisper.

'What do you think he said?' Sarah cried angrily. 'He said he was being blackmailed. He almost throttled me. Christ, Eddie, I've never been so scared in all my life.'

'Did you call the police?'

Sarah looked at him; could he really be that simple? 'Of course I didn't,' she explained tetchily. 'If the blackmail thing's true I'd be in even bigger trouble. And it is true, isn't it?'

Eddie drew back, perhaps because he feared that Sarah was going to swing for him. 'Sort of,' he said casually, smiling quite proudly, as if it were an achievement that he cherished.

'What the hell does that mean?' Sarah demanded.

'Calm down,' he pleaded.

He got up and went across the room to put the kettle on, an oddly domestic gesture that further infuriated Sarah. 'I don't know, Eddie,' she said, 'maybe I will go to the police. Maybe I will.'

'You can't . . .' he said, swivelling round quickly. 'You can't do that Sarah, you can't. It's not as simple as it looks.'

'It doesn't look simple to me. Tell me what's going on, Eddie. I have to know.'

He put the kettle on and leaned back against the sink, arms folded across his chest. 'Look, Sarah, it's like this. Thomas Russell . . .'

'That's not his name,' Sarah interjected sharply, staring him straight in the face.

'Thomas Russell is a kind of trading name,' Eddie explained smoothly. 'He and Westerham are old enemies, Thomas just wanted to kill two birds with one stone. Screen test you and get Westerham out of his hair at the same time. I'm sorry it turned out the way it did. If you'd kept out of Westerham's way then you'd have been none the wiser.'

'Eddie, what is wrong with you? What you've done is illegal, you've broken the law and you've involved me in it too. I don't care for Westerham or

168

for Bartlett, they've got nothing to do with me, or at least they were nothing to do with me. Christ, Eddie, I'm going to go to the police. What else can I do?'

He was silent for a moment, utterly appalled. 'You can't,' he said quietly, looking at her imploringly. 'Sarah, if you go to the cops it'll mean trouble for all of us. Me, you and Bartlett. You just can't, promise me you won't. Please, I've been good to you, don't do this to me.'

'But it won't be trouble for all of us, will it? It won't be trouble for Westerham, he's the victim here, him and me. How could you do it, Eddie? Did you get a thrill from hiding away and peeping at me and him?'

'No . . . It wasn't like that . . . Westerham's not the innocent victim he makes out . . . I'm sorry, I swear I only did it as a job, it was a film to me, that's all.'

'I don't believe you, Eddie,' she said coldly, sadly. He was quiet again, and she wondered whether she had shamed him into silence or whether it was because he was desperately searching for some excuse to save himself.

He was framed by the window, the tumult of wild vegetation behind him, the tall thistles, knee high grasses and weeds crowding the small enclosed garden, a garden he had locked the door on and turned his back to. She remembered the first time she had visited his flat, while she was still a student actress and in awe of him. His career was taking off then, he had just won an award for his camera work. It was a house-warming party, the rooms thronging with film and theatre people, larger than life and drunkenly happy. The door to the garden had been open then, she had stumbled out into the cool night

169

air, away from the throaty cigarette atmosphere of the house, away from the raucous laughter and pumped up music. She found him there, alone, sitting on the grass and looking up at the sky, she sat beside him and they talked for hours. That was the first and only time she had ever really spoken to him, to the man behind the dark glasses and leather jackets, to the character behind the superficial mask.

'Let me talk to Bartlett,' she said finally, wanting to put an end to his silent misery.

'Yes . . . Good idea,' he breathed again. 'I'll fix it up, he'll tell you what Westerham's really like. He's no angel, you shouldn't believe him, he's a butcher, that's what he is. His job is to go into companies and tear them apart. He has thousands of people laid off, wrecks lives by the dozen. Don't believe him, girl, he's not an innocent victim. We're the victims, the two of us.'

For a moment there was passion in his voice, and Sarah found herself wanting to believe him. 'Why are you a victim?' she asked, not with the intention of taunting him but wanting to hear for herself his version of events.

'I thought Westerham was a mate of Bartlett's, and I thought it was a weird kind of screen test. Bartlett was going to do his mate a favour and screen test you for this film at the same time.'

'Let me talk to Bartlett,' Sarah repeated coldly, finally grasping the fact that the Eddie who could stare at the stars with wonderment was dead and buried, and that the public image, shallow and conceited, was all that was left of him.

The car pulled up at a smart town house near Regents Park, along an avenue lined with expensive cars that gleamed in the dull grey afternoon. Sarah peered up at the houses, at the dead windows, dark with venetian blinds, at the brass name plates that announced anonymity with style. The leaves were thick on the ground, an autumnal tribute that was picked up by sharp gusts of wind and scattered across the wide pavement.

'Dead smart,' Eddie commented enviously. 'We're lucky he could spare the time to see us.'

'Of course he'd see us,' Sarah snapped irritably, 'he's on a potential blackmail charge.'

'No he's not,' Eddie replied stubbornly, 'that's not going to happen. This is all going to pass, you'll get a good part in the movie and . . .'

'We all live happily ever after,' Sarah concluded contemptuously.

'Wait here,' Eddie said, opening the car door and climbing out, 'I'll just check to see that everything's ok.'

Sarah watched him casually skip up the granite steps and press the buzzer on the heavy front door. He bowed his head slightly to talk furtively into the intercom, giving her a reassuring smile that failed to reassure. She wondered how Bartlett would react, and how she would react in front of him. He had to have seen the film, after all he had paid her a bonus so the results had to have been exactly what he hoped for.

The door opened and Eddie squeezed inside, looking back over his shoulder to make sure she remained in the car. Not for the first time she wished that Dominique was with her, or at least around to talk things through. Dominique seemed so sure of herself, and her pure confidence and powerful personality were something to aim at, a picture of how

Sarah might be, if she wanted to. And Sarah did want to be like that, she did want to have control, she did want to be herself and not a creature that other people had invented.

The door opened and Eddie emerged, a fixed smile breaking through the blank look he usually affected. It was bad news. Sarah recognised the familiar smile, a tightening of the face, giving the game away completely and undoing the work of the mirrored shades that were supposed to hide his feelings.

'What is it?' she asked, getting out of the car to meet him as he strode down the stone steps of the house.

'Don't get uptight, now,' he said, trying to pacify her even before he passed on the bad news.

'He's not going to see me,' she said, hazarding a guess.

'No, of course he'll see you. Only he's a bit paranoid, you can see that, can't you? Like I said before, he knows Westerham and doesn't trust him. And it's not as if he knows you either, you can see that, right?'

'Eddie, get to the point,' she sighed, exasperated.

'He thinks you might be wired, a tape recorder in the handbag or a hidden microphone or something. You can't be too careful,' Eddie smiled, amused by the incongruous circumstances.

'So search me,' Sarah suggested, lifting her arms, looking up at the house, certain that Bartlett was standing behind a blind, looking down with his dead grey eyes.

'Put your hands down,' he hissed, glancing nervously around the street. 'He'll see you, but first he wants you to lose your clothes. When we get in he wants you to strip off, and hand over your handbag, jewellery, the lot.'

She shook her head categorically. 'There's no way I'm going to give him any more cheap thrills.'

'Don't be stupid, girl,' Eddie cried derisively. 'There's a robe for you to put on, this isn't what you think. He just wants to play safe. Westerham's not the smartest guy in the world, but he's good with the women, maybe he's got you on his side now. Maybe he wants to have something on Bartlett to even up the score a bit.'

'You're sick, the whole bloody lot of you,' she complained bitterly. 'Go on then, lead the way.'

The door was open. Eddie waited for Sarah to go in first then followed her in. The hallway was long and narrow, a number of doors leading off from it, post boxes on one side, one wall covered in plaques carrying the names of the companies that used the building. The place was silent, lacking the bustle of activity, the hum of computer printers or the buzz of telephones. Sarah turned to Eddie and found him holding a rough terry robe in his hand, a blue bundle that he was offering to her.

'Better hurry up,' he urged. Her double reflection in the silver mirrors adorned his face.

'In front of you?' she asked distastefully.

'I've seen it all before,' he smiled callously.

She grabbed the robe, the anger swelling inside her with a heat and a violence that made her tremble. Her clothes were soon a tidy pile on the floor, dropped one after the other until she was naked and standing before him. The robe was rough and uncomfortable, but she wrapped it tight, cinching it at the waist, self-consciously aware that it barely covered her backside.

173

'Happy now?' she sneered contemptuously.

'Not half as happy as security,' he smiled, pointing out the security camera that had swivelled round to capture her in its single irised lens. It seemed to leer at her, the tripod a sick grin that supported the obscenely phallic eye.

'Bastards!' Sarah shouted angrily, more upset by the intrusion than she would have been prepared to admit. The skin on the back of her neck had prickled, and she felt sick at the intrusion, at the way her space had been invaded again.

'Mr Bartlett's waiting,' Eddie reminded her, gesturing towards one of the doors. He sounded more confident, as if being inside the house gave him an element of control that he didn't possess outside.

Sarah pushed through the door and then climbed the stairs that led up to a second door. Eddie was behind her, and she could feel his eyes on her long thighs, surveying the white flesh that he had caught on camera.

'Katya my dear,' Bartlett rushed across the room to meet her. 'I do so apologise for these unfortunate precautions.'

Sarah looked at him coldly, at the flat face crowned with thin white hair, at the eyes that were lifelessly grey. 'My name's Sarah,' she informed him, wanting to reclaim herself.

'Of course, my dear, and I'm not Thomas Russell of course. These games we play, they make life difficult, but what's life without difficulty? Still, we're not here to talk about life are we?'

'I'm not sure why I'm here,' she told him, pulling the robe tighter, aware of the way his eyes were scanning her emotionlessly. 'I ought to go to the police.'

'I would suggest that that is not the best course of action in this case,' he sniffed, turning and walking back across the plush office, an office as grey and neat as he was. The room was sliced with thin striped light that flickered through the venetian blinds, the walls painted off-white and decorated with large monochromatic prints.

'Then what would you suggest?' she asked, padding after him, hardly taking in the details of the room around her.

Bartlett sat behind the large white desk that dominated the room, leaned back and swivelled round in his seat. 'I wish there had been some other way, but Mr Westerham is a very difficult man to accommodate. He likes to think of himself as pure; in some distorted way he imagines himself to be an idealist. Do you see him in that light?'

'I don't see him in any light,' Sarah replied, shivering slightly in front of the desk.

'Are you working for him?' Eddie demanded, coming up behind her unexpectedly, his voice thick with menace.

'Of course not,' she responded, facing Eddie, making it clear that she wasn't going to be frightened by Eddie or anyone else. 'But I'm not working for you either,' she added, turning back to Bartlett.

'I think that you are, or perhaps that's how the police will view it my dear. You deliberately seduced Westerham, had sex with him while your boyfriend filmed it, and then you received payment for your services,' Bartlett smiled, enjoying the look of shock on Sarah's face. 'Isn't that what happened?' he suggested persuasively.

'No . . .' she said softly, horrified because Bar-

175

tlett's story was immediately credible, the ring of truth starkly clear.

'I think we should forget about the police, don't you? You have been working for me, and I see no reason why you should stop. You are a very capable young woman, a little naive but talented nevertheless.'

'Don't forget the film,' Eddie whispered, as if that still mattered.

'What do you want me to do?' Sarah asked, a sense of defeat pushing her to edge of despair.

'What does Westerham think of you?' Bartlett asked, swivelling round in his seat to look through the blinds at the street below. 'I understand he attacked you, are there witnesses?'

'No. We were in a lift.'

'What story did you tell him?'

'The truth. That I'd been used.'

Eddie laughed softly, but he fell silent when Bartlett turned around once more. 'Did he believe you?'

'I think so. At least I hope so,' she mumbled.

Bartlett smiled, his thin lips parted in a mask of satisfaction. 'Good. I want you to persuade him to give up. He can't beat me, and if he's not careful he'll lose everything he's ever worked for. I have it in my power to ensure that he never works again, if you'll forgive the cliché. I can't make that clear to him, but you can, he'll listen to you.'

'No he won't,' she disagreed, turning away from the steely grey eyes that watched her intently.

'He will, the evidence is there on the film. You've reached into him, my dear. There's a key, a secret key in every man, hidden, obscured, but there waiting to be turned. It's our good fortune that you've found the key, a happy accident but one set to favour us. He'll listen to the woman that beats him, you know the game, you played it so well.'

'And if I don't play?' Sarah asked, but there was nothing but the sound of defeat in her voice, the defiance she sought was gone.

'Be dispassionate, Sarah, this is business, don't let yourself be side-tracked by your finer feelings, commendable though they may be,' Bartlett urged, smooth and persuasive. He was leaning across the desk, hands together under his chin, looking up at her with a look of sweet reason, as if he were trying to help her, as if he really were on her side.

'What do I have to do?'

'Tell him that your life will be ruined if the film is released. Tell him that he has to salvage what he can for himself. Offer to come back to me with a deal. And if he wavers, use the cane on him, use a whip, do whatever it is that he wants, and do it well.'

'You know it's the only way,' Eddie whispered from behind her, a shadow presence that seemed to hover on the edge of her consciousness.

'And if it works?'

'He might come out of this with a career that's salvageable. In a few years he'll be back where he was before he meddled in my affairs. And you,' he smiled to her, 'you my dear will have a brilliant career in the cinema.'

'Do I get to do my film?'

Bartlett's smile was even broader. 'Sarah, my dear, I think we ought to discuss that very project.'

'I'll be waiting in the car,' Eddie said softly. Sarah turned, saw him backing quickly towards the door and realised that a prearranged signal had passed between the two men.

177

'What's going on?' she asked, trying not to let the panic show. Eddie disappeared, closing the door and leaving her to face Bartlett alone.

'Let me begin by saying how impressive your performance was,' Bartlett said, standing up and walking across the office to a dark mahogany cabinet. 'Eddie assured me that you were acting, but I have to admit that I found that very hard to believe. Which of us was right?'

'What's going on?' she repeated, standing stock-still, watching Bartlett with naked suspicion. He had opened the cabinet and was pouring two drinks from a cut glass decanter.

'There is a film,' he continued, oblivious to the stern look on her face or the distrust in her voice, 'though I'm sure you imagine that Eddie was stringing you along. He's a good technician, but nothing more. I do believe that he once had a future, but that died some time ago. In this case he was telling you the truth, or at least a version of the truth. You look cold, my dear, I'm sure this will warm you up.'

Reluctantly she took the proffered drink, half a tumbler of spirit, making sure that the robe was tight around her chest, and sipped a drop. 'These films, Westerham says they're made illegally, is that true?'

'Let's just say that the whole thing is rather grey in the eyes of the law,' he smiled and moved back to his desk, keeping a distance between himself and Sarah. 'Westerham had a future once, but like your friend Mr Watson, he seems to have lost his way recently. But you, you intrigue me,' again a smile, his eyes fixing upon her. 'Are you a method actress? Do you like to get under the skin of your characters?'

'I want to go home,' she said sullenly, taking another mouthful of the drink, the intoxicating

178

warmth of brandy smoothing its way through her body.

'The film is about a politician and his involvement with a professional lady. But the film is not a conventional drama, the sexual element predominates, it is the core of the film. Eddie once called it erotic cinema, and I think that's as good a description as any I can think of.'

'You mean a dirty film,' she said quietly, but there was no surprise; rather she felt a strange kind of relief, that at last her suspicions had been proved correct. She was feeling tired; all the standing up, the tensions, the early start, the toll was mounting up, and the generous measure of brandy was adding to it.

'Not in the sense you mean,' he explained matter-of-factly. 'These are not back street productions, nor are they seedy, disgusting or cheap. The films are high quality products, with real actors and actresses, professionally filmed, with real scripts and real dialogue.'

'But they are sex films?'

He nodded. 'Erotic cinema, it's a pleasant enough euphemism to differentiate what I do from the trash produced with a home video camera. But the sex is explicit, it's central, the key ingredient. Your performance with Westerham would have made an excellent denouement to one of my films, a perfect ending if you like.'

'That's not how Eddie explained it,' she complained softly.

'I am surprised,' though his expression said otherwise. 'He rarely needs to resort to subterfuge, the money is normally enough of an inducement. May I assume that you are still interested?'

179

She paused, her hesitation making Bartlett lean well back in his chair, a self-satisfied grin on his face. 'I might be,' she finally admitted, allowing a shy smile to warm her face. The drink was making her feel light-headed, and the tiredness was wearing down her resistance.

'The story has changed,' Bartlett explained, standing up and going to the window. 'The powerful politician being beaten by a slut is no longer interesting, one can read about that in the Sunday newspapers. It lacks depth. One can almost sympathise with him, the burden of power and responsibility being lightened with a few sexual games and fun. Don't you agree?'

She shrugged. 'So how do you see the story now?'

'How much more interesting is the politician who finds that the abstract power he wields is strangely unsatisfying?' He parted the blinds with his fingers and let a triangle of light strike his desk. 'Imagine a man who must supplement this power with real domination, sexual domination. A man who is excited by power for its own sake, a man who needs to dominate in every way. It makes a more interesting story, don't you agree?'

'Yes . . . Yes I can understand that,' she agreed, certain that she was being lulled into a false sense of security, but unable to see where Bartlett was taking her.

'I'd like to try you for one of the central roles, if I may?'

'I'm not doing another scene with Westerham,' she warned.

Bartlett laughed. 'No, I wouldn't dream of that. You've shown you can dominate,' he let the blinds go, the clatter filling the room. 'Now I want to see if you can submit. Remove the robe,' he ordered coldly.

Sarah stood and looked at him blankly, as though she hadn't understood him. He marched round the desk and tore at the robe suddenly, unexpectedly. It fell from her shoulders and slipped round her ankles. She was naked, her hands instinctively trying to cover her nakedness in a futile series of gestures.

'How very modest of you,' he sneered, his eyes wide, lips thin and stretched into a sneer of pure disgust. 'On your knees!'

'Why are you . . .' she started to complain, her reactions slowed by the drink and by the feeling of weariness that had being sneaking up on her.

'On your knees, bitch!' he swore, his voice loud and angry. He raised his hand and smacked her across the face, a fire that burned her cheek with a white hot flame. She fell to the floor, clutching her cheek, too shocked for words.

'What should I do with you?' he hissed, walking round her slowly, eyeing her nakedness from every angle.

'I don't want to do this film,' she whispered; she was shaking, and her eyes had filled with tears.

'Shut up. You wanted to fuck with Westerham, now you can fuck with me,' Bartlett told her. 'But unlike Westerham, I'm the one who does the fucking, understood?'

'Please . . . Please, let me go home,' she begged, looking up at him, unable to keep her eyes from the bulge in Bartlett's trousers.

'That's it,' he sneered, 'get a good look, where do you want it? Shall I stick it in your mouth, cunt or arse?'

'Please . . .'

'That's right, beg me for it,' he laughed again, the sound as cold and as cruel as polished steel.

'Why are you doing this to me?' she cried desperately, dizzy with trying to follow him as he circled round and round, a vulture waiting to swoop.

'An audition, my dear,' he said, and his voice was normal again, reasonable, calm, totally insinuating. 'You did very well, though not as well as you did in the other role.'

Sarah looked confused, her head felt muddled, foggy with exhaustion and alcohol. 'Can I get up?' she asked.

'I'd like to carry on, if I may?' he said, putting his heel on her shoulder to keep her on hands and knees.

'I don't understand . . .'

'Of course you do,' he insisted, as though talking to an idiot. 'I'm the master and you're my slave, it's quite simple, my dear. Think of it as a reversal of roles, you were on top and now you're on the bottom. What could be simpler?'

'Are you going to beat me?' she asked, her voice quivering.

'Beat you, and then fuck you,' he promised coldly.

Sarah couldn't tell what he was thinking, the ambiguity was there in everything he said and did. For the first time she realised that she was breathing hard, and that the warmth she was feeling was more than alcoholic. For a moment she saw herself on hands and knees, at Dominique's heel, and the sudden rush of excitement made her feel weak.

'Your nipples, they're hard,' Bartlett pointed out unemotionally. 'Are you wet?'

'I don't know,' Sarah lied, trying to stop herself

182

thinking about Dominique, knowing that Bartlett was reading the signals and getting a different story.

'Bitch! I'm going to make you beg,' he hissed.

She watched him walk calmly across the room, back to the drinks cabinet, with a slow measured stride that betrayed nothing of the excitement he felt; an excitement that she saw in the bulge of his prick. The lethargy that held her stopped her from getting up, it was in her power to put an end to the scene, but something stopped her. Dominique came to her again, the image of a strict young Mistress in red latex, cool and sexy, untouchable and cruel.

'Across the desk,' Bartlett instructed, turning to face her with a thick leather strap in his hand.

'What if I say no?' she challenged, feeling a little of her confidence returning.

'Then you walk out now and never come back,' Bartlett replied, but the smile on his face made it clear that he knew she was going to stay. 'Enough of that now,' he ordered when she made no move. 'You do as Master says from now on. Say, "yes, Master".'

'Yes, Master,' Sarah whispered, so quietly she wasn't sure whether she'd even said it.

'Louder.'

'Yes, Master.'

'Across the desk, now!'

She crawled across the office to the desk, aware that his eyes were fixed on her naked backside, on her long thighs and rounded buttocks. She stood and then bent over across the desk, pressing her breasts flat against the cool surface. Her legs were stretched tight, backside pulled taut, pussy slightly parted.

He was behind her in a flash and without warning the leather strap took a bite across her backside.

Her scream filled the room, made her struggle to get up, but he pressed her down with the flat of his hand. He was in control, and she had consented to it, allowed him to do this to her. The pain was a red scar that burned into her flesh. A second strap mark crossed the first, and her cry was raw and uncontrolled.

'Well, bitch?' he asked scornfully.

She tried to block his voice away. In her mind she heard the sultry tones that issued from the sweet lips of her Mistress. The pain was electric, and the reaction between her thighs was real, a naked sexual response that made the nectar seep from her pussy. Two more strokes of the strap touched her behind, just at the top of the thighs, where her thighs joined her arse-cheeks. She sighed, pulled her belly down and pressed her rear side higher, opening herself to the strap that touched her so violently.

She was delirious, the images filling her mind, the pain a stimulus that seemed to feed her imagination. She saw Mistress, saw the slave Vincent, saw herself kissing Mistress's heels, saw Westerham. Her nipples were hard points that grazed the smooth surface of the desk, and the sensation was too much. Instinctively she took her nipples in her fingers and squeezed and played.

Bartlett grabbed her by the shoulder and pulled her round. 'So you want to play,' he laughed. 'Cup your nipples, the strap is hungry.'

Sarah obeyed without question, half out of her mind with pleasure. 'Yes, Mistress,' she whispered, and the words were part of her breath, part of the sigh that Bartlett barely noticed. He raised the strap high and brought it down viciously, the snap of leather merging with the scream that tore from her vivid red lips. She arched her back and climaxed instantly, a shuddering explosion of pleasure that had her babbling wordlessly, a high so intense she lost control of herself completely.

She moaned, moved down, opening herself to the pleasure in her sex. Bartlett was inside her, thrusting his prick deep into her sex while she held him round the shoulder, her head resting on his chest. He was fucking her, and she had no memory of him first entering her. She was on the edge of the desk, wet with pussy juice that ran in rivulets from her sex clamped tightly round Bartlett's prick.

He grabbed her by the hair and pulled her head back so that she cried out with pain and discomfort. Her body was throbbing, smarting with red strap marks, her nipples pulsing like tiny hearts. He cried out suddenly, dug his prick as far into her as he could and pumped thick wet come into her sex. She climaxed too, aching with pleasure and pain that took her over the edge.

'You can go now,' Bartlett sighed, turning his back to her so that she couldn't see the expression on his face.

Sarah reached for the robe and wrapped herself tight. She still felt weak, but now it had nothing to do with the drink. Her body tingled, the pleasure she had enjoyed had been intense, but she knew that at the moment of orgasm the image of Dominique had been strongest in her mind. Bartlett had had his pleasure, but he was mistaken if he believed that she had yielded to him: she had yielded to no one but Mistress.

10

What was Tony thinking? It was obvious that her sudden departure had something to do with Westerham, no matter how Louise had tried to hide it. She had rushed in to Tony and given him a stupid story about a sudden phone call from her sister. It was patently false and in the end she had clammed up, preferring silence to telling more lies. Tony hadn't said anything of course, that wasn't his way, but Louise saw the hurt in his eyes, and also the fear. With the protracted manoeuvring between Bartlett and Westerham, normal circumstances had ceased to exist, for both of them.

She kissed Tony on the mouth before leaving hurriedly, and not for the first time, she felt the disloyalty as a bilious taste that rose up in her mouth. Westerham always made her feel that way, and the memory of the two of them together was a dark cloud that she tried to cover herself from. She had promised herself never to have anything more to do with him, and whilst she knew that Tony would never forgive her, she had also promised herself that once the dust had settled, she was going to tell him what had happened. But now Westerham had phoned, unexpectedly, and hinted that he had the tapes in his possession. There was no need to say which tapes he meant.

Trafalgar Square was almost deserted; a few tourists taking grey photographs, some sullen looking youths hanging around aimlessly, the pigeons waiting hopefully for the tourists to dish out some bird seed. The traffic was a riot of sound and motion around the island, sad looking buses blocking the way of the black cabs that tried to cut from lane to lane. It had been her choice. It was far from his hotel and that made her feel safe, because, despite herself, she was drawn to him. Westerham was a bastard of the first order, but there was something disturbing about him, and something attractive, in a dark brooding kind of way.

When he called he had sounded as confident and as arrogant as ever, even though everyone knew that he was losing. Even when she had taunted him he had laughed it off, brushing her cutting remarks away with a certainty that, for a moment at least, made her doubt the received wisdom that he was on his way out.

He had given her no time, no time at all, and when she had hesitated he had threatened her with going direct to Tony. She couldn't allow him to do that, and he had counted on it. She was shivering, standing under one of the lions at the foot of Nelson's column, her thin jacket doing nothing to keep out the cold that was channelled by Whitehall and swept up through the square.

A cab pulled up suddenly, swerving across the flow of traffic with typical abandon, and she saw Westerham getting out. From a distance there was nothing remarkable about him, he wasn't the sort of man to get a second look, certainly not from Louise. She waited, not moving, unwilling to rush across to meet him. He had called, it was his turn to come to her.

'What made you choose this place?' he asked by way of greeting, and his eyes were fixed on her.

She shrugged. 'It's neutral,' she said, looking down at her feet rather than face those eyes that seemed to see more than she wanted him to.

'You mean I can't touch you here,' he laughed, and it made her angry because that was exactly what she did mean.

'What do you want?' she demanded, sinking her hands deeper into the pockets of her jacket.

'I know about the video,' he said casually. 'The tape that keeps Tony Christie at Bartlett's beck and call.'

'There's no such thing,' Louise countered with all the confidence she could muster.

'If there was no such thing you wouldn't be here, would you? But there's no need to be embarrassed, Bartlett has caught me in the same trap.'

Louise looked up sharply. If it had been anyone else she would have doubted what she had heard, but not Westerham, he was too straight to stoop to the level of tricks. He was calm, almost blasé, as if the prospect of blackmail left him completely unfazed. 'I'm surprised,' she admitted, finally.

'Not as surprised as I was,' he smiled, and for a moment Louise was sure he was going to burst out laughing.

'Why are you telling me?' she asked, recovering slightly, slowly realising that he was letting her into a secret, and that by telling her he was giving her part of the power that Bartlett had claimed.

'It's too cold to talk here,' he said, 'let's go somewhere else.'

'Where?' she asked suspiciously.

'You choose,' he said, smiling again, amused by her obvious suspicion and the fear that informed that suspicion.

'It's nearly lunch-time, let's find somewhere to eat,' she decided, starting across the square in the general direction of Covent Garden.

They settled on a shabby looking trattoria just off the Strand, tucked away in a quiet backstreet away from the traffic and the crowds of people that thronged the busy main thoroughfare. In the walk from Trafalgar Square they had been largely silent. Louise was torn by a desire to know more about what had happened to Westerham, and a wish to draw a discreet veil over her own situation with Tony. And what was Westerham after? The question was central, he wanted something in return, there was no way he had revealed his own predicament just for the fun of it.

Westerham suggested a table in a quiet alcove, nestling in a corner under the signed photographs of actors and actresses from the fifties; black and white portrait photographs of flawless people with flowery autographs that flourished under their bright smiles. He refused a menu, preferring a glass of wine while Louise perused the menu, his silence unnerving her slightly. Looking at the photographs on the wall she could imagine that the place had been fashionable once, but that its star had faded like so many others.

'So, why did you tell me about the video?' she asked after they had ordered. She sipped from a glass of red wine that Westerham had recommended, doing her best to hide the smile of satisfaction that came naturally to her lips.

'Because I wanted to confirm that Bartlett had

used the same trick on Tony Christie,' he smiled. 'And you've done that. I'm certain now, not that I had any real doubts about it.'

'What are you going to do?'

'That depends,' Westerham said, leaning back in his seat, looking sombre, his eyes ringed with darkness. There was a weariness there that Louise had never seen before.

'Depends on what?'

'On you, I suppose,' he said without smiling. 'If I have to, I'll take my video to the police. I'm going to get Bartlett, no matter what. I have no compunction about doing that, and if that happens there's a good chance that any other blackmail attempts will come out as well. How would you feel about that?'

'If I didn't know you better I'd say that was a joke in poor taste,' she replied quietly. The waiter arrived, served the food quickly, as though he sensed the heavy atmosphere across the table, and departed with a quiet wish that they enjoy the meal.

'What was on your tape?' Westerham asked, ignoring the food before him and concentrating all his attention on Louise.

'What was on yours?' she responded quickly, her face colouring just a little.

'You want to trade?' he smiled, though the humour was forced. Louise flicked back her fringe with her fingers. Her heart was racing suddenly, something had passed between them, an implicitly duplicitous agreement to be honest no matter what. She nodded and accepted the trade.

Westerham smiled, a sideways kind of smile that Louise returned at once, knowing that there was to be no turning back. 'I was set up, one of Bartlett's men arranged for an out of work actress to meet me

190

at my hotel. We went up to my room where she put on a black leather outfit and proceeded to beat me with a whip.'

Louise almost choked on her wine. Westerham watched her impassively as she struggled for breath. 'She whipped you?' she asked incredulously.

'Sleazy, isn't it?' he said, looking away for a moment.

'I would have thought that you'd be the one doing the whipping,' Louise said softly, hardly able to believe what she had just heard.

Westerham seemed to notice the food, his attention turned to that rather than continue the conversation. Louise felt a twinge of sympathy, something she'd never imagined herself feeling for Westerham. It had to be difficult for him, a man who made a virtue of being in control, of dominating every moment and every situation, to suddenly find himself on the receiving end. She had to admire his courage, or perhaps it was simple stupidity, in coming out with the truth no matter what the consequences.

For a while they ate in silence, each of them lost in thought. Louise understood now why he had stormed into Tony's office and why he had been so violent. His reaction, impulsive, impassioned, was in stark contrast to the silence and defeat of Tony's. The two men were so markedly different, and yet they had both suffered the same treatment from Bartlett.

'Do you think it's funny?' he asked after a while, picking up the conversation where it had left off.

Louise shook her head. 'No, it's not funny, but I find it hard to imagine the scene. If it goes to court they'll have to show some of the film as evidence.'

'I know, but if that's what it takes . . .'

'Westerham, how could you let that happen? Don't you care?'

He smiled. 'I'm a sad bastard, remember? Why should I care what people think of me?'

'I'm sorry for saying that,' she said softly, 'but you made me so mad.'

'What's on your tape?' he asked, pouring more wine into her empty glass.

'Nothing, just me and Tony making love,' she said, taking a deep breath.

'So what's the big deal?'

She exhaled slowly, felt herself sinking into her seat. It was all so complicated, and Westerham was the last person in the world she saw as a shoulder to cry on. 'Nothing, there is no big deal.'

Westerham wasn't happy with that. 'I was honest with you Louise, at least repay the compliment. If it's no big deal how come Tony Christie toes the line?'

'Because Tony Christie's a fine man. He's not like you or Bartlett, he's not made from the same stuff as you two. You wouldn't understand him, he's sweet and gentle, and he cares about people.'

'Thanks,' he said flatly.

'You know what I mean,' she said defensively. 'Look at yourself Westerham, you're willing to pull yourself down in the mud so long as you take Bartlett with you. You'd rather sacrifice yourself than sacrifice your pride. Tony isn't like that, he's not like that at all.'

'He's scared,' Westerham said softly, and then, more insistently, 'What's on the tape, Louise?'

'If you must know it's just me and Tony having sex in his office. Over the desk. He comes on my breasts and sucks it off,' she stopped, the tears glittering in her eyes. 'Satisfied?'

'I had to know,' he told her. 'So why's he afraid of that?'

She paused, and looked at him through the tears. 'Because Tony loves his wife and kid too much. He loves them Westerham, and they love him. His wife adores him as much as he adores her. And I love him too, not that you'll understand that. I love him.'

'Who got you the job with Christie?' he asked, oblivious to the tears in her eyes and the quivering of her voice.

'Bartlett of course, he set the both of us up. I'd worked with Tony before, when I was still on the other side of the camera. Bartlett saw the way Tony was looking at me, the bastard knew what would happen if we were forced together for any length of time. He cut me out of the films for a while and got me a job working as Tony's assistant. Once he'd caught us he offered me a job in films again, but I decided to stick with Tony.'

'He's quite a matchmaker,' Westerham whispered to himself.

'What?'

'Nothing. Do you think that Tony can be persuaded to help me get rid of Bartlett for good?'

She shook her head instantly. There was no way that Tony would jeopardise his family, they were everything as far as he was concerned. Louise knew that: it hurt her, it caused her more pain than anyone knew, but she had to accept the fact.

'Louise, I'll be honest with you,' Westerham began softly, taking her hand in his, 'I mean to destroy Bartlett. Now I'm trying to get him without using the tapes, but if I have to, I'll tell the whole story. I'll put myself and Tony Christie on the line, do you understand that?'

'Please, don't do that,' she said softly, her voice filled with hopelessness.

'I have to,' he said sternly, and she could see the pain in his eyes too. 'How many more lives does Bartlett get to destroy before someone stands up to him?'

'No, no,' she pushed her food away angrily. 'It's nothing to do with standing up to him, is it? There's nothing noble about what you're doing, you want to get him because you want to win. Your pride can't take defeat, you're no better than he is.'

'Calm down,' he hissed, looking round at the other guests staring at their table.

'No, I won't calm down!' she shouted hysterically. 'You bastard, how dare you try to blackmail us too. That's what you're doing, you're using the same tactics as he is.'

'Come on, let's get out of here,' Westerham told her, hurriedly throwing a handful of ten pound notes on the table, rising from his seat and taking Louise with him.

She allowed herself to be pulled through the restaurant, her face streaked with tears of anger and frustration. She was vaguely aware of Westerham glaring at the other diners and at the waiters. They were in the street and she was crying still, then she was bundled into a taxi and they were alone.

'Why are you doing this?' she sobbed over and over again, her head on his shoulder while he smoothed a comforting hand through her hair. He was warm and strong, holding her tightly while the cab rocked her gently so that her tears gave way to a silence that hovered on the edge of sleep.

He led her into the lobby of a hotel and she followed, dazed, mute. They went up in an elevator and he took her to his room, opening the door and guiding her in.

'You've changed hotel,' she said absently, looking up at him pouring drinks at a small bar on the other side of the room.

'Drink this, it'll make you feel better,' he told her, passing her a glass.

'Do you have a real home?' she asked, taking the drink, wanting to make small talk so that she could avoid the pain bobbing below the surface.

'No. I move from place to place, wherever I'm working,' he explained emotionlessly, sitting beside her on the edge of the bed.

'Don't you belong anywhere?'

'No, I don't belong anywhere. I'm sorry to have upset you,' he said softly, his voice tinged with feeling. 'I'm a sad bastard, you've told me often enough.'

'I'm wet,' Louise said, surprised at herself, surprised at her physical reaction, at the heat between her thighs and at the feelings she felt for Westerham. He was so different from Tony. Perhaps it was that stark difference that she wanted, the strength, the will, the pure blind belief in himself; sometimes she missed that.

He took her in his arms, pulled her close and pressed his mouth to hers, forcing her lips open and his tongue into her. She yielded, let the feelings overwhelm her. Her sex was wet, and the ache she felt was dark and throbbing, an animal reaction that Westerham always engendered in her.

He released her and she watched him undress, stripping before her so that she could see him for

195

what he was, his prick thrusting from the dense black hair between his thighs. He was so strong, so masculine, so powerful, it was hard to see him being whipped, allowing himself to suffer willingly at the hand of another.

'This was where it happened,' he said, reading the expression on her face.

'Did you enjoy it?' she asked, doing her best to visualise what had occurred.

He nodded, a guilty smile on his face. 'I can't explain what happened,' he added.

Louise stood up and began to unbutton her skirt. He was on her in an instant, holding her in his arms and sucking from her mouth again, sucking away her breath, her will. She felt his prick rubbing against her skirt, a hardness that she wanted buried deep in the wet wound between her thighs, as if he could cure the ache inside her, soothe the emotions that seethed under the surface.

He lifted her skirt and slipped a hand under her silky panties, explored the shape of her behind and the sticky wetness between the thighs. She arched her back slightly, stuck her backside out so that her pussy lips opened and his finger touched her tantalisingly. She sighed, fell against his chest, and opened herself to his touch, wanting him to go deeper.

'Fuck me,' she sighed, wrapping her fingers around the hardness that teased against her clothes. She no longer wanted to think, she wanted to lose herself in the pure physicality of sex, to let the sensations of pleasure sweep away the anguish.

Roughly, Westerham turned her round and made her bend over at the waist, her skirt pulled up so that her long thighs and silky panties were exposed to his devouring eyes. He pulled the panties up between her thighs, forming a thin sliver of silk that parted her arse-cheeks, defining the shape of her behind, and rubbing deliciously tight against the wetness of her pussy and against the throbbing of her cunt-bud. He held her for a moment, eyeing her while rubbing the stretched panties up and down slightly. Each movement echoed back as pleasure that made her sigh.

'Please . . . please . . .' she sighed, bending lower so that her legs were taut, her high heels making every muscle and sinew tight, thighs apart as Westerham manipulated her using the panties he held tightly in his fist. He pulled the panties down suddenly, the wet bundle stretched tight across her knees, a thin trail of honey streaking down a length of thigh. She felt exposed, the tissues of her pussy stroked by the slightest breeze in the room. Two fingers went deep into her sex, stroked her slowly then withdrew with a thick pool of pussy juice, a prize that he offered to her parched lips. She sucked her essence from his fingers, tasting herself and enjoying it, feeling the nectar running from her pussy even more.

Louise cried out; he held her by the waist and pressed his thick rod into the wet heat of her sex. He filled her, stretched her velvet softness with his hardness. They held the position for a moment, enjoying the feeling of sharing and then he began to move inside her, gliding his prick into her wetness. He sighed, moaned, his whispers of sound merging with her own sighs. Her arms were stretched out before her, balancing herself as he thrust down, pushing herself back against him, feeling his stomach mash up against her arse-cheeks.

She climaxed quickly, and fell forward, flat on the

bed. He knelt before her, used his fingers to open her pussy, and kissed her softly under the sex, his tongue moving slowly; an exploratory tool that made her writhe. He licked away the thickest stains of her nectar, swallowing the seeping honey directly from between the fullness of her pussy lips. She turned over, lay on her back, looking up at the ceiling as he buried his head between her thighs. She closed her eyes, lost to everything but the feel of his tongue snaking back and forth over her pussy bud. She wrapped her thighs around him, trapped his head so that his breath grazed her sex as he sucked her. His tongue loved her, touched her, ministered perfectly to the desire that swept through her like a fire.

When she cried out again, climaxing forcefully, he moved beside her and kissed her hotly on the mouth. She could taste herself on his tongue, on the sweat of his lips. He moved around her, over her, offered his prick to her delicious red lips. She looked at his prick, at the thick rod, veined red and purple and glistening with the sweetness from her pussy, and the silvery essence that escaped from the glans. She licked it softly with the tip of her tongue, felt him tense, flex his cock and urge it into her mouth. She lapped at him slowly so that he moaned, tried to force himself into her mouth.

'I could beat you now, if I wanted . . .' she whispered, the idea coming to her suddenly. He responded by taking her head and forcing it down on his prick. She opened her lips and took the length of cock and swallowed it, sliding her tongue over the fleshy hardness. He tasted good, and she knew that she was going to swallow his come with pleasure. He rolled under her, making sharp thrusts with his hips, fucking her in the mouth just as he had fucked her cunny. She took him, playing her tongue over him as he penetrated her mouth forcefully. She slipped a finger into herself, and found the wanting was still there, her fiery bud alive to the pleasure.

She tried to frig herself with his rhythm, realised that she couldn't and so stopped him, deciding that she would take him as she wanted. He lay back, whimpering, sighing wordlessly as she moved her mouth up and down, round and round, using her fingers and every part of her mouth, while she fucked herself with the fingers of her other hand. He could take the pleasure no longer, he cried out, forced his prick deep into the back of her throat and unloaded wave upon wave of thick juice. She swallowed it eagerly, lost in the pleasures that erupted deep inside herself, climaxing even as her mouth was filled with his come.

'Please, Westerham,' she said later, riding down in the escalator with him, her body still glowing with pleasure, 'think about what you're going to do. Don't ruin everything for me and Tony.'

'You're too good for him,' he sighed sadly.

'You don't know him. I love him too much to want to hurt him.'

He looked at her for a long time, as if trying to work her out. 'Does he love you?' he asked finally.

'Yes,' she said sadly, 'but not in the way he loves his family. Please Westerham, if not for him then do it for me.'

'You're asking me to give up everything,' he said gravely, walking her through the hotel lobby. 'If Bartlett succeeds in getting my contract terminated then I'll lose everything I've ever worked for. My reputation is the only thing I've got.'

'Please . . .'

They pressed through the entrance of the hotel and out into the grey drizzle of the afternoon. A taxi cab was waiting, the doorman hurried forward to get the door for Louise.

'Please . . .' she repeated, looking into Westerham's eyes for some form of hope.

'I'll do my best,' he assured her, 'but I can't promise you anything. I'm sorry.'

'I'm sorry too,' she said, choking back the pain. 'I don't ever want to see you again, ever.'

The cab door slammed and she watched Westerham standing forlornly on the pavement, a solitary figure under a grey sky. The anger was part of the pity, was part of the desire, and all were expressed in the bitter tears that Louise cried.

Sarah found Westerham in the pool, swimming back and forth with a slow measured pace. She saw him looking up at the attendant, a leggy blonde sitting on a stool at the poolside, reading a paperback and barely paying him, or any of the other bathers, any attention. Sarah watched for a while, entranced by the play of light on the water, and the slow steady movement of Westerham's body through the water, head ducking under with every stroke, arms powerfully pushing the water aside and propelling himself forward. There were others swimming too, but none with the same determined air; he was the only one moving back and forth across the length of the pool without wavering or varying his pace.

Sarah stood by the entrance for a while and then walked in, her heels echoing through the building, harsh notes above the background of rippling water. The attendant looked up as she approached, a friendly smile on her face. 'Going in for a quick swim?' she asked, putting her thick paperback down and walking over to Sarah.

'No,' Sarah smiled, 'I was just looking for him.'

'Oh, well now you've found him,' she said, her smile evaporating. 'There's a viewing gallery upstairs,' she said, pointing to a door that led off from one side of the pool, 'you can watch from there.'

'Thanks,' Sarah smiled, turned and walked down the length of the pool, taking a certain pleasure in the sharp sounds of her heels and the way all eyes followed her. She caught Westerham's eye and he smiled, stopped for a moment and then swam for the edge of the pool.

'How'd you find me?' he asked breathlessly, brushing his wet hair back from his face.

'I asked at the front desk,' she explained, looking down at him and wondering how far up her skirt he could see. She was aware that several of the male swimmers were still looking at her, swimming slowly past so they could get a better look at her long bare legs. 'How's your day been?' she asked.

'Pretty shitty,' he complained, 'and yours?'

'Very strange,' she said, noticing the attendant shaking her head and pointing to the gallery. 'Blondie doesn't want me here; if you want to talk, I'll be upstairs.'

'I'll be along in a minute,' Westerham agreed and then ducked under the water.

The gallery was up a flight of granite steps and through another door. It was a good vantage point. Sarah stood at the edge and looked down at the pool, holding onto the guard-rail and smiling sweetly to the attendant who had returned to her stool and her book. Westerham was swimming the length of the pool again, his body a shimmering, hazy shape under the cool blue water.

She stood for a while before noticing that a couple of the men were treading water at the poolside, floating beneath her and surreptitiously looking up at her. Her skirt was short but loose, and, standing right up close to the rail, she knew that they could see the full length of her thighs and the dark shadow between them. It made her feel strange, knowing that she was being watched and yet that she was safe and in control of the situation. It hadn't been like that at Bartlett's office. She shuddered at the memory of stripping off under the leering mechanical eye of the security camera. There it had been an invasion, something stolen from her, now it was different, now it was something she could give, a sight of her body as she wanted it to be seen.

She leaned across, balanced her heel on the lower rail, a few centimetres from the ground, and straightened her other leg, giving a clearer view of her thighs. The men below floated in the water, pretending to rest while secretly enjoying the view, *stealing pleasure*, just as Dominique had explained. Sarah liked the idea, it added an extra thrill, made her nipples begin to pucker up and the feeling of excitement warm her pussy. She was Mistress, and was allowing her slaves below to look up at her with desire in their eyes and the painful knowledge that she was unreachable.

Westerham climbed out of the pool, raining water as he walked across to pick up a towel. He smiled to her as he patted himself dry, his hair plastered on his head and on his face. Sarah swirled round, leant against the rail, arms crossed over her chest. She was waiting for him and giving the men below a rear view, her bottom pressed against the thin rail, her skirt pulled up slightly and legs parted.

'They're still looking,' Westerham assured her, padding across the gallery to stand beside her.

'I know,' she smiled, 'how much can they see?'

'Enough to make swimming extremely hazardous,' he laughed.

'Kiss me,' she said quietly, 'kiss me on the mouth and run your hands under my skirt.'

'Another of your games?' he asked, his voice suddenly low and almost fearful.

'Do it!' she hissed, opening her arms to him. He was still damp, and the chlorine from the pool scented his body, a masculine scent that she breathed deeply. His arms were around her and his lips were cool against her own. She moved off the rail and enjoyed the feel of his hands sliding down her back. A breath of air and then his hands were at the top of her thighs, squeezing, stroking, gently pulling her bottom cheeks apart. She wrapped her arms around him, kissed him harder.

'Taste my wetness,' she whispered, rubbing her nipples through her top against his chest. She offered her backside to him, pert, round and keenly watched by the eyes below. His hands were cold against her skin, it felt good when his fingers slipped under her damp panties and brushed roughly through her pussy hair. She sighed, and glued her mouth to his lips as his fingers stroked the dampness inside her sex. His fingers played in and out, a slow deliberate touch that had her squirming. He tickled her rose for a moment then brought his fingers slowly to his mouth; they were dappled with wetness that he touched softly to his lips.

She breathed deeply, checking her growing excitement and looked down at the half dozen men in the pool. She saw them turn away guiltily and laughed, her power to arouse and control a delight that was still new and exciting.

'What next?' Westerham asked hotly, taking her hands and putting them on the wet bulge in his swimming trunks. Sarah stroked him a for a second, wondering what it would be like to have him kneel before her in public.

'I haven't decided, yet,' she smiled, teasing him a little. She released his prick and leant back against the hand-rail, smoothing her skirt down as a signal that the show was over.

'In that case tell me,' he said, becoming more serious, 'what was strange about today?'

'I met Bartlett, and he gave me a message to pass on to you,' she said, choosing her words carefully.

'What was it?'

'He wants to deal. He says you have a choice, either do a deal and save whatever you can of your career, or lose everything.'

He shook his head emphatically. 'That's not a deal. Either way I come out of this badly. Is there anything else?'

'Yes,' again she paused. 'He wants to use me as a channel of communication, he thinks I can persuade you to give it all up.'

'Crap. Anything else?'

Sarah shook her head. All day she had been pondering telling Westerham about her strange ordeal at Bartlett's hands, but now she couldn't. 'So why was your day so bad?' she asked, swiftly changing subject.

'I found out that Tony Christie, he's Director of Operations, is being blackmailed too. Unfortunately, I also found out that he's too frightened to do anything about it himself. It means that if I expose Bartlett as a blackmailer I'll end up ruining Christie's life as well.'

'But you're not going to expose him as a blackmailer,' Sarah said, making it a statement and a question at the same time.

He turned, leaned across the rail and looked down at the water, the light dancing on the silver surface. 'What else can I do?'

'Why can't you go to the police with what you've got?'

'I've got nothing, nothing that'll turn this into a police investigation. And what I do have will get me nowhere with the other directors; they all know that Bartlett's skimming money somehow, but they're too afraid of him to raise their heads above the parapet. Unless I get documentary evidence against him, I'll have no choice but to use the video tape.'

'You can't . . .' Sarah insisted, appalled at the idea of it.

'We can try the same thing on him,' Westerham mused, turning back to Sarah. 'Do you think you could do what you did to me to him?'

She smiled. 'No, he's paranoid about you now. He only agreed to see me on condition I was stripped first, and no, it wasn't like that. I was given a robe to wear, but it meant that he was waiting for you to try to blackmail him back.'

'Call him tomorrow,' Westerham suggested, 'tell him I'm willing to listen to any reasonable offer. It'll have to be cash, and a substantial sum, otherwise the video goes to the police.'

'Do you think he'll fall for it?' Sarah asked doubtfully.

'Fall for what?' he asked, his voice barely a whisper. 'It doesn't look as if I have much choice. It's either that, or ruin too many other people's lives.'

11

Sarah lay in Westerham's arms, sleeping, her face still, soft and innocent. Her breath was a whisper against his chest, an unfailing rhythm that Westerham could lose himself in. He stroked her hair, the smooth skin of her back, enjoyed the warmth of her body moulded to his. Why had he let her get so close? The question came to him again and again, but there was no answer to it. And now, now that she was close, he felt weak; Samson without his hair and still in thrall to Delilah.

Disengagement had been a vow, a promise he had made to himself long ago as an adolescent growing into a man. He could remember trying to explain it once, to put into words the thoughts and feelings in the deepest part of him. He had tried to explain it to Diane, typically a school friend's mother, in a rambling post-coital discussion; the sort of discussion that always brought the darkest part of him to the surface. He had talked about existence, about futility, about the pure meaninglessness of it all. Sartre and Camus came to his lips as he tried to explain to her that he was going to go through life alone, because that was the essence of the human condition. Alone, without excess emotional baggage, without the encumbrances of relationships, he'd be able to face the world and do the right thing. With only himself to worry about he'd never have to compromise, never.

Diane had laughed. She imagined that he was rambling, a morose adolescent who'd been reading too many books, so overcome with sex that he saw it as revelation. He'd silenced her by forcing his mouth over hers, burying his hard prick into her luscious sex. She was wrong. Westerham meant every word he said, he was alone because that was how he felt, that was how he wanted to be.

He dropped his first name soon after. At first it was merely an affectation, but in time it was natural, so that he was always Westerham, one unit, one word, one thing. But now the walls so carefully erected had been breached, and the heartlands invaded. Sarah and Louise had touched him, had reached inside and squeezed hard. The feeling of disengagement was a memory already, the exile had come to an end and he was weak and vulnerable, afraid just like everybody else. Like everybody else. God, that was strange, to see himself in those terms, to see that he could bleed with emotion like any other man. And that he could hunger for it too.

Sarah stirred, moved her lithe body against him, her scent filling him with renewed desire, a desire to lose himself in her sex, to blank out everything but pure physical pleasure. Better not to think, better not to brood, better to just fuck like a beast. That was what had pacified him the night before. Sarah had put a stop to his agonised complaints, silenced his despair with her body, drawing him closer so that his mouth was part of hers and his body merged into her body. They had made love like animals, dark, intense, wordless. How good it had been, and then, at the height of passion, to feel her in control, commanding, demanding, controlling. He had yielded to her, let her beat him with her hands, and force him to the ground so that she could ride his mouth and then his prick.

Now, with the new day at hand, Westerham had much to do. Like it or not he had to make as graceful an exit as possible. Pride dictated that death was better than dishonour, but pride had never been a prime motivation in his life. In the cold light of day, it was better to take Bartlett's tainted money and disappear from the scene as quietly as possible. The alternative was to go down floundering, wailing and screaming as he was dragged down to oblivion. In Westerham's world, word of mouth was everything. He worked on the very fringes of commerce, a shady area where the law was grey and the shadows welcome. If word got out that he had failed in an investigation then everything would be lost. If, on the other hand, a decent cover story could be arranged, then there might still be some mileage left in his career.

It was the sort of emotionless decision that he had trained himself to take, but it was painful never the less. The deal would have to be carefully worked out, but he knew that Bartlett would have an edge on him forever now, the threat of blackmail hanging over him always. Westerham consoled himself with the thought that after the pay-off he'd have the time to work out a suitable policy of revenge, some way to disable Bartlett for good.

'What are you thinking about?' Sarah asked sleepily, opening her eyes and kissing him softly on the chest, her lips wet petals against his skin.

'Nothing,' he said softly, stroking her again, glad for the warmth of her body and the evident concern in her voice. Did she feel close to him the way he did to her? Did she feel the way he did? These were questions that he knew he'd never be able to get answers for; he could never know what went on behind her brilliant blue eyes. There was no way you could ever measure the sincerity of another's words, it was easier when it didn't matter.

'Have you changed your mind?' she asked, sitting up in bed, her naked breasts rubbing softly against his chest, her nipples little buttons of flesh that he loved to suck and tease.

'No,' he replied flatly. 'I was just looking around the room,' he said, an open hand panning across the hotel room, taking in the dreary monotony and dull anonymity.

'What about it?'

'Maybe it's time I bought myself a place,' he said, making it up as he went along, but realising that the idea was good. 'After this I want to take a break from work. Buying myself a place might do me some good. What do you think?'

'Good idea,' she agreed, yawning, her open mouth inviting a kiss. He touched his lips to hers softly, and turned her yawn into an embrace.

'Would you help then?' he asked, his heart racing. Why should she help him? He held his breath, afraid that she'd shrug, that his previous indifference had infected her in some way.

'Of course I will,' she laughed. 'And when you find the right place, I can help you decorate it, otherwise it'll end up looking like this place.'

'Thanks,' he kissed her again, relieved, feeling elated by her answer.

'Well, what's the next step today?' Sarah asked, her hand moving across his chest to touch his left nipple, still red and sore. He winced – his flesh was still tender where her teeth had bitten into him – but the pain, raw as it was, seemed to connect with pleasure. Sarah threw the cover aside and uncovered his prick, hard and strong, throbbing as she teased his nipple in her fingers. 'Did Mistress hurt you?' she asked, toying with him, making him tense suddenly.

'Yes, Mistress,' he said softly, the words falling naturally from his lips.

'I'll have to tie you up one day,' she commented. 'I mean tie you up properly, in a chamber, so that Mistress can prove to you just how much she loves you.'

'And I'll show you just how good a slave I can be,' Westerham whispered. He was shaking, afraid of the power that Sarah held over him, and of the depth of his submission.

'When this is over,' she promised. 'Now, what do we have to do today?'

'Two phone calls. First I want you to call Eddie Watson and arrange a meeting with Bartlett. I'll have to face the bastard one day so it may as well be now. Then I'll call Louise and tell her that she and Tony Christie are safe; I've caused her enough problems as it is.'

Westerham and Sarah waited by the river, Westerham lost in contemplation of the muddy swirl of the Thames, while Sarah idly watched the tourists streaming in and out of the Tate gallery. Bartlett had responded almost immediately via Eddie. The impromptu meeting beside the Thames was his idea, so hurriedly agreed that there could be little time for Westerham to do anything tricky.

211

If the phone call to Eddie had brought immediate results, the same could not be said for the call to Louise. She had slammed the phone down twice, letting it ring and ring after that. It was a bitter blow but Westerham could understand her reaction; why should she listen to him after he had tried to black-mail Tony Christie himself? It hadn't been meant as blackmail, rather it was a desperate gesture to try to force a frightened man into action, but blackmail was what it came out as.

An elderly BMW car pulled up at the kerbside; the paintwork gleamed but the body underneath was past its prime.

'It's Eddie,' Sarah said, turning to face him, but introductions were superfluous. Westerham eyed him warily; swarthy appearance, slicked-back hair, sunglasses, despite the grey sky, and a leather jacket with designer frays.

'Mr Westerham, Sarah,' Eddie nodded to them, curt introductions, a hand offered in greeting.

'This isn't a social call,' Westerham said coldly, ignoring the proffered hand. He felt in control, his anger held in check, the desire to throttle the man before him balanced by his other considerations.

'Where's Bartlett?' Sarah asked, clinging to Westerham's arm.

'Who? I don't know who you mean,' Eddie exclaimed, grinning inanely. 'I understand you are willing to listen to reason, Mr Westerham,' he added, stepping closer to the embankment wall.

'You could call it that,' Westerham agreed, lean-ing against the wall, speaking out across the river.

Eddie adopted the same attitude, looking straight across the brown expanse of water. 'What is it that you require, exactly?' he asked.

'It's very simple. I want money and the master copy of the tape.'

'How much money?'

'Six times my current fee,' Westerham said, turning to Sarah who nodded her agreement.

'I'll pass that on,' Eddie said generously, a slight smile breaking through the solemn features.

'And we want an assurance that we'll have all the copies of the tape,' Sarah added, speaking from Westerham's side, her arm on his shoulder.

'My client's an honourable man,' Eddie smiled, as though he were happy to be quoting from a gangster movie. 'You'll get the master copy, you already have the only other copy. My client will give his word that this matter will be forgotten, it's just a misunderstanding.'

'For a moment I thought you were going to say a matter of respect,' Westerham said, unable to ignore the farcical nature of their meeting. For a moment he wanted to laugh loudly, but he knew that once he started, his laughter would turn to rage and then . . . and then Eddie would have to beat a retreat, or find himself on the receiving end of a smack in the mouth.

Eddie saw the joke, and smiled broadly. 'It's nice doing business with a man who's got a sense of humour.'

'I presume Tony Christie's humour's not as good,' Westerham remarked sourly.

'I don't know who you mean,' Eddie explained, affecting a look of innocence. 'I'll speak to my client and get back to you today.'

'There's one more thing,' Westerham said as Eddie turned back to the car at the kerbside.

'And what's that?'

'I shall have to complete my investigation of course,' he paused, and waited for the confusion on Eddie's face. 'I shall require from your client a breakdown of figures, something I can present to the Board of Directors. This breakdown will show that, in some cases, the film studio has been overcharged on various items. I want a list of these items. I accept that there is no evidence of major fraud, that perhaps accounting procedures have been a little lax, but that this is not down to any particular individual.'

Eddie nodded. 'My client is glad that you can give a clean bill of health to his operation. I'm sure he'll agree with you that there are some minor details that you can report on. Well, if there's nothing else, I'll be off.'

'There is one other thing,' Sarah said, stepping forward.

'What's that?'

She dealt him a stiff slap across the face, a hard open handed smack that had Eddie almost doubled over with pain and shock. 'That's for setting me up twice,' she told him coolly. 'And you can tell Bartlett that he can stuff his bloody film.'

'That was uncalled for,' Eddie complained, manipulating his jaw with his hand.

'We'll wait to hear from you,' Westerham smiled, wrapping his arms tightly around Sarah, an act at once protective and possessive, and yet somehow insecure.

Eddie slammed the car door shut and then joined the steady stream of traffic heading down the embankment towards Chelsea.

'Well, that's it then,' Westerham sighed, feeling relief and apprehension and disgust in equal measure. A cover story had been arranged, a start made on arranging the money, and a false assurance given on the tape.

'Not yet,' Sarah smiled sadly. 'You better make your peace with Louise, she's as much part of your decision as I am. I've got to go and see somebody.'

'May I ask who?'

Sarah smiled. 'No one that you'd know,' she said casually.

Westerham smiled too. There was something transparent in Sarah's manner, as if she could no more lie than he could. She was going to see someone important, someone connected with what was going on, but he knew not to push it. If Sarah had wanted him to know she would have told him, and difficult though it was for him, for the moment his curiosity would have to remain unsatisfied.

Where to begin? With Eddie and the film; Westerham at the hotel; the blackmail; being chastised by Bartlett; or with Sarah's burgeoning sexual experience as a Mistress? Sarah had sought the beginning, struggling to find the opening that would unravel neatly into a coherent story. But once started, it had become a problem of where to stop; the words flowed naturally as she told the story to Dominique. Even the minor details, such as the discovery of her exhibitionist feelings at the poolside, came out in the torrent of words that she had been saving up. Telling Dominique was the most natural thing to do; it was not so much a confession, more of a report to her best friend and teacher.

Dominique listened patiently, never hurrying the story along or asking unnecessary questions. Her eyes sparkled as she listened, sometimes smiling, sometimes frowning, her head held tilted slightly to one side, her long black hair framing her face.

The story finished, Sarah sat back in her seat waiting for Dominique's response. Dominique's tidy little flat was home; she felt comfortable there in the living room or seated at the kitchen table. As always, there was an undercurrent, an unstated agreement between them that Dominique could become Mistress and Sarah the grateful slave.

'Your friend, Westerham, you make him sound like quite a strong person; is he?' Dominique finally asked. She was wearing tight black leggings that stretched as she tucked her feet under her bottom.

'That's the weirdest part,' Sarah admitted. 'He is so strong, yet he does submit, he submits completely. He even calls me Mistress,' she hastened to add proudly.

'What about you? Don't you ever feel a desire to submit before him?'

The idea was strange. Sarah seemed genuinely intrigued; it had never occurred to her. Her role had been assigned by Bartlett and yet there had never been any doubt in her mind that it was right. 'He tried to resist once,' she remembered. 'The only thing he feels is guilt, and he seems disturbed that I don't feel that too.'

'But you do,' Dominique reminded her, 'you feel guilt when you've been a bad girl and I've to punish you. You feel guilt in being my slave, but no guilt in being his Mistress.'

'Why? I don't understand why?'

Dominique laughed. 'How many times must I tell you? There are no answers, you have to learn to accept yourself for what you are. You are dominant with men but submissive with women, is that really so awful?'

'You make it sound so normal,' Sarah sighed, unable to accept things so simply, and certain that such an explanation would do nothing for Westerham. It's not an explanation, he would tell her, and he'd be right.

'So, is it all over now?'

Sarah stood up and walked through to the kitchen. 'Westerham's admitting defeat, but that's not the end of it. He's hurt by it, I can see that, no matter how hard he tries to convince me. It's my fault, if I'd been more careful I'd never have put him into this position in the first place.'

Dominique followed, and put her empty coffee cup in the sink. 'If it hadn't been you, it would have been someone else,' she said, doing her best to soothe.

'That's not true,' Sarah responded sharply. 'If it had been someone else she would never have gone for the full dominatrix thing, she'd have just had sex with him and left it at that.'

'What makes you think you're so special? Westerham was waiting for this to happen. From what you've said he sounds cold, another stupid man intent on stamping his authority on the world. You've done him a favour, you've shown him a better way.'

'Please, Mistress, beat me,' Sarah begged softly, turning to face Dominique, the pleading clear on her face, her large eyes burning with desire. Her breath was sharp, shallow, the air scarcely touching her lungs.

'What's this,' Dominique said coolly, eyebrows

raised questioningly, 'a penitent waiting divine retribution?'

'Please, Mistress . . .' Sarah sighed, falling to her knees and planting soft kisses on Mistress's bare feet.

'Do you really think I'm going to whip you to expiate the guilt you feel for getting Westerham in trouble?'

'It's not like that, please, Mistress, I've been dreaming of this . . . All the time Bartlett was using the strap on me I thought of you, imagined I was being punished by my Mistress.'

'But you're a Mistress too,' Dominique taunted, standing before Sarah, hands on hips, looking down, a wicked smile on her unpainted lips.

'Not for you, Mistress, I'm your slave, I'm yours completely,' she begged, kissing Dominique's toes again.

'Stop that! If I want Westerham, will you give him to me?'

'Yes, yes,' Sarah grovelled. The idea had been in the back of her mind for some time, it was something that she had planned for later, when the mess with Bartlett had been cleared up for good.

'And if I beat you in front of him? If I turn you into a slave before your slave?'

'If that's that you want, Mistress. You know I'm yours, you can do what you like with me, I'm nothing . . .'

'Get up,' Dominique said softly, breaking into a smile, relaxing, losing the hard edge of her Mistress voice.

Reluctantly Sarah complied. Her pussy was wet with desire, a desire that Mistress refused and so further inflamed. It was torment, agony to be so near Mistress and yet not to be her slave.

'I've got something to show you,' Dominique said mysteriously, reaching out to massage Sarah's breast, her palm smothering a nipple that was hard and sensitive.

'Hurt me . . .' Sarah moaned, closing her eyes and crushing Dominique's hand onto her breast.

'Enough of that,' Dominique said softly, removing her hand and breaking the spell. 'Sit down, I've got something to show you, something I'm sure you'll be interested in.'

Sarah went into the other room obediently, the disappointment making her feel stupid, and yet she still felt ready to obey, the hope still flickered that she would be chastised. Westerham felt no need to beg, but then she was always so eager to punish him, ready to punish him on the slightest pretext. Dominique had no need to prove herself, she felt secure in her power, and Sarah's impassioned pleading was the obverse of that; the more she begged the less need there was to punish.

Dominique returned from the bedroom a few minutes later, carrying a video cassette in a plain white cover. She flicked on the television and put the tape into the player.

'What is it?' Sarah asked, walking across the room to examine the white slip-case.

'You'll see in a second, just watch, don't say anything,' Dominique instructed.

'What's it about?'

'Just listen!' Dominique snapped irritably, her face had reddened slightly and her eyes were cold with anger.

Sarah sat down sulkily, at a loss to understand

why Mistress was acting so strangely. Had she done something wrong? Had she transgressed some unwritten rule?

The film began, a single title screen appeared above sombre music, red gothic lettering flickering as the sound deepened and grew in volume. The legend said 'Elixir Productions' and below that, in much larger lettering, was the title, 'Passion Flower'. The titles faded and a picture emerged, a bedroom, white walls, white furnishings, the sun streaming through an open window.

A woman was standing at the window, the net curtains held by a breeze, her golden hair flowing over her shoulders. The room was scanned, from the mirror on the wall that framed a reflection of the young woman, to the door that was locked.

The door opened suddenly and another woman entered; tall, brown hair in tight curls, dark eyes, dressed in white t-shirt and shorts. She crossed the room and went to the other woman at the window, putting her arms on her shoulders and kissing her softly on the neck.

'Have you been crying?' the second woman asked, and her voice was clear, the recording obviously of good quality.

'What if I have?' the first woman asked, turning to face the camera. She had dark eyes that contrasted with the golden hair, her face was painted; vividly red lips, eyes lined with pencil.

'Don't cry,' the second woman said softly, taking the blonde by the shoulders and kissing her on the mouth.

The blonde accepted the kiss, opened her mouth to it, but kept her arms at her side, as though she were afraid of going too far. 'Why shouldn't I cry?' she

220

contended. 'My brother-in-law has just asked me to suck his cock and then you, my only sister, ask me to go along with it. He's your husband Christine, do you really want me to do that to him?'

Christine gazed into the blonde's eyes for a second and then pulled her close. They kissed again, more passionately, and this time the blonde held her sister in her arms. Soon the two women were naked, their beautiful bodies caught by the sun that shone through the room. They were kissing and sucking, their sighs and moans of passion clearly caught on film. There was no doubt about the sighs, they were for real. Close-up shots caught the blonde expertly sucking Christine's sex, her pink tongue going in and out of the dark-haired labia, slipping deep into the pussy that dripped with glistening droplets of juice.

The two women brought each other to climax; they were entwined, head to pussy, exploring each other and giving pleasure that was real and not make-believe.

'No . . . Terry . . .' the blonde cried suddenly, looking up to find a naked man standing beside her, his thick prick standing stiff and ready, only inches from her mouth.

'Let him, Roseanne,' Christine urged her reluctant sister, using her fingers to persuade her to give in.

'No . . . no . . .' Roseanne cried, thrashing her head from side to side deliriously, while her sister frigged her wet pussy with her fingers.

'If that's the way you want it . . .' the man said darkly, striding across the room to the dressing table. The camera lingered for a moment on his stiff cock, the thick glans an enticing delicacy waiting to be enjoyed. The picture cut back to the two women; Roseanne was on her back, her thighs parted, and

221

her sister was kissing her all over her body, raining down kisses on her sex, thighs, belly and breasts. Roseanne climaxed again, pinching her nipples in her fingers and screaming forcefully.

The man returned just as Christine squatted over Roseanne's face, opening her pussy lips so that Roseanne could lick and suck. Terry lifted Roseanne's legs high, holding her by the ankles with one hand. The camera zoomed in on the open pussy lips, swimming with flowing honey, the clitoris swollen and red, a pink jewel in a bed of flesh. The picture zoomed out slowly, the dark bud of her behind was exposed, and then the full shape of her backside.

Suddenly the soft white flesh was touched by something black and hard; the snap caught a loud retort that was followed by a cry that turned into a sigh. Terry was holding a black hair brush, and smacking Roseanne with it on her behind, beating her rhythmically, her skin becoming pink and then red as the camera homed in on every inch of her punished backside. In the background, the cries had turned into soft sighs and then into delirious moans. A long shot was cut in; it showed Christine climaxing forcefully over Roseanne's mouth while Terry chastised her with the brush. Roseanne climaxed again, forcing her mouth into her sister's sex.

Christine rolled away and Terry dropped the brush; even from a distance it was possible to see where her flesh had been spanked deep red. Terry sat astride the young woman who tried to resist feebly, she tried to get up but he was too heavy for her. The picture changed, her face was in close-up, and just above it, Terry's hard prick. A hand was on it, Christine's hand, masturbating her husband's prick over her sister's face. The camera lingered on his prick, hard, *powerful, the feminine fingers working it lovingly. He climaxed, thick jets of cream arcing down onto Roseanne's face, over her lips, chin, cheek, eyes. She was crying out, but it was no longer clear if it was pleasure or denial. Terry rolled away and the scene ended with Christine sucking her husband's come from her sister's face.*

'You're Roseanne,' Sarah whispered, turning to look at Dominique for the first time.

'Don't look so shocked,' Dominique whispered guiltily.

Sarah turned back to the film. She watched in silence as the story unfolded; the reluctant sister forced to have sex with her brother-in-law. She was begged, cajoled and frequently chastised, punished in graphic detail while her sister aided or watched her husband. And yet, despite the spankings and the other punishments, Roseanne managed to retain a degree of innocence no matter what she was forced to endure. And Christine, the wicked sister, seemed to enjoy her sister's tribulations, always finding her pleasure, being sucked and kissed, caressed and stroked by her sister while Terry did as he wished.

At last, towards the close of the film, which lasted about an hour, Christine relented. She kissed her sister on the mouth and promised to stop Terry, tearfully admitting that she had only agreed to Terry's plans because she wanted to test him, to see if he loved Roseanne and not her. She begged forgiveness for using her beloved sister in such an awful way. Tearfully Roseanne gave forgiveness, saying that she had hoped that Terry had passed the test, that she was sure Terry's interest was aroused only by the abstract idea of taking innocence, and that he loved his wife above all.

223

The sisters at peace, the final scene opened in a darkened room. A body was heaving, the camera catching the firm white flesh, glistening with sweat. Very slowly the picture zoomed out, the abstract segment of flesh turned into a torso and then a female body. A body that moved, tensed, relaxed, moved again. The soundtrack caught indistinct voices, sighs and moans that were part pleasure and part pain. Suddenly the dark scene was alive with light, two bodies caught in a harsh electric glare. A cry, a scream of despair, a wail that drowned out everything. The body was Roseanne's, stretched naked on the bed, and on top of her was Terry, driving his thick hard cock in and out of her anal hole.

A final picture of Christine's despair, and the sounds of Roseanne's orgasm, the final betrayal, and the film was finished.

'I didn't know,' Sarah said finally, turning from the blank TV screen to Dominique.

'That's how I know Eddie Watson,' Dominique explained softly, her face flushed pink with shame. 'He was behind the camera, he got me the part. A big production, a proper story, psychological impact, lots of sex. He sold me the same package deal that he sold you.'

'Why didn't you tell me?'

'I didn't think it was important. I mean there was never any hint of foul play when I was involved, certainly no blackmail attempt or anything like that. I needed the money, it paid well and so I did it.'

Sarah turned back to the screen, still able to see the pictures, the image of Dominique being fucked in the arse sticking in her mind. 'Did you know the films were being made illegally?'

Dominique shook her head. 'No, it was filmed in a proper studio, with real lights and technicians. I was told they were for abroad, so there was never any chance that we'd walk down the street and get recognised.'

'Are you ashamed of it?' Sarah asked, certain now that what she was seeing was Dominique's own package of guilt. It was reassuring in a way, as if it confirmed that guilt was a necessary part of being, an essential part of being alive.

'What you saw there,' Dominique explained, talking very slowly, every word carefully chosen, 'is my first experience of sexual pleasure-pain. During the film I realised that pleasure and pain were linked, and that pain enhanced the pleasure. When I climaxed after being beaten, it was for real, and as much a surprise to me as it was to you.'

'If only I'd known . . .' Sarah repeated, shaking her head sadly.

'This is a gift,' Dominique told her, looking up suddenly. 'If your friend Westerham can use this film in some way, then he's welcome to use it. You said he had no physical evidence, well now he has. This was filmed in the studio, on the same set they used for a real production; they used it during the day and we used it at night. They can be matched up, I'm sure of it.'

'Are you sure?'

Dominique smiled. 'There's a brush in my dresser, in the bedroom,' she said, 'get it.'

'I'm serious, Dominique. If you want to keep the film quiet, I'm sure that . . .'

'On your knees!' Dominique cried, her voice hard and sharp, her eyes glittering.

'Yes, Mistress . . .' Sarah sighed. She was wet,

the film had kept her excitement on the boil, and now she could feel a wet trickle of pussy honey dripping down her thigh. And Dominique looked so much more powerful than she had done in the film, black hair suited her, it made her look much sterner, more commanding.

'I'm going to beat you with the brush,' Dominique said, following Sarah as she crawled into the bedroom, 'and then fuck you with the handle till you scream like a bitch.'

'Yes, Mistress,' Sarah sighed, breathless, almost faint. She moved across the floor, on all fours, the rubbing together of her thighs sending spasms of pleasure through her. Her mind was blank, her body tingling with the terrible anticipation of punishment and release.

Westerham hardly bothered to murmur a greeting when Sarah returned. He looked up at her sharply, his dark eyes fixing on her aggressively. He had been waiting for hours, trapped in his room, waiting for Bartlett's messenger boy to call.

'Any news?' Sarah asked, her bright smile an irritant, acid in the eyes.

'No,' he answered sullenly.

'Have you called Louise?'

'I've tried to,' he hissed angrily, turning away so that he wouldn't have to look at her. She was glowing, her skin flushed, her manner relaxed, lips freshly glossed and achingly kissable. Where had she been? The question had been gnawing at him all afternoon, eating away like a cancer, and yet he could not ask her, could not bring himself to voice his anxiety. He wanted to know, *had* to know, but she had to tell him of her own accord, she was the one who had to broach the subject.

'Tetchy, tetchy,' she scolded, her subtle laughter getting under his skin, making the adrenalin pump as if he'd been beaten around the head.

'Call her up for me,' he ordered, striding across the room to grab the phone.

'Calm down,' she said softly, perhaps only then realising that there was no humour left in him.

He glared at her silently, the question on the tip of his tongue but he would not release it. He tapped the number quickly and passed the phone to her, his eyes heavy with barely suppressed rage.

'Hello? Is that Louise?' she asked, nodded emphatically to signal that it was. 'I have someone here who would like to talk to you. Don't put the phone down on him, please. He's been trying to talk to you for hours. Please . . . Just listen to what he has to say.'

He took the phone, a measure of relief flooding back. 'Hello, Louise, I must talk to you,' he said softly, afraid that a harsh word would cause her to slam the phone down again.

'You have five seconds,' Louise warned coldly. He could imagine the stern look on her face, eyes glittering icily and her lips shut tight.

'You and Tony Christie are safe,' he explained quickly. 'I won't be going to the police about the blackmail attempt. I've decided that there's too much at stake, I don't see why you and Tony should suffer because of my ego. I'll be taking Bartlett's poisoned money instead, it's the only thing I can do,' he paused, waiting for a reaction. 'Are you still there?'

'What about you?' Louise asked, the hostility in

her voice replaced with a tenderness that he'd never imagined hearing.

'I'll take his money and try to repair my reputation as much as I can. I can't pretend it's easy Louise, but this isn't just about me. You're right, I'm a cold bastard, but maybe I'm warming up,' he said, a forced smile on his face. Sarah came up behind him, kissed him tenderly on the face.

'Thanks,' Louise said, and then added, 'I'm sorry there isn't any other way. Bartlett's the real bastard, not you. I'm sorry for all the things I've said about you.'

'I deserved it. You can tell Tony Christie too, apologise to him for me. Now,' he sighed. 'I'll get out of your life forever. Bye, Louise.'

He passed the phone to Sarah, slumped back into the nearest seat. He looked drained, emotionless, as though the phone call had sucked away the last reserves of emotional energy in his body. Even the anger had faded, now he felt numb. He had expected elation, a certain satisfaction in doing the right thing, but he felt none of that, he didn't even feel glad that Louise had taken back all the things she'd said about him.

'You look like you need a drink,' Sarah said, kissing him on the top of the head.

'I feel dead,' he complained wearily.

'When this is over you ought to go on holiday,' she said, trying to cheer him up. The cocktail cabinet had been restocked; she poured him a whisky, but the smile on her face, etched in vivid red lip gloss, was tonic enough for him.

'Would you go with me?' he asked, and though it was meant to be a flippant remark, he knew that it hadn't sounded that way.

She turned, cocked her head sideways, thinking the suggestion over. 'It depends where you want to take me,' she smiled, walking back across the room with his drink.

'Wherever you wanted,' he said quickly, afraid that she'd change her mind.

'Sure,' she agreed readily, sitting on the floor beside him, resting her head on his lap.

They were silent for a while, as if the peace in the room was too precious to be shattered. He stroked her face softly with his hand, her warmth slowly bringing him back to life. He had lost to Bartlett, but perhaps he had won something in return, something of far greater value. Or, the unreconstructed part of him decided, that way of looking at things was merely an attempt to come to terms with an outcome he'd never bargained for.

The ringing of the telephone startled them both; Sarah laughed and picked it up. She listened for a second and handed it directly to Westerham.

'I've spoken to Mr Bartlett,' Eddie reported grandly, his self-important tone another irritant to get under Westerham's skin.

'And?'

Eddie paused before launching into an obviously prepared speech. 'He appreciates your goodwill in this matter, and is willing to come to an arrangement. The master copy of the tape will be delivered to your office tomorrow morning, along with documentation to help draft your report. The only sticking point is the financial arrangement.'

'How much?'

'Four times your agreed fee, payable after the delivery of the report,' Eddie stated, and Westerham could almost hear the pleasure in his voice.

'That's unacceptable,' Westerham stated bluntly, though he knew that he was in no position to negotiate.

'Three times the fee, half of it delivered up front,' Eddie offered, as though it were in his power to make the decision.

It was a final offer, take it or leave it, and Westerham had to take it. There was no doubt in his mind that the conversation with Louise had just been reported to Bartlett via Tony Christie. 'I'll expect it tomorrow,' he said drily.

'It's been a pleasure doing business with you,' Eddie laughed sharply before putting the phone down.

'That's it then,' Westerham sighed, turning to face Sarah, who was sitting on the bed. 'Tomorrow I get the doctored numbers and part of my bribe money. Then I turn round and deliver the word according to Bartlett, and watch everything I've ever worked for going down the drain.'

Sarah looked at him for a moment, her eyes filled with indecision, her lips twisted together in a frown. 'Perhaps not,' she told him, jumping off the edge of the bed and going across to the other side of the room.

Westerham lay back on the bed, arms out-stretched. 'What do you mean?' he asked looking up blankly at the dull grey ceiling.

She fished in her bag for a moment and found a video cassette which she solemnly handed over to him. 'This is one of the films that Bartlett produces. Do you think it can help?'

'Where did you get this?' Westerham asked, looking utterly stunned.

'From a friend of mine. She's willing to let us use it if it means getting him. Do you think it can help?'

'There's only one way to find out,' Westerham said, taking the video out of the case and slipping it into the hungry mouth of the player.

12

The narrow stairs curved upwards in a slow grim spiral that Sarah trudged without enthusiasm. Somehow she had expected much more, a receptionist perhaps, a plush carpet, an elevator at the very least. But Westerham's office was a garret in a dour looking building close to Blackfriars, near to the City of London. The only prestigious thing about it was the address, but Sarah could hardly imagine Westerham choosing a place to work on the basis of an address alone. No, she imagined that the very bleakness of the surroundings was what had appealed to him. Even the quality of light was dull; white, bare bulbs shining wanly on each landing, casting a sickly light on the stairs that carried on forever.

She stopped at the top of the stairs, almost dizzy from the climb. There was no name-plate on the door, but as there was no place else to go, she pushed the door and went in, promising herself breathlessly that she'd do more exercise in the future and that she really needed to get herself into shape. The office consisted of a single large room, but it was full to overflowing with paper; on bookshelves, on desks, on the floor, on the window-sill, books, magazines, correspondence, paper everywhere. In the midst of the chaos, surrounded by the acres of documentation, sat Westerham at his desk, hunched over a computer screen that cast a silvery light on him.

'Hi,' he mumbled, barely looking up from the flickering screen.

'This is a mess,' Sarah declared loudly, standing by the door and surveying the room in front of her. There was barely space to move. A narrow path had been hacked through the stacked shelves, cupboards, abandoned furniture and piles of dead office equipment to Westerham's desk.

'This is home,' Westerham objected, his eyes still fixed on the screen as his fingers made fleeting contact with the keyboard.

'How can you work in this mess?'

He shrugged. Perhaps it felt natural for him to work surrounded by so much disorganisation. Perhaps he knew where everything was, and what everything meant, but Sarah doubted it. She navigated through the office towards him, ignoring the long spool of paper that lay abandoned at the foot of a fax machine, avoiding the precariously balanced pile of documents by his desk.

'There's coffee over there,' he said, waving vaguely towards the window.

'You want one?'

'Sure,' he nodded, then looked up at her. 'What time is it?'

'Just gone nine,' she reported, realising that there was no clock in the office. Westerham had been up all night working but, apart from a slightly haggard expression, it was hard to tell. He didn't sound particularly exhausted, and there was none of the casual surliness that she knew he was capable of.

'There's no company registered as Elixir Produc-

233

tions, and none trading under that name, not in the UK or in Europe,' he reported, taking a break for a second. He stretched back in his seat, swivelling round to follow her as she negotiated her way to the window. 'I've also checked on Bartlett and Watson for directorships and things like that, but again I've drawn a complete blank.'

Sarah was slightly amazed that he'd managed to do so much just from his computer terminal during the night and early morning, but she felt disappointed too that the result hadn't been positive. She had been sure that the tape would be enough to pin something on Bartlett or Eddie. 'Where does that leave us?' she asked over her shoulder. There was an electric kettle and a bottle of mineral water on the window sill, jars of coffee and whitener were on the floor, a tube of plastic cups nestling between them.

'It's no surprise, I knew how well Bartlett had covered himself; I'd have been disappointed in him if it had been any other way,' he said without rancour.

'So there's no change then?'

'Not quite,' Westerham smiled. 'I did find a company called Alchemy Projects, with one Edward Tawson as managing director. That's T-A-W-son, as in Watson reversed. An elixir was a potion that alchemists used to prolong life, or turn base metals into gold. I'd guess that the names are down to Watson, I can't imagine that Bartlett would come up with anything so obvious.'

'So you have found something then?' Sarah laughed enthusiastically.

'It's not all there yet. Alchemy Projects haven't filed accounts for some time, and there's nothing that links them directly to Bartlett. Even the link to Eddie Watson is tenuous, despite the stupid anagram. If we had more time, another couple of days, then things might be different.'

'Could we delay?' she asked hopefully, for the first time glimpsing the possibility of victory.

'It's a race remember: my contract is due for termination, time is a luxury we don't have any more,' he explained philosophically.

It struck Sarah that during the night he had finally come to terms with his decision, he understood precisely what it meant and had accepted it with a cool detachment she could never have been capable of. 'If only Dominique had told me about the tape earlier,' she said, more to herself than to him.

'Well, it's no use worrying now. What's going to happen is going to happen,' he said stoically. 'But I'm not going to let it end there, once this is over I'm going to carry on until I have everything I need, and then it'll be the fraud squad he'll have to worry about, not his board of directors.'

Sarah made two cups of coffee, watery, foul looking liquid in plastic cups that were too hot to hold properly. From the window she could look down into an enclosed courtyard, a small rectangle of concrete that was shaded by the overhang of the building. She saw the motorbike drive in slowly, the messenger dressed from head to foot in thick black leather, his crash helmet a polished black dome. He stopped the bike and pulled a thick package from under his jacket and disappeared into the nearest door.

'Westerham, do you blame me for what's happened?' she asked, turning her back to the window to look at him, sitting at his desk and sipping the vile tasting coffee.

'Why should I? You were set up by them as well. Are you feeling guilty about it?'

She wasn't sure if he was kidding or not. Guilt had become a loaded word, linked in to everything they did together. 'Maybe it is guilt,' she admitted.

'There's nothing wrong with feeling guilty about things sometimes,' he said thoughtfully. 'I feel guilty about being your slave, but it adds to the pleasure. It's good to break taboos, there's a thrill in rebelling against things. A person without guilt is a person without depth, without character and without history.'

Sarah looked at him; it was one of those rare times when she felt that she could look into a person's eyes and see right down into their soul. His expression was grave, the weariness expressed in his eyes, and yet there was something joyous about what he was saying, something positive in the darkness. She knew that a feeling of guilt was part of him just as it was part of her, and although his struggle with it was far more intense than hers, it was a struggle she recognised. It was far better to accept the guilt, to turn it into strength, perhaps even to accept that it added a depth to the passion that it sought to deny.

They both turned to the door at the same instant and saw the motorcycle messenger appear, crash-helmet under his arm, looking up half apologetically as he came through the door. 'Mr Westerham?' he enquired hopefully, his eyes straying to Sarah for a moment.

'That's right.' Westerham stood up and threaded his way across the office to receive the thick parcel that the messenger held out for him. 'Do I have to sign?' he asked, taking the package.

'No, not on this one,' the messenger said, as if it were unusual.

'I thought not,' Westerham remarked, 'thanks.'

The messenger nodded, flashed another smile to Sarah, and left. Westerham walked back to the desk, carrying the package as though it weighed a ton. Sarah heard the roar of the motorbike as it came to life, filling the courtyard below with its harsh and powerful sound.

'Never thought I'd come to this,' Westerham sighed, sitting down behind the desk and gingerly opening the package.

Sarah watched him; there was nothing she could say, silence was what he needed rather than any vague words of comfort or consolation. She watched him thumbing through the sheaf of papers, a roll of computer print-out, a thick envelope full of money, the rectangular case containing the video tape. That it was the master copy was a fiction that none of them believed, but they went along with it because it was in the rules.

She was so caught up in her thoughts that the messenger walking through the door startled her. For a moment she thought that it was the same man, returning for some reason, but when he cast his eyes on her she realised that it was someone new.

'I'm looking for Mr Westerham,' he explained, looking around the cramped confines of the office.

'Yes?' Westerham rose again and crossed the room, a tinge of exasperation in his voice.

'Package for you,' the messenger said, pulling out a thick buff envelope from his crash-helmet and handing it over. 'You don't have to sign or anything,' he added.

'No? What a surprise,' Westerham snapped, drawing a sharp look from the messenger. Sarah smiled to him and he shrugged back at her before turning to leave.

'More crap from Bartlett, probably,' Westerham concluded, throwing the package down on the desk, sending bits of paper flying everywhere.

Sarah bent down to pick the papers up, sharing in his feeling of frustration but quite helpless to do anything about it. She rearranged the papers neatly on the desk and then picked up the package that had just been delivered. Westerham was staring fixedly at the screen, as if he could divine an answer from the rows and columns of numbers that were displayed in stark white on black. She opened the padded envelope and pulled the thick wedge of paper out. She stared at it for a while, then passed it silently to Westerham.

'It looks as though we're still in with a chance,' Westerham said, as though hardly able to completely believe it himself.

Sarah nodded. There was a simple note with the thick wedge of paper; a plain white slip of paper, the pure whiteness of it marked with a message that said 'Thanks, Louise.' The note was attached to a carefully folded pile of photocopies, page upon page of extracts from an accounts ledger, handwritten records that covered many months and which told a story that the computer records did not.

Westerham flicked through quickly, scanning the tiny writing until he came to the entry he was looking for. 'Here it is,' he said quietly, 'a series of payments to Alchemy Projects for undisclosed production services on *Passion Flower*. I can cross-refer this to see what real production was on at the time, to see where these costs were buried.'

'You might even be able to compare the films, to see if the same props and sets were used,' Sarah added, hardly able to believe that things had changed so suddenly.

'That would clinch it,' Westerham agreed calmly, his manner betraying none of the elation that Sarah suddenly felt swell up inside her. They had won, they had done it!

'Aren't you happy?' she demanded, almost jumping up and down with joy. She couldn't understand why he wasn't laughing, why he wasn't deliriously triumphant.

'There's still a lot to do,' he reminded her, allowing himself the luxury of a smile. 'But you're right, I do feel very relieved.'

'Relieved? Relieved? Honestly, Westerham,' she sighed heavily, 'sometimes I just don't understand you.'

He looked at her and smiled. 'I've still got a lot to do,' he said, spreading the photocopied pages out in front of him.

The security guards stepped back as soon as they saw the uniformed police, following in Westerham's wake as he moved through the lobby towards the stairs. A secretary snapped out of the stunned silence that had fallen over the lobby like a sudden paralysis, and reached for a telephone. Westerham saw her from the corner of his eye, snapped his fingers and a young policeman jumped forward to snatch the phone from her hand.

Westerham felt powerful, assured, totally in control of the sitation, and it showed. His stride was purposeful, almost a swagger, an air of command about him, the detectives a pace behind merely his

239

lieutenants. He looked back, saw other uniformed officers spreading out through the building, ready to begin taping up the filing cabinets, impounding documents, already warning staff not to touch their computers or destroy any documents.

He raced up the stairs, excitement kept firmly under control, his face set with determination. It was what he had been building up for, the final confrontation with Bartlett, and he was savouring every sweet moment of it. Other cases had ended with the police, but none felt as satisfying, in none had the element of personal victory been so pronounced. It was also true that none had been wrought at such a high cost, his life had changed and was still changing.

He was followed up to the first floor by several officers from the fraud squad, taciturn men who moved with a practised ease through the building, taking control of the situation with minimal fuss and maximum effectiveness. Westerham had used up a lot of favours to get them to move so quickly, but they knew and trusted him; he had never let them down before and so they had listened when he outlined the case against Bartlett. They were thick-set men, naturally cautious, instinctively wary, and the case seemed far too routine to warrant the special action that he was asking for. Finally, to persuade them to move when he wanted them to, he had been forced to suggest that the case might fall under the jurisdiction of another force.

The boardrom was on the first floor, through an ornate double door, the way barred by a pretty young secretary who looked askance at the policemen that swarmed in front of her.

'How long have they been in there?' Westerham demanded, stepping round behind her desk to stop her using the intercom to warn those inside. She reminded him a little of Louise, the same icy expression but lacking that element of passion and intelligence that had first attracted him to her.

'Half an hour, Mr Westerham,' she told him, the shocked expression making the two detectives with him smile to themselves.

'Time to meet Mr Bartlett, I think,' one of the officers told her, his sombre expression melting into a smile as her mouth dropped open.

'Is it a full meeting of the board?' Westerham asked, and when the woman nodded he turned to the police and nodded his assent.

Together they marched to the doors and pushed their way in, three dark-suited men, avenging angels come to punish the wicked. They stood in the doorway for a moment, acknowledging the stunned silence that greeted them. Bartlett was standing at the head of the table, an unfinished sentence still on his lips. His eyes locked into Westerham's and he understood what had happened, a look of defeat tearing away at the arrogant self-confidence that had been his public persona.

It was Gilder that broke the silence, and in so doing, he was announcing his ascendancy once more, reclaiming the intiative that Bartlett had held for so long. 'Mr Westerham, I trust there is an explanation for this intrusion?'

'These gentlemen are from the Metropolitan and City Police Company Fraud Squad,' Westerham announced. The men on either side of him straightened up. 'They have come to interview a member of this board of directors.'

'I assume this has some connection with the investigation you have been conducting,' Gilder said, his redundant words spoken with all due gravity, though Westerham was sure that there was a smile of satisfaction hiding behind the grey impassive face.

'Mr Bartlett?' One of the officers stepped forward.

Bartlett cleared his throat. 'Am I to understand that I am being arrested?' he asked, trying to summon up the self-control he was famous for.

'No, sir, you are not,' the officer replied. 'I am merely requesting your help in an enquiry we are currently undertaking.'

'Officer,' Gilder interrupted, 'are there any other people here that you wish to interview?'

'No, sir, not at this juncture,' the second officer replied stiffly, but the implication that others might be involved caused a sudden intake of breath around the room.

'May I call my brief?' Bartlett asked, sinking down into his seat.

'Yes, sir, of course. If you'd like to join us we'll arrange for him to meet us at the station,' the first officer suggested.

Bartlett nodded, stood up and walked across the room. He stopped in front of Westerham, their eyes met for a moment and then he turned away, meekly following the two policemen out of the room. In that brief moment, a split-second, Westerham saw the defeat in Bartlett's eyes, the look of a man whose faith in himself had just collapsed. If Westerham had been inclined to gloat, to revel in his enemy's downfall, it was dispelled by the thought of how close the victory had been. If it had not been for Louise's last minute intervention than the board meeting would have sealed his defeat, and he would have been the one to be pitied.

'Mr Westerham,' Gilder said, snapping Westerham back to earth, 'would it be possible to have a preliminary report of your investigation so far? Or is the matter now *sub-judice*?'

'I am afraid that my study has yet to be fully completed,' Westerham told the board, momentarily catching a pleading look from an ashen Tony Christie. 'There are still a few areas that require further investigation, and I presume I can count on the cooperation of everyone here.'

'Of course, I can assure you of our undivided support in this matter,' Gilder lied, a murmur of assent a guilty echo to his words.

'A full report will be delivered in due course, the Crown Prosecution Service permitting,' Westerham told the board. 'Now, if you'll excuse me, gentlemen, I too will be helping the police in this enquiry.'

Westerham withdrew, closing the doors on the stunned boardroom. As an exercise in hypocrisy, it was no better or worse than he had expected. It left a bitter taste in the mouth but it was a taste he had grown accustomed to, no matter how distasteful. He smiled a goodbye to the secretary, now being chatted up by two bored looking policemen, and raced down the stairs to catch Bartlett and the others.

The case was far from over, the nitty gritty work was still to be done; the mulling over of records, the tracking down of bank accounts and off-shore funds, but the hard work had been done. Bartlett was history, no matter how good the lawyers. Westerham had turned the tables; the blackmail tape was now to his advantage, because to reveal it would add a multitude of new charges and destroy any credibility that Bartlett had left.

Westerham stepped out into the street and breathed sharply. The moment of elation had gone

243

and now he felt empty, drained of everything but a weariness that he felt to the core. He had won, he had got what he had aimed for, and as had happened so many times before, he was struck by the realisation that what he had been aiming for was hardly worth the effort. Like climbing across a border and finding the other side was no greener, it was the sense of emptiness that followed every victory.

'Where do I belong?' he asked himself, pulling his long overcoat tightly around his waist, hoping to keep out the cold he knew came from within.

13

The room was luminous when Westerham entered, bathed in a brilliant white light that shone from the walls and through the large rectangular windows. It was their room, his and Sarah's, the centre of the house that they had chosen together, and always, even on the darkest of days, he felt that it was alive with a light that danced with a radiant intensity that existed nowhere else in the world. Sparsely furnished, at first by accident and then by design, there was space to hold the light, and the combination of light and space was all that could be desired. The white walls looked down on a bare floor of stripped pine, a large square carpet in the centre of the room, two sofas facing each other under the unshielded windows.

Sarah looked up at him sharply, a fleeting look of guilt on her face replaced by a nervous smile. She was dressed in a short black skirt and black top, her bare thighs tucked under her skirt where she sat on one of the light grey sofas. Beside her there was another woman, young, jet black hair, looking up at Westerham curiously, as if she knew him. Westerham closed the door behind him; the room was a private domain, a new universe, and he felt a sense of intrusion, a discomfort that the space so carefully carved out had been invaded.

He and Sarah were lovers, and, sometimes, he was her slave. Always on the edge of renunciation, on the brink of denial, he submitted to Mistress totally, unable to resist the delicious confusion of the senses that was total submission. When he tried to talk about it, when he wanted to understand what it was that was being enacted, Mistress would silence him. Sarah called the room her chamber, and as Mistress, she explained to him that all doubt was banished and pleasure put in its place.

'This is Dominique,' Sarah said softly, her eyes widening and then turning away from the questions she saw on Westerham's face.

It was no surprise; Westerham had guessed the identity of the woman, and he was afraid of what her presence signified. Dominique was part of Sarah's secret life, the strange source of power that Sarah drew on. Sometimes she would disappear for days, leaving him to suffer agonies of doubt and withdrawal, waiting for eventual return. And when she returned she was replenished, refreshed, powerful. It was an unspoken rule that he could not question her about where she'd been, she was a free agent and he had no right to know, no matter how painful the not knowing might be.

'Aren't you going to say something?' Sarah asked, her eyes on Westerham as he walked across the room, his own eyes fixed on Dominique. There was a half smile on her lips, an unspoken challenge, quiet confidence in her eyes, amusement too.

'I'm sorry,' Westerham smiled, stopping behind the empty sofa, his back to the window. 'Please forgive me, I wasn't expecting you.'

'Evidently not,' Dominique returned the smile. 'How's Bartlett?'

The question was unexpected. Bartlett had long ago ceased to be central to Westerham's life. The police were working through the case slowly and methodically. The police, with more resources and less personal interest, were digging deeper into the tangled web of his financial dealings. In the process Bartlett had become an empty shell, hiding behind lawyers in an effort to retain some substance, as if they could anchor him in the world of reality that he no longer controlled. 'Bartlett should be appearing in court some time in the next year,' he reported. 'Thanks for your help, it made all the difference.'

'I know,' Dominique smiled confidently.

Westerham looked at her, trying to reconcile the peroxide blonde who had screamed in ecstasy as she was arse-fucked in 'Passion Flower' with the dark-haired young woman before him. She seemed unnaturally calm, almost still, oozing confidence, a sardonic smile permanently on her lips.

'Dominique likes our room,' Sarah remarked, her tone suggesting that the momentary silence unnerved her.

'There's a certain quality about the light and space,' Dominique explained. 'It suggests serenity and innocence, don't you agree?'

'That wasn't entirely deliberate,' Westerham said guardedly.

'It may not have been intentional,' Dominique said, leaning across to stroke Sarah's hair, 'but it was deliberate. We all have an ideal image of the world; some of us manage to carve out an approximation in the real world. My chamber is in the darkness, as Sarah will tell you.'

Westerham watched silently, fascinated by the seductive way that Dominique was running her hand through Sarah's golden hair. There was a possessiveness about the gesture, and a sensuality that he could see reflected in Sarah's half closed eyes and the rhythm of her breath.

'Do you like watching me touch Sarah?' Dominique asked suddenly, her hand tracing a line through Sarah's hair and down to her thigh, resting lightly on the knee.

'Does she like it?' Westerham asked, swallowing hard. Sarah's eyes were half closed, fluttering, her face flushed red. He knew the answer, he could see the desire and the response.

'She likes it alright, but you? Do you like it?' Dominique repeated, her rosy lips parted in a delicious smile. 'Don't analyse!' she snapped. 'Answer. Do you like it?'

Westerham's heart was pounding, the fire burning on his face too. He nodded, unwilling to deceive the confident young woman in front of him. Yes, he liked it, his prick was stiffening, the desire beating from his heart through to his belly. Yes he liked it, yes, yes, yes.

'Please . . . Mistress . . .' Sarah sighed, her voice barely audible, a fluttering sigh that shook Westerham with all the force of a scream.

Dominique laughed, leaned across the sofa and drew Sarah's mouth to her own, pressing their lips together in a long slow kiss that Westerham watched in confused silence. 'She tastes so good,' Dominique said, looking up and smiling.

'I don't understand . . .' Westerham whispered.

'Show him,' Dominique ordered sharply.

'Please . . .' Sarah turned to Dominique, her face a picture of supplication, eyes filled with fear, her lips quivering.

'Do it, now,' Dominique ordered, her voice utterly cold.

'I'm sorry . . .' Sarah whispered, turning to Westerham for a moment. She stood up unsteadily, eyes averted. Her skirt was loose, revealing less thigh now that she was standing. Reluctantly she turned her back on Westerham, turned her face towards Dominique who was looking at her coolly, as though measuring the reaction. Very slowly Sarah reached round and lifted the hem of her skirt, exposing her bottom completely to Westerham's view.

He looked for a moment, unable to quite grasp what was going on. His eyes took in the picture of Sarah's reddened arse-cheeks, finger marks still clear on the firm flesh, without understanding.

'I had to punish her,' Dominique stated calmly. 'I put her across the sofa and spanked her hard. She likes that, she likes being spanked, don't you?'

'Yes, Mistress,' Sarah agreed, her voice an appalled whisper.

'But . . . You can't . . . She's . . . Mistress.'

'I'm her Mistress,' Dominique announced proudly. 'Bend over, display yourself properly,' she commanded, proving the point completely.

Sarah obeyed without question, without a murmur of complaint or a word of protest. She parted her legs and bent over, her skirt pulled up at the waist. Westerham could see how well she had been punished, her beautiful backside was tanned red, finger marks on each arse-cheek, the top of her thighs equally as red. Her pussy was exposed, the pink flesh glistening within, a droplet of essence smeared down the inside of her thigh. She had enjoyed her punishment, the pain and the pleasure as one, the same sensation, the same desire.

'Why are you here?' Westerham finally asked, tearing his eyes away from Sarah's punished form. The desire was intense, an ache in his balls, his prick as hard as stone, but tempered by the confusion he felt, a confusion that he didn't want to feel. The chamber had been free of questions, free of doubt, the domain of nothing but pleasure, but now the sanctity he had sought had been invaded.

'Tell him,' Dominique ordered. Sarah started to straighten up, letting her skirt cover her behind. 'Stay where you are,' Dominique snapped. 'Touch yourself, I want him to see you fingering yourself while you explain.'

Westerham took a deep breath. Sarah's fingers showed snow-white against the reddened flesh of her backside; she touched herself gently, her fingers lightly caressing her pussy lips before going deeper. 'I wanted you to know,' she sighed. 'I wanted you to know that I too had a Mistress. I wanted you to know about Dominique . . .' she sighed, two fingers were moving into the wetness of her pussy, her fingers glistening as her love-juice was drawn out slowly.

'What does this mean?' Westerham demanded angrily, his vision of heaven sullied by Dominique's presence. Sarah was Mistress, not the slave, she was to be obeyed without question, her destiny not to submit.

'How tiresome you are,' Dominique declared airily. 'Tell him, what are the rules in my chamber? What are the rules you follow without question?'

Sarah sighed; she was finger-fucking her pussy, the love-juices flowing freely down her hand, the smarting ache of her backside mingled with the spasms of pleasure that she stroked from her pussy-

bud. 'Subservience . . . Obedience . . . Submission
. . .' Each word was a whisper, followed by a pause
and then a sigh. Suddenly she arched her back and
exhaled forcefully, her rear side pressed out, her
fingers deep in her sex, she shuddered, cried out,
climaxed. For a moment she looked unsteady, as
though about to collapse, but then she steadied, her
body locked tight.

'Clean her fingers,' Dominique ordered, her smile
directed at Westerham, at the look of horror and
fascination on his face.

For a moment he looked at Dominique, eyes filled
with anger and rage, disgusted that she should sully
his sanctuary. Always on the verge of renunciation,
but the pleasure could not be resisted. With a start
he realised that now he had another Mistress, and
that he would obey her as he obeyed Sarah. Instinctively he fell to his knees, to his natural station. He
crawled across the room, across the carpet patterned
with light, towards Sarah.

Dominique smiled indulgently, her eyes glittering
with a pleasure that could not be denied. Westerham
felt the shame rise up in him, a wave of self-disgust
that was washed away by an even bigger wave of
desire. Sarah's fingers were coated with thick pussy
honey, scented by her body. He touched his tongue
on her fingers, lapped her honey into his mouth and
held it for a moment, savouring her taste, letting it
fill his mouth. He swallowed, licked some more,
assiduously working his tongue up and down her
fingers in an effort to eat every last drop of her
secretions.

'Enough,' Dominique declared. She stood up,
sharp-heeled boots placed firmly on the ground. 'I'm
glad that you understand,' she smiled. 'You see, she

is still your Mistress, you are still her slave. But now you're mine too, she belongs to me, and you belong to me.'

'Yes . . . Mistress,' Westerham said shakily. The questions swarmed in his mind, insects in flight, a dark seething mass that clouded everything. Too many questions, too many.

'Strip off, I want you naked,' she snapped. She reached out and smoothed her palm against Sarah's punished bottom-cheeks, her hand moulded firmly to the soft rounded flesh. Sarah sighed, moved perceptibly closer to her Mistress.

Westerham undressed quickly, his eyes meeting Sarah's for a moment, meeting her hooded glance, the desire so clear to see, so clearly physical, sensual, complete. In a moment he was naked, sitting beside Sarah, waiting for Mistress to command.

'Does he colour well?' Dominique asked, a finger rubbing tantalisingly over Sarah's pussy lips, dappled with droplets of sex-honey.

'Yes, Mistress, he colours very well,' Sarah reported breathlessly.

'Beat him for me,' Dominique ordered, as though seeking proof of the assertion.

Sarah straightened up, her skirt falling into place, covering the redness of her behind. She bent down, picked up Westerham's trousers, and unthreaded the thin leather belt. He watched her, knowing what to expect, fearing it and welcoming it with the same breath.

'Bend over, hands and knees,' Sarah directed quickly.

Westerham did as commanded; he sat up on all fours, looked straight ahead, and tensed his body for the blow. The snap of leather and flesh filled the room, a brittle sound that seemed to hang in the air. Another snap, the leather tongue licked across the buttocks, biting deep into his side where it stopped. A flurry of blows, snapping repeatedly, making his body burn and ache with pain. And then silence, a silence that was filled with the stinging of his body, a smarting of the flesh that made his prick throb. It could not be denied, the pleasure could not be disavowed.

He turned suddenly at the unexpected feel of flesh on flesh. Dominique was standing over him, looking with studied interest at the strap marks that were red imprints on his white flesh. Her finger tips were cool against his skin, magically drawing away the worst edges of the pain. She smiled, satisfied with what she saw and felt.

'Is he good, Mistress?' Sarah asked, her voice filled with an almost childish wish to please.

'What about here?' Dominique asked, her hand parting Westerham's arse-cheeks. He tensed, a finger tracing down the cleft, touching him under the balls and then moving up, probing gently, lingering for a moment at the tightness of his anal-hole.

'Please!' he hissed sharply, moving forward to escape Dominique's exploration.

'You'll pay for that,' Dominique promised, whispering seductively in his ear.

In a moment the belt was around his neck and being drawn tight, Sarah pulling it so that she held him, effectively leashed like an animal. He struggled to see what was happening, aware vaguely that Dominique was behind him.

'Stop that!' Sarah warned, her voice full of the unmistakable sound of Mistress in command, ordering him into place. She placed a knee on his lower back, pressed down, pulling tight on the belt at the same time. He stilled, fought for breath, fought for control.

'Obviously the strap was not enough for you,' Dominique said harshly.

Westerham felt her warmth, she touched him again, the silken feel of her fingers across the stripes on his lower back. Her fingers touched him between the rear cheeks again, traced along the crack, tantalisingly soft, and then she pressed a finger into his behind. He closed his eyes, felt sick, felt a spear of pain and then the first inklings of pleasure. She rested her finger in his behind, buried into the tightness of his anal-sheath.

'Tight, very tight,' Dominique concluded, speaking to Sarah.

Sarah moved and allowed him room to look back. Dominique was squatting down, examining his backside with an almost impersonal curiosity. She smiled, taunting him with her delicious red lips and glittering eyes. Sarah leaned across, and looked at him too. Very slowly she sucked a finger in her mouth, wet it liberally with spit and then she too took her turn in entering his behind. He froze, overwhelmed with shame that he should be used, and yet he felt the pleasure too, a pleasure that he had been entered, a pleasure that he was being degraded.

'Have you ever used him, here?' Dominique asked, patting Westerham's arse-hole after Sarah withdrew her finger.

'No, Mistress, never,' Sarah replied earnestly. Westerham swallowed hard, afraid that Dominique might take that as an invitation.

'Has he ever used you?' Dominique asked, smiling wickedly.

254

'No, Mistress.'

'I want to see him fuck you in the arse,' Dominique told her coldly. 'Would you like that?'

Sarah shook her head, her voice suddenly losing its power. The leash around Westerham's neck loosened, her hold on it no longer secure.

'On the floor, across the sofa,' Dominique directed without hesitation. Sarah obeyed, she fell on all fours, crawled forward miserably, rested her chest and head on the sofa, her backside sticking out. She looked beautiful, long shapely legs, tight round backside, her quim swimming with juices. Westerham' prick was throbbing, dribbling a thin stream of silvery fluid, as he eyed her intently, awed by the pure sexuality of Sarah's prone position.

'Wet her arse-hole,' Dominique ordered crudely, relishing the look of anguish on Sarah's face.

Westerham crawled forward, his backside still stinging where he'd been beaten and then fingered. Sarah closed her eyes and he didn't know whether it was from a sense of shame or because she felt so good, the pleasure too much to take. The light suffusing the room bathed their bodies, touched their skin with a golden tone that made everything seem too real, too perfect. He kissed her lightly on the thigh, barely touched his lips to her smooth flesh; he felt her tense, as though his mouth were electric.

The whistling of the belt was unexpected; the blow cut across Westerham's thighs, two red lines drawn across his skin. He kissed Sarah more insistently, his tongue tracing a line under her buttocks, moving directly towards her exposed pussy, the pink flesh wet with her love-fluid. He tasted her sex on the tip of his tongue, the taste of Sarah, the taste that was her and no one else. His tongue pressed between

255

her swollen pussy-lips, touched the raw flesh within, a long slow stroke of the tongue and then a touch, tantalising, teasing, against her clitty. She sighed just as Mistress let loose another blow with the strap, cutting Westerham across the lower back, a red stroke of pain that made him sigh with pleasure and pain.

'Suck her, in the arse,' Dominique urged impatiently, the belt stretched tight in her hands, ready to land more blows should her slaves displease her.

Sarah moaned softly, pressed her backside out, opening herself for his tongue, deep in the velvet heat of her pussy. He was sucking and licking, playfully caressing her rosebud with his tongue, making love to her with his hot wet mouth. Mistress didn't want love-making, her command was more direct. Westerham used his hands to gently part Sarah's backside, pulling her arse-cheeks open and incidentally parting her pussy lips to expose the swollen pinkness of her clitty. Her rear hole was a tight round bud, set between the perfect globes of her arse-cheeks.

He kissed her softly on her arse-hole, his lips resting for a moment on the forbidden orifice. He could feel her tensing, afraid of the violation that he was to perform on Mistress's direct orders. Westerham licked her slowly, up and down over the flexing rear opening, and then the tip of his tongue pressed into her, forcing its way into the tightness of her anus. He withdrew his tongue, tasted her in his mouth and then tongued her again, enjoying the feel of pressing into her tight little bum-hole. She sighed as he played his tongue slowly around the sensitive ring of flesh and then entered her again, deeper than before.

For a minute he tongued and kissed, wetting her hole and enjoying every second of it. In all their games together he'd never really tongued her behind so fully and with so much pleasure; but the pleasure he felt was matched, she sighed and moaned softly, her initial reluctance transformed as she opened herself more, pressing her backside into his face so that he could penetrate deeper.

'Fuck her, now,' Dominique ordered, smiling wickedly.

'Yes, Mistress,' Westerham complied. He touched his lips once more to her behind and then withdrew. He took her by the waist, pulled her lower, moulding her body to his. His cock was hard, sticky with his own lubrication. He took his prick in his hand and guiding himself, he stopped, his cock pressed against the impossibly tight rear hole. He looked up and Mistress Dominique nodded, a faint smile still on her lips.

Sarah screamed, her harsh cry of fear and pain lost in the light and space of the room. Westerham pressed himself in slowly, his prick opening her, penetrating deep into her anal passage. He stopped, half way in, and waited, she was tense and tight, and he feared hurting her.

'All the way in,' Dominique told him, moving round so that she had a better view of what was going on.

Westerham pushed in hard, felt her body expand to take his length. She was tight and warm, her arse-hole clenched tight around the base of his hardness. He was inside her, in her arse just as Mistress had commanded. For a second he was afraid that Sarah was going to scream, but she stopped herself. He could sense her trying to relax, trying to accustom herself to anal penetration.

'How does that feel? Do you like having it in the arse?' Dominique asked, bending down low to kiss Sarah on the mouth. Her voice was tender, almost loving, and yet the undercurrent of cruelty was still there, adding an ambiguity to her concern.

'Yes, Mistress, it feels . . . good,' Sarah whispered, her body unnaturally still, as though she feared every movement.

'Fuck her,' Dominique said smartly, looking up at Westerham

He began to move in and out slowly; she was so tight that every movement felt like heaven, sending spasms of sensation pulsing through his body. The feel of her backside as he pressed down was fantastic, her opened body impressed on his abdomen as he thrust into her. He could hardly control it, the blissful energy was too much. He held her tightly, pulling her down hard on his cock, his rhythm slow and hard but becoming faster. He looked up and saw Dominique smiling approvingly.

Sarah was moaning, babbling deliriously. She allowed herself to be manoeuvred, controlled, her body an instrument to be used as Mistress demanded. She and Westerham were being choreographed, performing as Mistress desired and for her desire alone. Westerham looked up and saw Dominique unbuttoning the front of her long black skirt. Her legs were bare under the loose folds of material, smooth thighs, an enticing vision of soft white skin against the black material.

Westerham and Sarah were moving together, their bodies working to the same motion. He could feel the heat of her sex, her pussy juices were dripping from her cunt, down over thighs and onto him. She was frigging herself with one hand, teasing her clitty as he drove into her behind.

Without a word Dominique stepped onto the sofa; her skirt hung open from the waist, the dark hair between her thighs leading to bulging pussy lips, parted slightly. She sat in front of Sarah and opened her thighs, her pussy fully exposed. Without prompting Sarah moved forward, buried her face in the sweetness before her. Dominique sighed, wrapped her hand in Sarah's hair and pulled her closer. Westerham watched silently, his body still pumping hard, on the verge of climax. He could see the fleeting look of pleasure on Dominique's face, her eyes fluttering as Sarah sucked her expertly.

'Kiss my heels,' she managed to gasp, wrapping her legs over Sarah's shoulders, her sharp-heeled boots offered to Westerham's hungry mouth. He hesitated, but the pleasure of submission was too great to resist. He began to suck and lick her heels, running his tongue up and down the sharp leather heel, worshipping Mistress as he obeyed her every command. The three bodies moved together, as in a dream, two slaves wrapped in the same pleasure as their Mistress. The moment was electric, a white heat of passion that seemed to explode blissfully. Sarah cried out, her body froze and shuddered, her tongue buried deep in Dominique's pussy. Her climax was the trigger. Westerham could hold back no longer; he mashed his lips against Mistress's heel and then he was spurting thick jets of come into Sarah's tight bum-hole, the feel of her backside pressed tight against his belly.

'Bitch! Bitch! Bitch . . .' Dominique cried, both

hands holding Sarah's head, forcing her slave to suck up the waves of pussy honey that flowed with climax. Her cry hung in the air, and then there was silence.

Westerham lay flat on his back, bathed in sweat and come, breathing hard and almost dizzy. He felt empty and yet strangely fulfilled, and then, thinking without words, he realised the truth. Dominique had not come to destroy the chamber, she had not invaded the sanctuary as he had feared. Her pleasure was their pleasure, she belonged in the white room, had been a part of it long before her visit.

Sarah moved, tried to sit up but Dominique shook her head. 'He's not finished,' she said, her voice almost cracked.

'What is it, Mistress?' Sarah whispered, her question punctuated by kissing Dominique's fingers.

'You need to be cleaned,' Dominique smiled. Her voice was calm, clear, relaxed.

Westerham understood. His body ached as he moved, his prick was slick with droplets of come, the echoes of the beating still impinging on consciousness. He moved forward, and parted Sarah's arse-cheeks once more. Her rear hole was a tight button, trailing a thin white line of semen, dripping down her crack into the redness of her pussy. He was going to suck her clean, suck his juices from her anal-hole and then suck her pussy free of her own emissions. He was the slave, he had to obey, he belonged now, the man who had never belonged before. He belonged to Sarah, and they in turn belonged to Dominique, both of them.

He pressed his tongue into the welcoming tightness of Sarah's behind, felt the desire explode again, his prick impossibly hard. At last, the questions were stilled.

Letter from Esme

Dear Readers

Oops! Excuse me while I stretch. I've just got up, you see. January's always been my favourite month of the year: but not because it's the first of the twelve months, when you're keeping all your resolutions. It's not even because it's named after the Roman deity Janus, god of passages. No, it's because all this cold weather gives me the ideal excuse to stay in bed! I know it annoys the publisher, but he soon forgives me after a flutter and a wiggle. After all, I do some of my best work in bed!

Nexus's New Year opens up with *Heart of Desire*, in which we meet Sarah, an actress researching her role as a dominatrix. But before punishment can be dispensed, it must be received, as her zealous instructress soon demonstrates.

The Passive Voice tells the story of Harriet and Hilary, two girls tied to each other by something stronger than mere sex or love − bondage. My, my, some of the things those vixens get up to . . . But my lips are sealed. As indeed are Hilary's most of the time!

Good news for our female readers − our Black Lace books have been so successful that from now on, we're bringing out two a month. The first of these is *Outlaw Lover*. It's the year 2075, and society has been divided into communities of rich and poor. Fee Cambridge is one of the lucky ones. She's got all she could wish for − except a decent sex life. Her frustration leads her to make a daring incursion into the wilderness, where she gets a little more excitement than she bargained for . . . (NB: *Outlaw Lover* is a close relation of the old Nexus title *Wicked*, so it's probably not worth getting both.)

The second title for January is *Odalisque*. Auralie is a designer, and belongs to a powerful sophisticated family. It soon becomes clear that she has other designs − on her innocent cousin Jeanine. Why is she persecuting this beautiful young thing? And is Jeanine really as virtuous as she seems?

Looking ahead to February now, and there are yet more exciting developments − a brand new image for Nexus. We've revamped the cover design to give them a more chic 'n' moody look − the gorgeous girls are still there, but you'll find the shots are more stylish, and framed in a sexy peek-a-boo panel.

But while the covers have changed, the stories are as steamy as ever . . . as I found out when I read *Stephanie's Trial*, the fourth sexual adventure for the popular dark-haired enchantress. The story begins with Stephanie taking a well-deserved break from her exertions at Devlin's castle. She leaves as a domineering mistress, but returns to find that the tables have turned, and before long she is standing in the dock at the mercy of all her former slaves . . .

Following close on its heels will be *New Erotica 2*, which I especially enjoyed − and not just because it was edited by me! Last year's *New Erotica 1* proved so popular, we just had to do it again. Like the first book, *NE2* is a tightly packed compilation of extracts from 13 of the best recent Nexus (and Black Lace) titles, and this selection includes *Web of Desire*, *Linzi Drew's Pleasure Guide*, *Paradise Bay*, and *The Dungeons of Lidir*. All with a special introduction from yours truly! I must admit, I'm very proud of the way I've picked out the very horniest moments from our books. Mind you, I've had worse jobs.

The girls of Black Lace have done themselves proud this month, not least with *The Senses Bejewelled*. The sequel to *The Captive Flesh*, it picks up the story of Marietta, now safely installed in the harem as Kasim's favourite. But her tranquillity proves short-lived, as she becomes the victim of a kidnap organised by her master's greatest rival. In his wicked clutches, she is subject to all sorts of abuses − and she can expect no sympathy from her fellow slave, who she jilted in favour of Kasim.

Finally, it's back to mediaeval England for *Avalon Nights*, where we join King Arthur and his famous Knights in a tale of saucy sorcery. A new arrival causes great disarray at court, and the noble lords end up competing for a prize beyond their dreams. Sometimes I wish I was alive in those times. Being a bondsman sounds like fun! Recognise the plot? Then you must've read *Knights of Pleasure*. If so, save your money for next month's scorchers!

Well, time to snuggle down in front of the fire now, and read through a few possibles for future Nexus books. I know it sounds like a cushy job, but it can get a little lonely sometimes. Maybe I'll invite some of our authors round.

They've done some great stuff for us lately; I think it's about time I congratulated them in person . . . See you next month!

Love,

Esme

THE BEST IN EROTIC READING – BY POST

The Nexus Library of Erotica – almost one hundred and fifty volumes – is available from many booksellers and newsagents. If you have any difficulty obtaining the books you require, you can order them by post. Photocopy the list below, or tear the list out of the book; then tick the titles you want and fill in the form at the end of the list.

CONTEMPORARY EROTICA

AMAZONS	Erin Caine	£3.99	
COCKTAILS	Stanley Carten	£3.99	
CITY OF ONE-NIGHT STANDS	Stanley Carten	£4.50	
CONTOURS OF DARKNESS	Marco Vassi	£4.99	
THE GENTLE DEGENERATES	Marco Vassi	£4.99	
MIND BLOWER	Marco Vassi	£4.99	
THE SALINE SOLUTION	Marco Vassi	£4.99	
DARK FANTASIES	Nigel Anthony	£4.99	
THE DAYS AND NIGHTS OF MIGUMI	P.M.	£4.50	
THE LATIN LOVER	P.M.	£3.99	
THE DEVIL'S ADVOCATE	Anonymous	£4.50	
DIPLOMATIC SECRETS	Antoine Lelouche	£3.50	
DIPLOMATIC PLEASURES	Antoine Lelouche	£3.50	
DIPLOMATIC DIVERSIONS	Antoine Lelouche	£4.50	
ENGINE OF DESIRE	Alexis Arven	£3.99	
DIRTY WORK	Alexis Arven	£3.99	
THE FANTASY HUNTERS	Celeste Arden	£3.99	
THE GIRL FROM PAGE 3	Mike Angelo	£3.99	
HELEN – A MODERN ODALISQUE	James Stern	£4.99	
HOT HOLLYWOOD NIGHTS	Nigel Anthony	£4.50	
THE INSTITUTE	Maria del Rey	£4.99	

LAURE-ANNE TOUJOURS	Laure-Anne	£4.99
Ms DEEDES AT HOME	Carole Andrews	£4.50
Ms DEEDES ON A MISSION	Carole Andrews	£4.99
Ms DEEDES ON PARADISE ISLAND	Carole Andrews	£4.99
OBSESSION	Maria del Rey	£4.99
PALACE OF FANTASIES	Delver Maddingley	£4.99
PALACE OF SWEETHEARTS	Delver Maddingley	£4.99
PALACE OF HONEYMOONS	Delver Maddingley	£4.99
QUEENIE AND CO	Francesca Jones	£4.99
QUEENIE AND CO IN JAPAN	Francesca Jones	£4.99
QUEENIE AND CO IN ARGENTINA	Francesca Jones	£4.99
SECRETS LIE ON PILLOWS	James Arbroath	£4.50
STEPHANIE	Susanna Hughes	£4.50
STEPHANIE'S CASTLE	Susanna Hughes	£4.50
STEPHANIE'S DOMAIN	Susanna Hughes	£4.99
STEPHANIE'S REVENGE	Susanna Hughes	£4.99
THE DOMINO TATTOO	Cyrian Amberlake	£4.50
THE DOMINO QUEEN	Cyrian Amberlake	£4.99

EROTIC SCIENCE FICTION

ADVENTURES IN THE PLEASURE ZONE	Delaney Silver	£4.99
EROGINA	Christopher Denham	£4.50
HARD DRIVE	Stanley Carten	£4.99
PLEASUREHOUSE 13	Agnetha Anders	£3.99
LAST DAYS OF THE PLEASUREHOUSE	Agnetha Anders	£4.50
TO PARADISE AND BACK	D.H.Master	£4.50

ANCIENT & FANTASY SETTINGS

CHAMPIONS OF LOVE	Anonymous	£3.99
CHAMPIONS OF DESIRE	Anonymous	£3.99

CHAMPIONS OF PLEASURE	Anonymous	£3.50
THE SLAVE OF LIDIR	Aran Ashe	£4.50
DUNGEONS OF LIDIR	Aran Ashe	£4.99
THE FOREST OF BONDAGE	Aran Ashe	£4.50
KNIGHTS OF PLEASURE	Erin Caine	£4.50
PLEASURE ISLAND	Aran Ashe	£4.99

EDWARDIAN, VICTORIAN & OLDER EROTICA

ADVENTURES OF A SCHOOLBOY	Anonymous	£3.99
THE AUTOBIOGRAPHY OF A FLEA	Anonymous	£2.99
CASTLE AMOR	Erin Caine	£4.99
CHOOSING LOVERS FOR JUSTINE	Aran Ashe	£4.99
EVELINE	Anonymous	£2.99
MORE EVELINE	Anonymous	£3.99
FESTIVAL OF VENUS	Anonymous	£4.50
GARDENS OF DESIRE	Roger Rougiere	£4.50
OH, WICKED COUNTRY	Anonymous	£2.99
THE LASCIVIOUS MONK	Anonymous	£4.50
A MAN WITH A MAID 1	Anonymous	£4.99
A MAN WITH A MAID 2	Anonymous	£4.99
A MAN WITH A MAID 3	Anonymous	£4.99
MAUDIE	Anonymous	£2.99
A NIGHT IN A MOORISH HAREM	Anonymous	£3.99
PARISIAN FROLICS	Anonymous	£2.99
PLEASURE BOUND	Anonymous	£3.99
THE PLEASURES OF LOLOTTE	Andrea de Nerciat	£3.99
THE PRIMA DONNA	Anonymous	£3.99
RANDIANA	Anonymous	£4.50
REGINE	E.K.	£2.99

Please send me the books I have ticked above.

Name ....
Address ....
....
.... Post code ....

Send to: **Cash Sales, Nexus Books, 332 Ladbroke Grove, London W10 5AH**.

Please enclose a cheque or postal order, made payable to **Nexus Books**, to the value of the books you have ordered plus postage and packing costs as follows:

UK and BFPO – £1.00 for the first book, 50p for the second book, and 30p for each subsequent book to a maximum of £3.00;

Overseas (including Republic of Ireland) – £2.00 for the first book, £1.00 for the second book, and 50p for each subsequent book.

If you would prefer to pay by **VISA** or **ACCESS/MASTERCARD**, please write your card number here:

Please allow up to 28 days for delivery

— — — —   — — — —   — — — —   — — — —

Signature: _____